Silverleaf Rapids

Kensington Books by Jodi Thomas

Ransom Canyon Novels
Silverleaf Rapids: A Ransom Canyon Prequel

Someday Valley Novels
Strawberry Lane
The Wild Lavender Bookshop

Honey Creek Novels
Breakfast at the Honey Creek Café
Picnic in Someday Valley
Dinner on Primrose Hill
Sunday at the Sunflower Inn

Historical Romance
Beneath the Texas Sky

Anthologies:
The Wishing Quilt
A Texas Kind of Christmas
The Cowboy Who Saved Christmas
Be My Texas Valentine
Give Me a Cowboy
Give Me a Texan
Give Me a Texas Outlaw
Give Me a Texas Ranger
One Texas Night
A Texas Christmas

Silverleaf Rapids

Jodi Thomas

kensingtonbooks.com

KENSINGTON BOOKS are published by

Kensington Publishing Corp.
900 Third Avenue
New York, NY 10022

Copyright © 2025 by Jodi Thomas

All rights reserved. No part of this book may be reproduced in any form or by any means without the prior written consent of the Publisher, excepting brief quotes used in reviews.

All Kensington titles, imprints, and distributed lines are available at special quantity discounts for bulk purchases for sales promotion, premiums, fund-raising, educational, or institutional use.

This book is a work of fiction. Names, characters, businesses, organizations, places, events, and incidents either are the product of the author's imagination or are used fictitiously. Any resemblance to actual persons, living or dead, events, or locales is entirely coincidental.

To the extent that the image or images on the cover of this book depict a person or persons, such person or persons are merely models, and are not intended to portray any character or characters featured in the book.

Special book excerpts or customized printings can also be created to fit specific needs. For details, write or phone the office of the Kensington Sales Manager: Kensington Publishing Corp., 900 Third Avenue, New York, NY 10022. Attn. Sales Department. Phone: 1-800-221-2647.

The K with book logo Reg. U.S. Pat. & TM Off

ISBN: 978-1-4967-4816-4 (ebook)
ISBN: 978-1-4967-4815-7

First Kensington Trade Paperback Printing: June 2025

10 9 8 7 6 5 4 3 2 1

Printed in the United States of America

The authorized representative in the EU for product safety and compliance is eucomply OU, Parnu mnt 139b-14, Apt 123
Tallinn, Berlin 11317, hello@eucompliancepartner.com

A spring that flows through Ransom Canyon
Deep in the Heart of Texas

Folks say about the big ranches from Wyoming to the Rio Grande that the first settlers fought for their land, the next few generations built, pouring their blood and sweat into the soil, but then the bloodline began to thin, weaken, and eventually dissipate.

But the Kirklands' ranch stood strong over the generations. The Kirklands believed in doing what was right and leaving the land better than it was when they took the reins.

Now one boy has to grow into a man before daylight on a ranch calculated in thousands of acres. His worth will be measured in honesty to his friends, a pledge to his family, and one forever promise made in love.

Chapter 1

Fall in Sorrow

October 1991

Staten Kirkland

For a moment, with his eyes closed, Staten Kirkland could see prairie grass spread out as far as he could imagine while wind whistled over land that had never been broken by a plow.

He thought back to the generations of Kirklands who had ridden over his land and been buried beneath it. They had bled as they'd built one of the biggest ranches in West Texas. And today as the chaos of reality rolled in, Staten feared it all might fall and he, at nineteen, couldn't do anything to stop the panic.

At this moment the youngest Kirkland wasn't on his land. He was fenced in with sterile white walls and huge lights above. The smell of sage had been replaced with cleaning products. No breeze. No stars. The sound of night was gone and rolling carts, clinking trays, and beeping machines seemed to bounce off the walls. He tried to think; he had to do the right thing.

Not quite a boy and not fully a man, Staten struggled to stop shaking as he tried to stand straight, alone, waiting.

His great-grandfather had fought outlaws and diseases that killed hundreds of cattle. His grandfather faced grass fires a mile long and a winter that froze the cattle as they stood on the plains.

In the 1920s the whole world seemed to turn brown. Livestock and people died. Ranchers and farmers had sorrow baked in their bones.

Staten rarely thought of the graves of the first settlers buried where they were on high land with the sounds of rapids below whispering in the wind. The first Kirklands rested near the back of the family cemetery now, shaded by hundred-year-old oaks and bordered by three other family plots where the neighboring ranches met.

Today, his grandfather James Ray Kirkland, known to most as J.R., had almost joined the family plot. With all the battles he'd fought, a stroke took the old man down at sunset after he'd worked a twelve-hour day.

Staten was told his grandfather stepped into the kitchen of his home and said, "I made it in before dusk, honey."

Tabitha, his wife of forty-seven years, managed to reach James as he fell. She was screaming as he closed his eyes.

A hundred miles away Staten had just walked into his dorm at Texas Tech when he'd gotten the news. He'd run directly for his truck, knowing he had to get back to Crossroads as fast as he could, then turn on miles of rough road to make it to the headquarters of the Kirkland ranch, named the Double K.

He was raised on the ranch and it was changing. He hated change. Going to college or taking a vacation was fine, but he was always ready to turn around and head back home. Now, he stood perfectly still, wanting his life to settle.

Without a thought, the youngest Kirkland had rushed back

to Crossroads. With the midnight dark smothering him, he'd raced at top speed, knowing the patriarch of the Kirkland clan was fighting for his life.

As he drove, he'd made a mental list. Whatever happened, Staten would have to be prepared. The work on the ranch had to continue. A dozen people needed to be notified before dawn.

As it happened, the old man had been fortunate his stroke hit today. The clinic's pop-in doctor's weekly visit had been extended while Betty Ann Hampton, the new banker's wife, didn't seem in any hurry to deliver baby number four.

By the time Staten parked and ran into the clinic, the doors five feet away had been closing. He was left alone in what looked like a hallway. The emergency doors on one side had signs that read DO NOT ENTER. On the other side were a few folding chairs. A small desk with a wire basket had another sign that read FILL OUT FORM BEFORE RINGING BELL.

Staten wouldn't have been surprised if he saw DON'T DIE OR BLEED ON THE FLOOR WHILE YOU WAIT.

Muffled sounds and commands came from the two tiny emergency rooms beyond the doors. He smacked the DO NOT ENTER sign with the palm of his hand. He might be only a freshman in college, but he was tall and football player solid.

Staten took one step inside and immediately spotted his grandmother. She had ridden in the ambulance, refusing to part with her husband as the EMTs struggled to keep the only father Staten had ever really known alive.

Moments later every nurse within yelling distance was ordering Staten as well as his grandmother to leave the ICU.

He looked at his granny. As always, she faced trouble with her chin high and her eyes without tears. "I'm staying with my James," she told the nurse.

Amidst the chaos Staten lifted the corner of his lip in a tiny grin. No one fought Granny. The nurse backed off. Maybe she didn't want to argue with someone twice her age or maybe she feared being beat up by a senior citizen.

"Let her stay," the doctor said as he came through the door. "Mrs. Kirkland knows more about doctoring than all of us put together. She was a nurse in the war. Delivered half the babies in the county before we got a clinic, and she did everything right on their ride in from the ranch."

"She was a nurse in Vietnam?" someone piped up. "I thought she was a history teacher."

"No, before that. Now, shut up and get to work." The doc glanced at Staten. "Get out, kid. Unless you've got some kind of medical training I don't know about, you don't need to be here."

Staten moved toward his grandmother.

One nurse rushed forward but just as she started to speak, Granny cut in. "I'm not leaving him tonight, but, Staten, you have to. The men will need orders before dawn."

Staten wanted to protest, but he recognized the steel in her eyes. "I'll be home before dawn, but I'll be waiting out in the hall for the next few hours. Keep me informed."

Granny gave a two-fingered salute. She was wearing her "everything is going to be all right" smile, but this time the message didn't reach her eyes.

He paced in the tiny emergency room hallway for hours before the doctor finally came out.

Staten didn't even notice the doctor coming in until his hand was on Staten's shoulder. "Son, your grandfather is going to pull through, but he won't be the same. He had a stroke and needs to rest now, but you can visit him tomorrow."

Staten nodded as if he understood what the doctor was saying. As if he understood anything that was happening.

When the doctor walked away, Staten stood and turned to face the glass door. He stared at the darkness before dawn. He repeated the words that his grandfather said every morning, "It's time to saddle up. There's work to do."

He silently added to himself, "But what to do first?"

He still had not figured out the answer to that question, when a tall, thin cowboy stepped through the doorway, a dusty hat in his hand and spurs clinking with every move. "How's J.R.?"

"The doctor says he'll be fine and Granny's staying here with him."

Jake Longbow looked down and twirled his hat with his scarred and calloused hands. "It's almost dawn, and there's work to do. We got cattle to move. The trucks are lined up at the corrals and every hand on the place is wearing out the clinic's grass outside."

For a minute the two men looked at each other. Jake was the foreman of the Double K and had been as long as Staten could remember. Jake knew what to do but he waited for a Kirkland to make the order.

A part of Staten wanted to run or cry or break down in tears, but he couldn't do any of that. It was time to grow up. The boss of the Double K had always been a Kirkland and Staten was the only one around to take up the reins.

He nodded grimly and walked to the front door with the old cowboy by his side. Thirty men waited outside, still in their work clothes from yesterday and worry in their tired eyes. Staten took a deep breath and pushed on the door, which felt heavier than usual.

Jake put on his hat and said in his low tone, "I got your back, son, and I always will. Right now you're the boss until J.R. recovers. Somebody has to run the ranch. And there's no days off to think about it."

Staten nodded again and stepped out into his new world whether he was ready or not.

His voice was strong as he faced the men waiting outside.

"Thanks for coming out and showing your support. My grandfather is resting. In stable condition for now."

The cowboys whooped with the news. In the distance Betty Ann screamed and a baby started crying. The head nurse yelled out the window for them to be quiet or she'd come out and pop their hats off, and she wouldn't care if their heads were still in them.

As the noise died down, Staten went on. "While he's out of the saddle, we've still got cattle to load."

He moved to the side and let Jake give the individual orders.

All Staten could think about was that there was someone else who should be stepping into his grandfather's boots. Staten's father, Samuel Kirkland. All the old guy ever said about his only son and the ranch was that Samuel hadn't taken to ranching. Staten always grinned when his grandfather usually went on to add plenty about the women his father married.

Staten's dad had been too busy to make the trip home from Austin last night, but he promised to show up if the old man was still alive by the weekend.

"Okay," Staten yelled. "We'd better get back to the cattle or my grandfather will be cussing mad if we don't keep the ranch running."

Now that his panic had subsided, Staten needed to go somewhere to be alone and let the world slow down.

He hated change. He hated when his father remarried or when his friends moved away. He even hated when the seasons shifted. And he was definitely hating it that his grandpa was suddenly out of commission for an unknown amount of time.

Staten took a minute to go back and wave to his grandmother through the emergency room's window, then he squared his shoulders and went to work.

He got in the old pickup that his grandpa had taught him to drive when he was ten. Staten had done his duty. He'd given the orders and Jake would fill in the details, but Staten knew as long as he was home, he'd be the first up and the last to turn in. He was Boss.

Movement caught Staten's eye as Dan Brigman seemed to come out of nowhere and grab the pickup's door before it could swing closed. Adrenaline woke Staten's tired body.

The seventeen-year-old Eagle Scout stared with authority. "Your grandfather going to be all right, Kirkland?"

"I think so." Staten didn't have the energy to say more.

"Good." Dan patted the pickup like it was a horse. "Now on the drive home keep it under seventy. The sheriff told me to tell you that your grandfolks are going to need your help. No wrecks."

Staten almost laughed. Dan's voice hadn't fully changed, but he already sounded like an officer of the law.

"Will do, Scout." Staten waved and headed home. Dan might be a couple years younger than he was, but he wore a badge and that demanded respect even if he was a junior deputy.

Fifteen minutes later, as Staten pulled up to the barn, Jake had beat him home. He was standing with a paint already saddled. "Kid, your grampa likes to ride the land when he has thinking to do. So, I readied your horse just in case you'd like to do the same. We'll handle things here until you get back. I told the cook to keep food hot all day. We'll work in shifts."

Without a word, Staten swung into the saddle and took off at a full gallop, no speed limit to worry about now. He wasn't sure why, but he rode out to the highest ridge on the Double K Ranch. He'd heard his grandfather say many times that the first Kirkland men liked to watch dawn on that spot where Ransom Canyon shone in all its glory. He'd said that one piece of dirt was their cathedral.

Staten could see the river that cut through the otherwise unbroken land. He could see the pastures and the family cemetery. But best of all, he could watch the sun come up over land that had belonged to five generations of Kirklands. His grandfather said the people had Ransom Canyon dirt in their blood. Deep down Staten knew he and Amalah, his girlfriend since the second grade, would rest here together forever in the cemetery on the hill shaded by huge oaks.

As Staten stepped down off the paint and dropped the reins, he wasn't surprised the horse stayed ground tied. Jake Longbow had always been great at training horses. Staten had only been away at school a little over a month and Jake had done wonders with the wild paint.

Staten walked out on the ridge to face the sun and breathed deeply for the first time since he got the call from his granny that the man who'd raised him had collapsed.

As he took a deep pull of dawn air, Staten's muscles relaxed. He didn't have to be a man yet. The fate of the ranch wasn't on his shoulders. J.R. was going to pull through. He had to. Staten had to have time to get through college and see the world with Amalah before he settled down to work with his grandpa.

Though over six-four and solid as a rock, there was still a boy in Staten that believed the old man would live forever, but the man in him knew one day his hero wouldn't. Then, James Ray Kirkland would sleep with the ancestors.

Chapter 2

No Roots

October 1991

Dr. Charlotte W. Lane

Charlotte Lane drove through the tiny settlement of Crossroads, Texas. Like many areas in rural America, it was a town where most travelers wouldn't bother even to slow and look for the town's name. But this was her new home. She'd only visited it once while passing through on a research trip, but something about Crossroads had stuck with her.

All her life she'd lived in books, not in places, and she guessed here would be the same. What did it matter where she worked or lived? The minute she rested, she stepped into her real home: Fiction. Classics. Love stories. Science fiction. Mysteries. And her true love, Westerns.

She smiled a sad smile, thinking that she was like the town.

Nothing to see. Small and ordinary. Brown hair. Brown eyes. Middle age.

When she was little, she thought her parents gave her a plain name to match her face. All through school they told her how smart she was. Not once had they said she was pretty. She was plain, and now she lived in a plain town. A plain main street. One water tower. Two churches across from one another, and the local sheriff's office located beneath the local judge.

The summer weather had been hot and dry, leaving what had grown in spring already dead and turning brown.

Charlotte slowly passed a few dozen homes huddled together on short streets with bare trees out front. A ten-by-ten-foot shed of a post office, with a huge American flag waving at what had to be the center of nowhere. North, south, east, and west. The same view, no matter which direction you faced. Only four roads to escape.

She read that there was a lake nearby but she couldn't see it. And judging by the dead plants, she doubted the place saw much rain. She heard there was a canyon out here somewhere, too, but that was nowhere in sight either. It was flat land as far as she could see.

"It would be hard to get lost in this town," she said to her cat, Baylor, riding shotgun.

Charlotte made it a habit to name her cats wherever they were found. Denver, a midnight tomcat, moved in when she was growing up while her parents taught at the University of Denver.

When she moved to Sul Ross, she picked a white cat, named him Sul and lived with him while she got an undergrad degree. The day she packed to move, Sul decided to stay and disappeared. She waved as she drove away, but she didn't see him wave back.

Five years ago, she picked up Baylor while teaching a summer class in Waco. She talked to him, but he usually appeared bored or irritated that she was living in his house.

Baylor didn't even bother to look at her most of the time.

Charlotte gave up talking to the cat and mentally mapped the town. She drove ten miles an hour and took in Crossroads. If she was lucky the tour might last five minutes. The one main street had five open businesses. A café across from the post office. A funeral home with a TWO FOR ONE banner. A hardware store with overalls hanging in the front window and farm equipment spilling out the back. The bank was so small they probably had only one teller.

A short street behind Main had a two-door fire station and a clinic. Both looked more like storage buildings than emergency and rescue. The clinic had a five-foot sign that said OPEN 24 HOURS EXCEPT SUNDAY.

Half a mile down East Road was a big gas station. Charlotte thought of not bothering with it, but she decided she'd take the whole tour. Outside, the gas station had six vacant pumps. Inside there were restrooms, a lottery machine, and anything a traveler might need. Food, candy, hats, and stuffed animals.

As she walked down the back aisles, Charlotte was surprised to see canned goods, bread, wine, and even a long line of coolers with milk, ice cream, butter, and beer.

A man hovering near the 32-ounce drinks looked like he'd been living in the store for years. "Can I help you find something, sugar? I'm the owner of this place. I got anything you need. Got to drive thirty miles to find a Walmart to get something we don't carry. I've even got a hot bar up at the front. Got corn dogs already fried, barbecue, and tamales."

She thought about telling him that she was a vegetarian, but he really didn't look like he cared. Besides, she was a frequent backslider on her belief. Now and then she'd have to eat a cheeseburger with all the trimmings. She considered she was only half wrong; after all, the cow was a vegetarian.

Charlotte bought a Diet Coke and a small bag of popcorn. It was time to move along and find the house she'd bought from the town's only Realtor. As she headed off to first locate the school, she had to laugh. She must be crazy. She just uprooted her entire life, her career, and probably her sanity. For all she knew, everyone in this town was as crazy as the old man who'd just tried to sell her a day-old hot dog.

It was Miss McBride, the Realtor, who'd contacted her when she'd taken the job as the new high school English teacher. Miss McBride said she had the perfect house for Charlotte. Near school. Red door she couldn't miss. Furnished. Special price for teachers.

In the oil boom days of early Texas, school districts offered free or discounted housing to get teachers to come to isolated locations. Maybe Miss McBride found one still standing. Or maybe the house was so bad, the one Realtor in town always started there.

Charlotte slowed so she could find her new home. Third house from the school. Red door. After teaching at Texas A&M in College Station, one of the biggest universities in the U.S., this place seemed like a porta-potty.

But she couldn't stop smiling. She turned down West Road and saw a sign that announced the school zone. Behind the sign stood Crossroads's only K–12 school. Three stories of red brick and glass. But this town had something College Station didn't.

Peace, she thought.

The three-story school put her in mind of a mother hen with little houses around like chicks. A gym, an outdoor covered patio, a football field, and slides and swings for the younger grades. Bike racks for the middle grades and a parking lot full of more pickups than cars.

For years she'd taught English at the graduate level. The pace had been fast and exciting until one day she'd shattered and decided to take time to breathe. The truth was she'd been teetering on the brink of a breakdown for a while.

She'd started her teaching career at a little high school. She'd loved it but everyone had encouraged her to climb. She took summers of grad classes until she moved to a small college. Then a few years later A&M called. She was proud of the climb, but moving around left her with no friends, just colleagues.

Somehow, while she was following her career, she forgot about living her life.

Over the past five years, many of her Western Literature classes at A&M had been replaced with creative writing courses or film studies. Enrollment was low. The West was outdated and students didn't find it interesting.

She'd been forced to teach topics she had no interest in nor expertise. The stress of learning new areas of study had slowed her writing and her research, and in an effort to find a temporary escape, she'd taken a much needed sabbatical to reclaim her passion for the West. And Crossroads had seemed the perfect place for that.

Everything seemed to be moving in slow motion here. It would give her the time she needed to reset. Research, write, and maybe even help her relocate her love for higher education.

"If you knew how the story would end, would you read the book?" she whispered to herself. "Would you even start the path if you knew where the road would lead?" She looked up as if the answer might be just above her.

"I would," Charlotte said to her old black cat asleep in its crate. After all, she'd loved A&M before all of the changes. "I'll love the fight and growth, and the challenges will remind me I'm still alive."

Maybe she would suit up and battle again. Or would she turn another way? After all, there were four directions.

She passed the school windows decorated with a banner that

announced WE WELCOME GRADES FROM KINDERGARTEN TO SENIORS: GO WRANGLERS. Twice she circled before she found a small street called Campus Road.

Red door, three houses down from the school, with an old van parked out front. The Realtor hadn't lied.

The chubby young woman in her thirties climbing out of the van must be Miss McBride.

She had a name tag as big as her left breast. The moment she saw Charlotte, the only stranger in town, she started jumping up and down like a former cheerleader.

Three days ago, Charlotte had changed her life. First, she took the job as the high school's English teacher. Then she said yes to a chatty Realtor. House unseen. Now she was in the middle of nowhere, unsure of what she'd gotten herself into.

Miss McBride had claimed a dozen times she had the perfect house for Charlotte. In fact, she swore it was a miracle it had come open a week ago. The Realtor repeated it was a small cottage in need of paint, with a charming red door.

She added that the place also came cluttered with old furniture that she called "mid-fifties." No grass on the tiny yard, and a sidewalk made up of concrete crumbs. What looked like pumpkins growing in the abandoned flowerbeds.

Once Charlotte let her talk, McBride was like a book on tape. "It may not be the prettiest, but you must always think on the bright side, dear. The front yard could be props for Halloween decorations. Halloween is just around the corner. What a fun time to move into your new home."

Charlotte told her she didn't celebrate that holiday.

When McBride was silent, Charlotte thought she heard a sniff.

She tried to cheer up the Realtor by suggesting that it wasn't really a holiday.

Miss McBride rattled in her squeaky voice, "Everyone in

Crossroads celebrates and that makes it real. After all, it's on the calendar."

Charlotte thought about reminding her that St. Patrick's Day was also on the calendar, but Miss McBride didn't even pause to take a breath.

"Coach Biggers, our dearly departed teacher and coach, died last week, but he loved Halloween. He had his Dr. Seuss costume pressed yearly so he'd be ready. And, dear, don't you worry, he'd already bought his treats."

Miss McBride added, "He died of a heart attack, so he won't mind you passing the candy out." She raised her voice. "One piece per child, please. We don't go overboard on sweets. One of the PTA rules."

Charlotte held her smile in place and reminded herself that she'd moved here to start over. She could pass out some candy and pretend to enjoy the costumes.

Miss McBride continued. "Coach Biggers taught at the school for forty-five years. He's the only English teacher and coach anyone remembers. He was loved, funny, and dedicated, even left his house to the school to sell to his replacement. But the young girl who helped change over the deed to the house said most of the students thought he'd been dead for years, still standing in front of his blackboard. Can you imagine?"

Charlotte didn't like knowing that she was stepping inside a dead man's house. She hoped he was happy in the hereafter with no papers to grade. She preferred to think that they were both moving on.

Crossroads had one of the few openings in her field, so she had taken the job and the house for the price of the back taxes. How bad could it be? The high school needed someone fast to fill his shoes, so the house was a steal. Biggers had left all of his belongings for the next resident to clean up. But the part about keeping all the furniture seemed more a curse than a blessing.

After McBride handed her the key and left, Charlotte sat in the gravel driveway of the spooky little house, in her parked car loaded down with everything she owned in the trunk. For several minutes Charlotte just looked at the school a few lots down from the red door.

"This will work," she whispered to her cat. "I can walk to school every morning." She might even come home for lunch.

As the sun disappeared, Charlotte picked up her worn leather work bag, a purse almost big enough to fit her fat cat, and what she'd bought at the gas station. She squared her shoulders and marched up the three steps.

Charlotte stepped into the small living room that was exactly what she'd expected. A huge desk. Bookshelves on three walls. Worn rugs. An old box TV that probably stopped working a dozen years ago.

She walked through the four rooms, all the same size. The bedroom was the only room bare of old Biggers's personal things. Someone—maybe even Miss McBride—must have cleaned it. No clothes or sheets or pictures hanging around.

The kitchen cupboards were stuffed with canned goods. There was an ancient coffeepot and some old, chipped dishes. The bathroom could have been roomy enough, but the washer and dryer took up half the space.

Charlotte stared in the mirror over the sink and fought back a tear. She was tired, road-weary, and afraid. She looked more fifty-three than forty-three. She'd walked away from her colleagues, her job, and her home. Halfway through her life and here she was starting over.

She'd thought about telling everyone she was only leaving for a few years. But she'd hated all of it. Life had melted into Groundhog Day. Lectures, reading, eating alone, grading, meetings, more grading, and sleep.

She'd never stepped out of her routine. Her young dreams had faded away. She felt like she was on a merry-go-round, and she might change horses but she was still circling around.

Her life had become one old record that kept playing. All her studying and teaching and watching the same shows and listening to the same sermons and taking the same trail around the same park.

But her biggest fear was that she'd move to start over and make her new world exactly what her old life had been.

What if she couldn't change?

She stared at her reflection. "I will transform. This time I'll try to remember to live."

Chapter 3

Organizing a Life Amid Chaos

November

Staten Kirkland

All the horror of the past month had replayed in his dreams last night. Staten Kirkland stepped onto the porch of the little house his great-great-grandfather had built over a hundred years ago, trying to clear his head. He watched the sun come up as he waited for his coffee to cool down. Lately, the world seemed like one long day. There had been no weekends or time to even think. He just slept then woke up and got back to work.

He could imagine what life had been like before he was born. His mother pretending to want a rancher's life while she was pregnant with him. His father trying out politics in Austin with an eye for Capitol Hill.

The original plan was that both his grandfather and father would work the ranch together with J.R. running the place while Samuel was needed at the capital. Then when Samuel was home, Staten's grandparents would travel. Granny taught world history and she planned to see a bit of it.

Staten wished he could talk over the problems on the ranch with his gramps. He didn't want the old man to worry, but he was only nineteen. Too young to be in charge. Too young to grow up. Too young to turn into a man overnight.

As usual, his father was nowhere to be seen. No help at all. Too busy living his own life in his own world. Samuel never made it home except when he needed photos to prove he was a rancher. The capital's fast life and parties had roped him in.

Granny used to say that her son was always drawn to shiny things. That's why most of his ex-wives were platinum blondes.

The year Staten was born must have been a busy time. His father was the youngest state senator in Texas at thirty-five. At first, his mother stayed on the ranch and Samuel said he'd come home on weekends.

But it didn't work out. Staten took a swallow of his first coffee of the day as he remembered how Jake Longbow had described his mother. No extra words, just the facts. She was young, rich from birth, and bored. Ten years younger than Samuel. City girl who hated standing in the shadow of her husband. As she finished birthing Staten, she switched the baby to a bottle within three months, handed Staten to his grandmother, and headed to Austin. She wanted her share of the limelight.

Staten took another sip and remembered the rest. His mother never came home to the ranch or lived in the big house. His parents were always too busy to come back together, but somehow they managed separate vacations. Without him. They'd fly in to do photo shoots but his mother was just a lady who hugged him now and then. All he remembered of her was she had blond hair like the rest.

She divorced the senator a few months after he was reelected for his third term and never came back to pick up her son.

Then his father married again. Number two had darker hair

and a funny giggle that seemed to just bubble up like a burp. She built the big house and decorated it like a showroom for photo shoots. After his second mother left, it sat empty for five years as Staten learned to ride a horse and rope cattle in his grandparents' home.

Wife number three ignored Staten, which he didn't mind. She decided to change the big house too, but left when the remodel was finished. Granny said that wife forgot to come get him and take him to his dad. With her trips between Washington and Austin, then furniture buying in New York, Staten's young mind figured his third mom took a wrong turn somewhere.

After that his father seemed to form a pattern. Some he married, some he didn't. But no one ever moved into the big house.

It didn't matter. Staten and Jake just called them all "Miss Kitty" after the lady in *Gunsmoke*.

Staten tossed his cold coffee into the flower bed. His grandparents' little cottage was also meant to be their retirement home. It stood in the shadow of Samuel's big house built for show. But Staten always smiled because the morning sun shined on their small home and the open land. He loved living in the cottage. The people he loved lived there. From birth the cottage was his home.

Staten's girlfriend, Amalah, used to say they'd marry someday and fill the big house with children.

He agreed, but deep down his grandparents' cottage would always be home. Where love lived.

It had been over a month since the oldest Kirkland had been rushed to the clinic, but still things had not gone back to the way they were. No one on the ranch could accept that J.R. might die. How could the Double K run without Staten's grandfather stepping out at dawn yelling orders? Everyone still needed him.

Running his fingers through his hair, Staten realized he was in need of a cut and a shave, but that was the least of his problems. "It seems like a year since I came home," he said to no one. "How could it be only a little over a month since I drove a hundred miles an hour to get here? It feels like forever." He barked a laugh.

His hands had a few more scars now from hard work. His face was sunburned. His body ached.

He'd be looking like Gramps before Christmas. He was aging fast. The work around the place was never finished, and every night he sat with Gramps and talked until the old man fell asleep.

His grandfather had almost died a few short weeks ago. When Gramps came home, he was a shell of the man he'd been. Usually, Granny never spent money she could save, but she hired two nurses from Lubbock to help her take care of the old man. They slept in the big room downstairs from Monday to Friday and helped lighten Granny's load.

Staten's father never made it home from Austin, but his secretary sent flowers to the clinic. And Gramps's name made it in the newspaper, the *Austin American-Statesman*.

One line: SENATOR SAMUEL KIRKLAND'S FATHER HOSPITALIZED LAST WEEK.

It was a hell of a way to get more votes.

Staten noticed the three ex-wives didn't call, but the newest wife did send a gardener from Lubbock to replant the flowers in the bed at the front of the big ranch house. Time for more pictures, Staten thought.

Amalah called every night at ten. She talked about what was happening on campus, and he talked of how Gramps was doing. Every night he whispered, "Love you, Ama." And Amalah would say, "I love you, too. Come back to me. It's no fun at college without you."

"Soon," he answered, but with each day's passing he wondered when that day would come. Since the day he left campus Staten hadn't even opened a textbook.

Staten told her that no matter how early he got up or how

late he came in, the work on the ranch was never finished. He told his girl how he missed her, and she promised to come home every weekend she could. But there was always a football game, or she had to study, or the weather was bad.

Every night their talks grew shorter. He was tired. She had homework. He had to get up early or she had a test. Sometimes his grandfather had a hard night and Staten would take a shift sitting up with him. But as the weeks passed, he realized that he and Amalah had less to say. They loved one another but they were in two different worlds.

Amalah might not have grown up on a ranch, but she listened as he talked about things she didn't understand. And what hurt Staten the most was that she cried because he couldn't hold her.

They'd never been apart. He'd loved her for as long as he could remember. They'd planned for college. He couldn't make up his mind what he should major in, but Amalah knew from the first that she wanted to be a teacher and Staten's wife.

One night, as fall turned into winter, she mentioned he was far behind in his classes and he said slowly, "I don't think I'm coming back this semester. I'm still needed here."

He could hear her trying to hold back tears. He tried to comfort her. They would get together on weekends. He'd go back to Tech as soon as he could. She promised to come home when she had time, but she missed him and the crying continued. They both knew there were no weekends on a ranch. He had to work. Gramps and the ranch hung on every conversation. They'd be lucky to see each other once a month.

When he finally said goodbye, the "I love you" sounded hollow.

The truth was he hadn't had time to even think of her for days.

On the seventh Friday when Amalah couldn't come home, he stood tall and looked out into the night. The light from the little house glowed behind him and made his shadow stretch toward the big house.

All of the wives loathed the life out here; it was hard to be the center of attention when there's nobody around to be the crowd. What if Amalah hated it too? Staten was growing to love the ranch more every day. Something was changing as he took over. The land, Ransom Canyon, and even the rapids that turned silver with the falling leaves this time of year. The land was becoming a part of him. No. He was becoming part of the land.

Ready or not, Staten would hold the Double K together.

He looked back through the cottage window. Granny was laughing as she tried to shave Gramps. The old man watched her with love in his eyes.

His grandmother had met her love in Dallas. She wasn't raised on a farm or ranch, but they had lived out here for fifty years. Amalah would too. His Ama loved him; she'd stay with him. She'd never leave. She'd announced in the second grade they would marry someday and he'd agreed.

As Granny kissed her husband's bald head, Staten realized something. She didn't love this ranch; she loved her husband.

The thought made him smile. Maybe he and Amalah would be all right.

Chapter 4

Always Solitary

November 1991

Peggy May Warner

Peggy Warner climbed out of her ugly green Ford Pinto that was almost as old as she was. When she slammed the door closed, the handle came off as usual. At twenty-seven she thought she should have enough money to buy herself a new car or at least have a boyfriend to drive her around.

But no. She blamed it all on birth order. Peggy May was the baby in the family. She didn't get to go to college. The five other kids had drained their parents' savings before she got there. A few even begged to go to Europe after they graduated from high school and won out.

After all, they'd only used a little of Peggy's school savings, and she probably didn't want to go to college anyway. She was shy. The girl in the corner who forgot to go wild in her teens. Everyone in the family agreed that since she was reclusive, it was fine if she stayed home and read.

As the youngest she never got clothes with the tags still on. Hand-me-downs were good enough. She wasn't going anywhere anyway. Peggy was a homebody. They always said sweet Peggy wouldn't mind being left out. Someone had to stay home and feed the pigs and chickens.

But one thing did bother her. Her father had to call the names of all five siblings before he got to hers. She was "Hey you, kid" until she was ten. Then "Hey, missy" through her teens. Then began the roll call, and her name was always last.

About the time she thought of growing up and leaving the nest, her parents decided they were getting old. She couldn't leave home; she was needed.

Her folks announced they were tired of spending their money on their kids. By the time Peggy finished high school, Mom and Dad were saving for retirement. None of her kin thought she was smart enough to keep going. She'd be wasting money on more than a high school education.

With five older siblings and their mates, who were always around to tell her what to do, Peggy gave up thinking for herself. All of them thought their little sister was a bubble off of normal. They all agreed she needed to stay near home and with her family. One of her older sisters gave her a used computer and said the library would help Peggy take classes on every hobby she liked. Cooking. Quilting. Yoga. Speaking different languages. CPR.

Her oldest sister swore any of these classes would be more helpful than a college degree.

Before Peggy turned twenty, her role was set in the family. Peggy May Warner was the caretaker. She was the one who went to sit with great-grandmother in her last days—which lasted two years.

When her cousin broke a leg, Peggy went to take care of her four kids—for six months.

A sister's husband was deployed and her sister couldn't handle the twins and work all by herself. Peggy had to help. Another four months.

After that she stopped counting. She just kept a suitcase packed.

If anyone was moving, having surgeries, expecting a baby, or remodeling, Peggy was called in. Once the crisis was over, the family needed a long vacation while Peggy house-sat, fed the pets, and mowed the lawn.

When she first came everyone was excited. Then she fit in a corner. And after a few months, quiet Peggy became invisible. She rarely came out of her room if the family had company. Peggy would rather be alone than have to sit among people she didn't know.

She had over fifty relations, so someone always needed her. When she turned twenty she moved above the garage. Everyone agreed she didn't need an apartment. Usually when she returned from helping a relative, she spent the first few days tossing junk away that her mother thought she might want.

The family seemed to think Peggy was on vacation when she came back home between assignments. They'd laughed at her egg business she ran on Saturday at the farmers market. She always had fun but none of her kin ever had time to accompany her. At twenty-seven years old, plain, straight-haired, and no makeup, she figured in a few years she'd be truly invisible. She'd just float from house to house with no one talking to her.

Most of her kin forgot to pay her. After all, she was family. Or sometimes they'd pay her half the rate. Or worse, they'd pay her parents.

Her parents sometimes passed the money on to her, but not always. She still lived at home. She didn't really need to get paid.

But this cool fall afternoon Peggy stood beside her old car parked on the dirt road a few yards from the mostly forgotten family cemetery.

As usual she pushed her pity party aside while she pulled the shovel from the back seat. She used the shovel like Moses used his staff to get up the hill. There were jobs, like keeping up the cemetery, everyone assumed Peggy would do. After all, she didn't have a real job. So she was in charge of weeding the graves.

While she worked, she remembered the few dates she'd had. One of her brothers tried to match her up with his wife's cousin. The guy never stopped talking about himself or took the toothpick out of his mouth. She might have forgiven him, but every time he got near, he managed to brush against her chest. When he helped her with her coat. When he shook her hand as he leaned in to whisper "hello" like it was foreplay. When he pulled out her chair and patted her shoulder, his hand always went a bit low.

After she told her brother she wasn't interested in his wife's cousin, her sister-in-law was offended.

As Peggy made it up the hill on this cloudy day, she remembered the guy had apologized for bumping her breasts as their date ended, and then he'd brushed her blouse as if he planned to wipe his mistake away.

Peggy had jumped backward. "Excuse me, I have to go throw up."

Now she laughed at her fast thinking and the look on his face.

"Forget about that bad date," she whispered to the clouds. "I've got work to finish before it starts raining. What was I thinking, doing this on a cloudy day?"

She made it to the top of the graveyard, still talking to herself. "No one in the family has time to weed the community graves. They all have real lives."

The first cemetery was just outside Crossroads, and the

town paid her to keep it up. The small cemetery, called the Settlers' Rest, had dirt ruts rising above the county's only rapids that ran through Ransom Canyon.

This place was special. The first families lay among the trees overlooking Ransom Canyon. Four ranches met here. Four founding families and some cowboys, who worked on the land and wanted to be buried where only prairie spread beneath the sky, rested there.

Peggy started chopping weeds almost as tall as she was. All the weeds crowded around the gravestones as if protecting them. With each whack she politely said, "Sorry." Then she'd giggle. The day was perfect; the cloudy view was the best and she was alone.

Could this day get any better?

Near the top she stopped and smiled at the sun fighting to peep through the clouds. Looking down the hill at her work, she noticed there were several plots that had room for six graves, but the ground had never been broken. One lot not yet claimed by any of the Warner kin, though it was on the Warner fourth of the land set aside.

"This one must be mine," she announced. Hers alone, all hers.

She didn't want to be buried with others, with husbands and wives and children that were not hers. In death she wanted to have a place all her own.

She walked toward the empty space. It was perfect. Standing on the spot she felt at home. It might be fifty years before she was put to rest, but someday she'd be buried right here. If all her brothers and sisters got to pick their place, she should have one square too.

Peggy began to dig. Thanks to the rains, the ground gave easily, so she kept right on digging. It made no sense, but she wanted to dig a grave to try it out. She laid the shovel down and climbed in. She had to make sure it wasn't too short.

Covered with dirt, she scrambled back to ground level,

picked up the shovel and kept digging until the hole was two feet deep and just right from head to toe.

She climbed in again, lay in the hole and placed her hands on her chest. She looked up and saw perfect clouds. In the morning air, she could hear the rapids gurgling in the valley below. This one beautiful day, one place seemed made for her. When she died, this was where she wanted to rest forever. She closed her eyes thinking that she might never have a house of her own or time to herself, but she had a place to rest when her life was over.

Peggy was almost asleep in her paradise when she heard a horse.

Part of her dream, she thought. The jingle of spurs. The swish of leather. All at once the dream seemed real but she didn't want her fantasy to end.

Steps moved toward her and she sensed someone getting closer. The ground seemed to shift.

Be still, she thought. They might not notice her.

"Miss," a low voice whispered near as if he didn't want to wake her. "You okay?"

Peggy opened one eye. With the sun behind him, the man above was in shadow.

Low laughter floated between them. "Are you okay? I can see one beautiful blue eye looking up and hair the color of sunset. I hate to awake such a sleeping beauty."

For a wink she considered being afraid, then she realized she was the one acting crazy.

If anyone should be scared, it should be him. After all, who in their right mind would lie down in a two-feet-deep grave?

"I was just..." She couldn't think of anything that made sense. "I was just..." Her eyes filled with tears. Once he told this story in town, she'd have not just her family laughing, but the whole county would make fun of her.

He whispered as he sat near her, his long legs crossed and his worn hat pushed back.

"Stunning blue eyes shouldn't cry. That would be a crime," he said in a low tone.

"I was just measuring," she whispered. He probably thought she was nuts.

"That makes sense. It would be terrible if your feet hung out." Then he laughed as a chuckle burst out of her.

As she looked up at the cowboy, tears dropped off her chin.

He didn't say a word. He just pulled out his handkerchief and handed it to her. "Are you hurt, my sunshine lady?"

"No. I was just trying it out. I don't want to die. I just wanted to see the view from here."

To her surprise he spread out on the grass next to the hole she was in. He used his arms for a pillow and stared at the clouds.

"It's like the biggest canvas in the world. It is so peaceful out here. Quiet, cool."

Then the strangest thing happened: They began to talk. They saw shapes in the clouds and laughed about how one looked like Mickey Mouse and another looked like a dead rabbit with its tongue hanging out.

They were like two kids talking on bunkbeds. He made her laugh and they talked about their childhoods and future dreams.

After an hour, when rain threatened, he stood and bent down with both hands out. "Let me help you up, miss."

She saw the length of him. Tall. Thin. Tan hair that was not acquainted with a comb. Some might say he wasn't handsome but she saw kindness in his eyes and his laughter.

Without a word she stood, and he locked his big hands around her arms and gently lifted her out of the hole.

An inch away from him she could feel his warmth. "I don't even know your name and we practically had a date."

He looked down into her eyes, both clearly seeing each other. "I was hoping you were Peggy May Warner."

Peggy stepped back, surprised that he knew her.

The cowboy circled her waist to keep her from falling into her someday grave.

Words tumbled out as he settled her on solid ground. "I'm Duke Evans. I ride for the Double K, but you know all cowhands help out on other ranches when needed. I was riding fences this morning and thought I'd stop and eat my lunch up here."

When she didn't say a word, he continued. "Since you were cleaning the Warner plots, I assumed you were Peggy Warner. I've seen you at the library and a few times at the Saturday farmers market. You never noticed me but those blue eyes haunt my dreams. I didn't think I'd ever get to talk to you."

Peggy just stared. No one had ever said anything like that to her before.

When she still didn't speak, he tried again. "You're tall, Peggy Warner. You looked at my face, not the buttons on my chest, but you didn't talk to me. Shy?"

"Yes, I guess. I'm not usually around any people who aren't kin."

"Well, I don't want to be strangers." He offered his hand. "Hello, Peggy Warner."

She smiled as his palm covered hers. "Hello, Duke Evans."

His eyes never moved off her face. "Since this was an almost date, how about we have a real date tomorrow? We could go to dinner."

"I can't. I have to sit up with my cousin during the night. She's over nine months' pregnant. Lots of the family can stay with her in the day, but no one wants the night shift." Peggy felt like she might cry.

He stared at her and smiled as if he saw inside her. "How about we meet here at noon tomorrow? I like talking to you. We'll have a noon date. I'll even fill in your someday grave so we can have a picnic right here."

"I'll bring lunch," she said low, as if there might be someone trying to eavesdrop.

"A real date, blue eyes. Just me and you."

"Me and you." She whispered, "You mind if we add one small thing?"

"Name it."

She lowered her head as heat filled her cheeks. She couldn't look at him as she asked.

"Name it, Peggy."

She began to back up.

He didn't move. Just watched her as if watching a wounded animal.

She was ten feet away when she stopped and said, "This real date tomorrow ends with a kiss." She couldn't look at him. "Do people do that?"

The wind seemed to still as she waited.

He smiled. "Well, blue eyes, since I've already held your hand, I figure a kiss comes next." When he winked at her, they both laughed and nodded. It was a deal.

Chapter 5

Late November Wish

Friday

Staten Kirkland

Staten carried the dinner plates from his grandparents' bedroom toward the kitchen. Since the stroke, a new routine had formed with the three Kirklands in the little cottage. Staten tried to make it back to headquarters by dark. Granny didn't serve dinner until Staten was washed up and sitting on the left side of J.R.'s bed.

Lately he'd begun to call his grandfather by his initials like the ranch hands did. When Staten called him J.R., the old boss seemed to feel stronger, as if he were still running the spread. His gramps sometimes asked questions about what was happening in the pastures, or the numbers on stock prices and the chance of rain.

When Granny brought in dessert, she always smiled to hear ranch talk. It was almost as if things were back to how they'd been.

After her James got quiet, she'd collect the empty drinks and Staten would follow with the plates. The meals were almost normal except they sat around J.R.'s bed and the old cowboy came to dinner in his PJs, which he hated. Granny passed him pills now and then and always tried to get him to eat more. After dinner and the dishes were done, Staten and his grandfather would watch the news or football and Granny would knit.

Soon the old man would fall asleep. Staten would turn off the TV. Granny would kiss both her men, and Staten would step out of the room as she settled her husband for sleep. Most nights neither said a word. Granny and Gramps would just smile at each other as if both were silently saying, "Glad you're here with me."

As Staten did almost every night, he walked to the back porch of the cottage house that had always been his home. He saw nothing but the darkened land and a star-bright night sky. His first weeks back, he'd silently cried as if the world was too heavy on his shoulders. He knew he couldn't handle the load. Maybe at thirty, maybe at twenty-five, but not at nineteen. This was not where he should be. He wanted to go back to Texas Tech and to Amalah and the new life he'd barely gotten started.

People talked of their college days or Army years or their carefree summers when they explored and learned who they were, but somehow, in the blink of an eye, life was pushed forward by ten or twenty years. He worried about the weather and getting back before dark. Going into town for supplies and mail were now the highlights of his day.

Silent tears fell those first days as he stood every night in the midnight cold. But as weeks slowly passed, his feelings had numbed as he looked out on the open prairie.

Most nights he didn't think of anything; he was too tired. Or sometimes he made mental notes on what had to be done tomorrow.

Other times it seemed he could hear his grandfather whisper in his ear, "If a hand doesn't do something right, don't fire him; teach him." Or, "Don't order a man to do anything that you wouldn't do yourself."

Tonight, he stared up at the sky wishing life would slow down.

Suddenly the overgrown sage by the porch brushed his jeans, and he saw a shadow moving at the corner of the house. In a breath he stopped drifting in his mind and stiffened like a hunting dog on point.

Staten reached for his Colt that had been near all day, but it was gone. When he'd stepped inside before dinner, he'd taken it off along with his chaps and hat. Granny's rule.

The shadow moved closer.

In the two months he'd been home, he'd grown rock solid from constant work. The first one to saddle up and the last to quit. Even from the beginning, he pulled his share and more. He had to. It was the job of the one in the supervisor role, and on the Double K it was always a Kirkland. By the second week the men were calling him "Boss."

Whatever came around the corner, Staten would stand his ground. He took in air and waited. Reason told him one of his men would not be sneaking around, and a stranger on the Double K was trespassing.

The shadow seemed to wither back.

Staten took the two steps off the porch in one bound. "Who's there?"

He was about to charge when the shadow flew toward him crying his name. "Staten!"

He caught her a second before he realized it was his Amalah. His girl. His love.

His arms wrapped around her, and for a moment he just

held on hard, too tight. Inhaling the scent of her while her dark wavy hair flew out around her like a cape as he swung her around.

Amalah laughed and squealed then started kicking and wiggling. "Put me down, Staten. I can't breathe."

He didn't put her down. He didn't want to let her go. He couldn't. This was the only great dream he'd had in months. The only wish that had kept him going.

She started kissing him, her lips brushing over his neck, his cheeks, then finally meeting his. He let her feet touch the ground, and his hands plowed through her hair, then moved down her body that he knew so well. The memory of every day they'd been together floated around them.

They'd held hands in the third grade when no one was looking. He'd snuck a kiss in the fourth grade a few times. Mostly pecks on the cheek and then a kiss on the lips that ended in nervous laughter. By the time they were in the seventh grade they'd gotten to talk on the phone every night.

Granny's only advice about love was, "Go slow and enjoy every step. Don't fall in love; grow into it."

By the eighth grade, Amalah cooked dinner with Granny on weekends now and then, and Amalah often traveled with Staten and Gramps to stock shows and rodeos. Sometimes they even went to a fair in Amarillo or Dallas. Often, she'd invite him over to her house to watch a movie. And in high school, as soon as he got his driver's license, Saturday was date night.

Everyone knew they'd someday marry. They held a piece of each other already. They were meant to be together.

Staten had believed it, too, but now, for the first time ever, he wasn't so sure. His grandfather's stroke had changed more than just one life.

October and November had seemed like years without her, but it must have flown by for Amalah because she never had time to drive to Crossroads. He tried not to let it upset him.

When Staten left, she'd had to readjust her life just as much as he had.

The first few weeks after he'd left, Amalah had cried for him and wished she was home. But by the time the cold wind moved in, they talked of why she was too busy to make it back. When Thanksgiving came, her mother took her to Dallas for a big family reunion. No chance to make it to Staten.

He tried to understand, but he was too hurt. They'd never missed a holiday together. They'd never been apart for so long.

After that, Amalah only called every other night and neither of them seemed to have much to say. To pass the time, Staten worked harder, and sometimes when he had an hour alone, he rode the fence line as if looking for trouble.

But he knew the trouble was within him. He was starting to not care about anything outside of his world, outside of the ranch. He didn't have time to. The proof was that he had stopped counting the days before Christmas break and her return. And now guilt was setting in.

He wanted to talk about how he felt, but all he could do was hold her now. He could feel her heart beating against his. He felt whole again. Finally, she was in his arms. Maybe with her here, all his worries would just go away. Maybe they'd go back to how they used to be. Maybe everything would work out after all.

Wrapped in the blanket that always lay on the porch swing, they held each other. They traded sweet, slow kisses with hushed small talk. She told him all about her life at college. The football games and the dances and a hundred other things to do and learn. The plays, the protests, the parties that lasted all night.

He talked about what his life had become, listing what he'd been doing. Herding cattle, pulling a newborn calf by himself. Breaking up a brawl in the bunkhouse when two hands were drunk. Fighting a grass fire for three hours when it jumped the county road onto the Double K.

He told her the details. A fireman who'd played football with Staten last fall had stood beside him that night. As they fought flames, the new fireman never stopped yelling, teaching the rancher how to fight.

As fire melted to smoke, two men turned into boys for a moment as they yelled and cheered. No game this time, but they'd won.

As the night settled around them, Amalah leaned her head on his shoulder and closed her eyes. He realized she wasn't listening, but she was smiling. She didn't care about the fire or the cattle. But he knew she was happy; maybe because they were finally back together.

To be honest he didn't care about what was going on at campus a hundred miles away. She'd talked about people he didn't know and told him everyone at Texas Tech was so much more interesting than the people in Crossroads. She'd said, "Here they act like wild kids but at Tech they talk or debate about important things like world hunger."

Staten used one foot to swing them slowly as Amalah began to doze. Facts began to wash up on the shore of his mind. He couldn't remember a time he didn't love her. Snuggled against his side, she felt the same but something had shifted. She'd changed somehow and so had he.

He slowed the swing, running his fingers along her arm as if to prove she was really there. For the first time in his life, he wondered if they truly belonged together. Both were morphing into different people. Worrying about different things. Living different lives. Maybe she didn't belong on the ranch, even though that's where he did belong. Could she ever be happy here?

Staten could feel the doubt all the way to his heart even if his brain argued. If they stayed on the Double K, he couldn't offer her all the things she'd learned to love about Tech.

He kissed her forehead. "I love you forever and forever. I've been dying to hold you since I left."

She'd always been his gal. Somehow they'd get through this.

"Me too," she whispered, snuggling closer to his side.

As he moved in for a long kiss, she lifted a finger and stopped him. "I'm not staying the weekend though. I have to leave early tomorrow morning to get back to campus. I have a study group for finals. I can't miss it."

Staten didn't say a word. He just kissed her finger and let the swing move them slowly as she drifted to sleep. He couldn't feel her heart beating against his anymore and its absence was deafening. Somehow it felt like she'd already left.

He didn't let a tear fall. He was too old to cry over something like this. He didn't have time to be upset. Amalah was leaving in the morning, and he'd be getting back to work. They both had lives to get back to.

The night grew colder but he didn't wake her. Staten just pulled her closer to his side. He wished there was someone who would put out the fire burning inside him. He wished Amalah could. But she only seemed to make it rage hotter. In one semester he'd become dumb, not interesting, and talked about nothing.

Part of him wanted to go back with her to Lubbock. They'd planned for college together for years. Staten was the one who'd wanted them to go to Tech. He'd told her about how much fun it would be. Her dream was to be a teacher, and he figured he'd end up studying land management or something in agriculture.

But a bigger part of him longed for Amalah to come back home to him and stay. But if she did, she'd be giving up her dreams. She'd seen a bigger world and she might not want to settle here with him now. He couldn't take her dream away. He wanted her to be happy as much as he wanted to be with her.

But he was still needed here. As much as he wanted to go back to Tech with his girl, he had to stay. And she had to go back to

Lubbock. There was only one way right now, and it was breaking both their hearts.

As dawn rose, he was into "what-ifs." Maybe his gramps would get better soon. Maybe he could go back with her in January to start the new semester. Maybe his father would come home and help out. Maybe Amalah would decide to drop out and stay here with him.

Staten could almost see sheets of paper falling on the porch, each with a huge NO written in blood.

He knew there was only one choice. The right one. Right for her and right for the ranch. What was right for him would have to wait.

He lay his rough hand over hers. "I love you," came out with a frosty breath.

She pulled her hand away in her sleep and slipped it under the blanket.

Staten closed his eyes and thought only of the past as he realized they might not have a future.

Chapter 6

A Dreamer

Peggy Warner

All night Peggy sat in an old, uncomfortable rocker, half covered with one of the kids' blankets she borrowed from her cousins for warmth. Ashley-Lynn, in the bed five feet away, groaned every time she moved.

Peggy had sat with her before, during labor with her previous child. She remembered last time her cousin was pregnant, Ashley-Lynn insisted she needed to go to the hospital a hundred miles away in Lubbock. Three times she and her husband Fred had loaded up in the car and driven to the hospital because her cousin didn't want to deliver in the tiny clinic in Crossroads. False labor the first three times. On the fourth try, the baby finally arrived.

For this baby, her husband, sleeping on the couch tonight, swore he wasn't starting the car until he saw the baby crown.

Peggy didn't interfere with the couple's fights that seemed never-ending.

Her job was to get the mom-to-be, who was on bedrest, whatever she wanted during the night. Fresh water every hour, which she rarely drank. A towel after she spilled most of the water. Crackers for her indigestion. Pillows to prop up her huge belly just right. Sometimes Ashley-Lynn would demand that she turn the heater up or turn the heater down. Or the worst order, "Wake Fred."

Every night, Ashley-Lynn swore the baby was coming and Peggy would make sure they'd packed everything they'd need at the hospital. She'd wake Fred, and he'd tell the crazy, round woman she'd have to have the baby at the clinic in Crossroads. He wasn't driving a hundred miles in the middle of the night when there was a perfectly good hospital bed five minutes away.

Then the couple would wrestle Ashley's robe and slippers on and sit on the couch to watch TV until her water broke. After all, the clinic was almost within walking distance. They planned to leave the almost eighteen-month-old and the four-year-old with Peggy. They knew she wouldn't mind.

Tonight, Peggy would mind. "Actually, I can't stay here after nine, Ashley." She couldn't say she had a lunch date, so she said, "I will have been up twenty-four hours."

"So! I haven't slept for weeks." Ashley-Lynn's voice was somewhere between a whine and a snap. "You're not even making a baby. You can't be that tired."

"Come, Ashley," Fred said. "Peggy needs sleep too. Besides, both our mothers will be here around eight to get set up for the baby shower."

As Ashley-Lynn groaned again, Peggy whispered, "I'll leave when your mom gets here. I want to go home before the party starts."

Ashley-Lynn pouted, but then conceded, "Well, Mom will be telling everyone what to do the moment she walks in. Maybe you're right to leave when she gets here!"

Peggy rose from her chair. "It's been an hour. I forgot your fresh water. I'll get it right now." She was gone before Ashley-Lynn could say another word or hatch another plot.

Once she was in the kitchen, Peggy took her time filling a cup and making sure everything was in place.

By the time she went back to the living room, Ashley had waddled to the bed and fallen asleep. Another false labor alarm. No baby tonight.

Peggy sighed. She'd be back again tomorrow night. She settled back under her too-small blanket and waited for her aunt to show up and take over.

She'd gather up her things, go home to sleep an hour or two, get dressed, and then drive out to the cemetery for her first real date with Duke Evans.

For the first time in her life she didn't care about what the family wanted her to do; nothing was going to stop Peggy today. She had a real date. With a nice guy. For one moment in her life she was going to live for herself, and she might just go wild.

"Almost sunup," she whispered for the third time.

Fred called from the living room that his mother-in-law was stopping on the way to pick up a few things. "You don't mind waiting, Peggy, do you?"

Peggy watched the clock move past eight. Fifteen more minutes passed. Half an hour. Ten to nine.

The front door creaked open and Peggy's Auntie Ruth bumped her way in, making so much noise she woke Fred on the couch and one of the kids. Auntie Ruth called out, "Grandmom is here. Time to wake up."

Peggy stood, folded her tiny blanket, picked up her water, and looked around to make sure all was in place.

She was ready to leave when her aunt reached the bedroom. Ruth walked right past Peggy and tapped Ashley awake. "I'm here, my girl, and it's about time. This place is a mess. How do you two make such a clutter when all you have to do is sleep all night?"

Peggy was almost to the front door when Auntie yelled through the house, "Don't take a donut from the bakery box I set on the counter, Peggy. I just bought enough for the party. All the kin are coming over to wish Ashley-Lynn well. That baby is coming today. I can feel it in my bones."

The donuts. Peggy loosened her hold of the doorknob, walked back three steps to the counter and wrapped two donuts in a paper towel.

A minute later she was running to her car giggling. She was free and she had a date. And best of all she was a donut bandit. She'd have something to talk about with her cowboy.

He might think she was too wild for him.

Peggy drove over the speed limit just to prove she was going crazy. Then she pulled beside her parents' house and took her garage apartment steps two at a time.

She was too excited to sleep, so she took a shower, changed her clothes, and now and then stopped and thought about his gray eyes. He saw her, she decided. He really saw her.

Peggy packed a lunch. Nothing fancy. In her little garage apartment, she didn't have much. She didn't have enough time to go shopping, and she didn't dare go into her parents' house. They'd ask a hundred questions, or worse, they'd have a list of chores for her to do this morning.

Peggy slipped out feeling like a thief in the night.

She'd parked beside the garage just right so no one in the house would see her drive off. She had told her dad yesterday that she was going to have lunch with friends in town this week. Her dad never bothered to ask any questions, but she hoped he remembered.

As Peggy drove toward the cemetery, she practiced what she'd say to Duke.

But when she got to the hill, no one was there. She didn't see a person for miles. No cowboy.

Peggy pushed her bottom lip out like a child and tried not to say aloud, "Not again." In the school play she was the stand-in who never got on stage. She almost won the lottery once but she was off by one number. Her date to the prom got sick, and a hundred other things that almost happened. She almost got into the University of Texas. She almost got a job she really wanted, but her parents said Dallas was too far away from home.

Sitting down on the damp grass, she didn't despair. She could almost hear her father say, "Look, Peggy, when someone has a loss, it does make you stronger. No one gets everything they want."

She straightened like a wooden soldier. Tall. Stoic. "Another time," she sighed. But Peggy no longer believed in waiting. If he didn't come, it was his loss. She would enjoy herself anyway.

She walked to the old graves at the top where the oaks shaded the ground and the rapids babbled in the distance. She spread out a small tablecloth. Set out two sandwiches, two bottles of water, a small bag of chips, and two donuts.

The day was warm for November and no wind for a change. Lying on a wool blanket, she covered her legs with her coat. For just a few minutes she wanted to look at the clouds like they'd done the last time.

It crossed her mind that she might have dreamed her cowboy. Real or fantasy, she closed her eyes and dreamed of him again. He was kind. She remembered that he looked at her as if she was special. No one had ever looked at her as he did.

He'd stared like he saw the beauty in her.

Yesterday, she'd first thought he was teasing her, but as time went on, she recognized the honesty in his eyes. All her life it seemed she'd always been the plant, picture, or unseen ornament in the room, but she remembered that it had seemed she was all he saw.

"He was real," she said.

He'd told her, in a shy way, about growing up twenty miles

away. Duke was five years older than she was. His father had been the postman until he retired. He had two sisters and a brother. All married.

He said he'd ridden in the local rodeos in his teens and twenties, and he remembered her brothers riding too.

She laughed and told him her brothers' wives made them stop as soon as kids came along.

She remembered Duke talked slow and low. Within an hour of the first meeting, Peggy felt like they were old friends. Like she'd known him forever.

"He was real," she whispered.

Chapter 7

Teardrop Dawn

Saturday

Staten Kirkland

Staten hadn't closed his eyes all night. He slowly rocked the swing on the porch and listened to the darkness as Amalah slept against his shoulder. By dawn he hadn't figured anything out. It made no sense that a hundred miles could break Amalah and him apart. They knew they were in love. The forever kind of love. He wanted no one but her and he also knew she'd do anything for him. But neither wanted the other to give up their goals.

He didn't want Amalah to give her life at Tech away, and he had to stay here on the ranch. She loved this time of her life. He couldn't ask her to give it all up just because he was unhappy with his. Lately the only tranquilizer for his sorrow was work.

These days he told himself not to stop until he was too tired to think. From dawn until dusk all he thought of was the ranch.

Staten remembered stories of the first Kirkland in Texas, James Randall Kirkland. Staten's great-great-grandfather had ridden on horseback after the Civil War with only his father's broken watch, a horse, enough money to buy land, and a dream.

The first Kirkland traded his watch to the Natives for his wife, Millie. Then he bought land in the middle of Nowhere, Texas, and went to work building a ranch that would last for generations.

Staten didn't have it so bad, he said to himself. Amalah would be home again for break soon, and in the spring his grandfather might be better. And Staten could go back to Lubbock. He could go to college again. He could live his life with his girl like they'd always planned. Even if he lost a semester, he could make it up in the summer.

As the sun crawled up to meet the clouds, he kept thinking and worrying. There were too many ifs. Staten didn't know anything anymore. It seemed every day was a maybe.

Every minute he was more of a rancher and less of the kid he used to be. He was changing. He'd put on ten pounds of muscle. And his priorities had shifted. He now worried about things he'd never thought about. Right now, with Amalah next to him, Staten was organizing what he needed to do on the ranch today.

When he heard his grandmother starting breakfast, he woke Amalah with a kiss, soft and sweet, trying to memorize the feel of her lips. "Good morning."

She yawned, glanced at her watch and jumped out of the swing, running off the porch without looking at him. "Sorry, Staten. I'm late. I have to get back. I have so much to do at Tech today."

She was leaving already? She didn't even have time for breakfast?

He walked behind her to her car, trying to think of something that might make her stay a few minutes more. But nothing came to mind, and he knew he had a full day of work ahead of him too.

Amalah swung around, almost bumping into him as she remembered she'd forgotten something. Staten.

Then she smiled, love shining in her eyes, and Staten's world settled. For a moment they were like they had been before. She stepped on the running board of her Mustang so she'd be almost as tall as he was.

She leaned toward him, inviting him to close the distance. The kiss was short and sweet with little passion. Staten told himself that was all right. After all, Granny could see them from the kitchen window.

Amalah giggled and kissed him one last time on the cheek.

"Come back next weekend," he said so low he doubted she'd heard his wish.

For a blink he saw hesitation in her honest eyes. "I'll try."

They both knew she was lying.

He closed her door and stepped backward. She'd always smiled when she left or looked back to give him a sad puppy glance, or sometimes she'd make a funny face.

But, this time, she didn't look back to him.

Staten watched until she disappeared from sight. He wasn't hurt. He was just numb. Somehow, he seemed older. She'd told him all the fun things she'd do today, and his afternoon could be wrapped up in one word: work.

He turned back to the little house. He didn't bother to change out of yesterday's clothes. They were wrinkled now but he'd be dirty in an hour anyway. If he had time to come in for lunch, he'd change before he made the trip to town.

One day last week the postman told him he smelled like cow snot.

Staten didn't argue. He just smiled and walked out of the post office.

The postman had yelled after him, "Hope I see you before I smell you tomorrow."

After Staten put on his chaps, gun belt, and hat, Granny handed him a cup of coffee. "How's Amalah?"

"Busy." He kissed her cheek. "I got a long day but I'll try to be in before dark."

She patted him on his shoulder. "Don't overdo it. And make sure you eat."

"Granny, I'm a man."

She closed her fists on her hips and looked up at him. "You may be a man and the boss on the spread, but Granny outranks all."

Staten laughed and leaned down to kiss her graying hair. "Yes, ma'am."

He added what he always said as he walked out: "Remember, if no one is around and J.R. has trouble, shoot off three shots and everyone on the ranch will be riding full out to y'all."

"Of course I know."

When Staten looked back, Granny was already headed to the bedroom with Gramps's breakfast. He walked to the bunkhouse to eat with the men like he did most mornings, going over his list of what had to be done.

Halfway across the yard, Jake Longbow caught up with Staten and fell in beside him. "Morning, Boss."

"Why don't you call me by my name anymore?" Staten said in a hard tone. "You have known me all my life."

He wasn't ready to be the boss. He needed more time.

Jake straightened and announced, "You are the boss. When a man does the work of the boss, he deserves the title."

"But I'm only nineteen. You know a lot more than I do."

Jake answered, "You'll age, and I bet in five years you'll be the best boss around."

As Staten saddled up for the day, his mind whirled with thoughts of Amalah. He loved that she'd driven out to see him, but the truth was her quick visit had left a gaping hole in his chest that neither of them could fill.

He threw himself into his work, roping twice as many cattle. Riding out to check the farthest fence line of the north pasture. Double counting the new stock and checking all the inventory. When the hands paused for lunch, Staten kept on working.

He didn't want to think about the future or even remember the past. He didn't want to worry about how everything was changing. He just wanted to stay numb. Not feel a thing.

When he got back to the cottage, his body ached but he was too tired to think. He contemplated calling Quinn O'Grady. He knew she was going through something, and she seemed just as alone as he did. She might be half a country away in New York, but she'd always been his good friend.

His grandparents were both napping on the couch. He watched them as he ate. To him, these two were his only parents. The only people who mattered right now. Granny always made him clean his plate, and J.R. would discipline him when Staten acted up.

The rules were plain and Staten followed them. He would do anything for them. They loved him and he loved them.

When he stood to put his plate in the sink, Granny had woken up and was looking at him with sorrow clouding her eyes. "I'm sorry you're having to deal with so much so fast. I know you're missing out on being young and going to college."

"All the football and parties and stuff don't really matter. In truth, what I'm learning here every day is fun and probably more helpful in life." He was surprised that he believed his words.

"But it's not what you want."

"I just want Amalah. I miss our talks. Knowing about everything she's doing and thinking. For almost every day of our lives, we were close. We could finish each other's thoughts.

Did everything together. Now she's learning new things, living a different life, and I'm becoming an expert in cattle. I know it's important for the ranch, but no one wants to talk about it. It's like we're part of two different worlds."

His heart squeezed hard as he finally said what he'd been keeping inside for weeks.

"Try not to worry, son. A little space won't break you two if you're meant to be together. Life is full of difficulties and the couples who stick out the hard times are the ones who last." She looked to J.R. with a soft smile. "Just look at me and your gramps."

Staten knew she was right. He and Amalah would find a way to work everything out. They wanted to be together, and they would be again someday.

But he couldn't just sit around and wait. And he couldn't ask Amalah to wait either. He needed to do something now. He always felt better when he was in action. Moving toward a goal.

"If I could learn just one subject. It didn't seem important when I was at college for a few weeks but now, I think I'd listen," he thought out loud.

"I can't help you with that, son. I taught high school and I'm pretty sure you've got that done." Granny put his big hand in both hers. "You'll catch up. Don't worry. Nothing lasts forever. Things usually work out the way they are meant to."

He attempted a smile. That was the problem. Staten wanted him and Amalah to last forever.

Chapter 8

Wide Awake

Saturday

Peggy Warner

A crow cried overhead, startling Peggy awake. For a moment she didn't want to open her eyes. She let the warm sun lay over her like a blanket. The wind whispered through her hair and she could hear the oak tree's branches dancing above her.

Then a hand moved along her arm. "Sleep," a deep, low voice whispered in her ear. "I'll watch over you. That seems my new job."

Peggy opened one eye and found Duke Evans smiling at her. His gray eyes melted into her with what looked like real affection. As she rose to her elbows, she realized she'd been using his knee for a pillow and his hand rested on her shoulder.

No one but her kin had ever touched her, but with him it felt natural. Safe. Sweet.

"I'm sorry." She sat up, regretting the loss of his touch. "I didn't sleep much last night."

"Don't apologize; I liked watching you sleep. You are a real-life sleeping beauty." He moved her sunshine hair behind her ear, his fingers brushing her face. "Strange, I think I feel all is calm in the world when I'm near you. Would you mind if I claim that kiss you promised? Once you find out I ate both donuts you might be mad."

She couldn't think of what to say. She just laughed.

Her cowboy leaned closer to her and the breath caught in her throat.

Looking into his gray eyes, she wanted to tell him how long she'd waited to be kissed. She instead heard herself whisper, "I've been waiting for you."

Duke's eyes widened in surprise and then melted into something sweeter. Maybe he'd had his share of *almosts* too?

He lifted her head in his hand and slowly leaned down to meet her. His lips touched hers lightly and her heart fluttered. As he straightened, the corner of his mouth shifted to a soft smile.

It wasn't enough. For the first time in her life, Peggy knew what she wanted and she asked for it. "More, please."

Duke laughed and lifted her into his lap, pulling her against his chest. This time she met him in the middle, touching her lips to his as heat washed through her. The second kiss came daring. His hand cupped the back of her head, his fingers twisting in her hair as if he'd waited for this as long as she had.

Then he pulled away as if he'd been too bold.

As she caught her breath, she saw a question in his eyes. It seemed neither one of them had a roadmap on this new journey, but he continued to hold her close. And she loved the feel of his arms wrapped around her.

Duke might be unsure, but for once Peggy knew exactly what she wanted. She wouldn't back away from this adventure.

Her hand shook as she raised it to cup his cheek. "More, please," she whispered again.

He laughed. His third kiss came tender and longer. Their mouths moved together in a sweet dance as he taught her to kiss and showed her how much he felt.

She didn't know how much time had passed. It could have been hours or mere minutes. But, when they finally broke apart, he kept her on his knee and held her close against him. It was exactly where Peggy wanted to be.

He kissed her head, then spoke low as if afraid to disturb those laid to rest. "I've been wanting to kiss you since you left yesterday. I'm sorry I couldn't get here on time, but I loved seeing you wait for me. I wanted to wake you but I couldn't. We were alone. No one else around. You looked so beautiful. A perfect moment."

One tear drifted down her cheek to land on his blue checkered shirt. He must count in moments as she sometimes did. Not minutes or hours but only moments. They both were still, fearing if they moved, the magic would disappear.

Peggy leaned back, his arms still circling her waist, and put her hands on either side of his face. She kissed him lightly. "I feel like I've known you forever."

He held her so close their breathing joined. "I have the same feeling. It's going to be grand knowing you."

She shifted to the picnic blanket and passed him the lunch she'd packed. They laughed as they ate and told stories about growing up. Duke kept his hand on her knee and never stopped touching her. He wasn't bold, but gentle.

As the sun drifted behind the clouds, he stood and offered his hand. They walked down to the edge of the graves, then they ran down the hill to the rapids. By the time they reached the bottom, they were both laughing and gasping for air.

"I feel like a kid again." He picked up a rock and skipped it, as if proving his point.

"Me too. We're stealing time. I'll never forget this day."

"Me either. If I have this one afternoon with you or hundreds, I'll tuck each one deep inside me to keep forever. I'll always have this memory of a pretty girl walking with me to the water's edge."

They strolled hand in hand along the river, trading stories about childhood and dreams they thought were long gone.

"Tell me something you've never told anyone," Duke said. "I want to know everything about you."

She didn't know where to start, so she just said the first thing that popped into her head. She tiptoed near the splashing water. "If I ever killed myself, I'd jump in the rapids because I can't swim. I'd be gobbled up. But at least I would die with water singing to me."

He told her that when he saw his first colt born, he went behind the barn and threw up. "The other hands laughed at me and I started swinging. I hit a few, but not hard. They kept laughing and I kept swinging until Mr. Kirkland stepped into the fight and swung once. I tumbled like a tree falling in the woods, but I heard J.R. say, 'No fighting during work.'

"When my black eye finally opened, I asked the old man why he hit me. Kirkland said he wanted me to remember the rule."

She laughed, then covered her mouth.

With a big hand he gently pulled away her fingers. "Don't hide your laughter. It's perfect." Then he opened her hand and kissed her palm. "Keep this kiss to take home."

She let herself smile. She couldn't stop it from spreading across her face anyway. No one had encouraged her to laugh before. She closed her fist, wishing she could put the kiss in her pocket to keep forever.

They stood by the water, both sharing things they'd never told anyone. Then when both were silent, the river swallowed their secrets.

The wind brushed against her and she shivered. Without a word he put his arm around her and pulled her close under his coat. As his heart beat against her cheek, she felt as if her luck had just changed. She would never forget this day. Or this man. Or his kiss. If she never had another date, she'd cherish this time forever.

As he pulled her closer, she saw the same joy in his eyes that she felt. Some girls might think he was too tall, too thin, too plain, too shy, but to her he was perfect. He was kind and thoughtful. He saw her as no one ever had. And she saw him.

He thought she was someone to cherish. When he kissed her nose she giggled, and Peggy swore so did the rapids. She didn't say a word because his lips were moving to her mouth.

Her heart raced as the kiss grew deeper. She circled his neck with her arms as she realized a new dream. She wanted him close. Always.

She broke the kiss and whispered, "I think you're mine."

"No," he said. "You are mine. Maybe I've been trying to find you all my life."

"I don't think it happens so fast."

He lifted her off the ground and said, "What if it did? I think we've been waiting long enough, Peggy. Don't you?"

Before she could answer, he continued in a rush, "I know there is so much you don't know about me. I spent a night in jail once for being drunk. I own a truck outright, but I don't own a car. I work for the Kirklands, and Jake, the foreman, says I know enough to hire on as a foreman on any spread around."

"Is that what you want to do?" she asked as she grinned, because that was more words than he'd ever said before all at once.

"Maybe. Someday I'd like to go back to my folks' place. It's small but it's quiet. My dad used to play around making belts and chaps. He was good at making them but he never got into selling them. Gave most of them away." He smiled down at her. "I guess it's not much of a dream."

"I think it's grand."

"Well, now I got a problem. Since I found you in a grave I started on another goal."

"What's that?"

"Kissing you every time I see you. One kiss today and I'm addicted."

Before she could answer, he kissed her again. Hard this time, and long.

Then suddenly he pulled away. "I'm sorry. I didn't mean to kiss you full out."

She fisted her hands in his shirt, looked right at him and said, "Again. We've waited long enough, remember?"

His words were brushing her lips. "I'll never hesitate with that order. Will you let me take you out? I don't care where we go, as long as you're with me."

"Oh," she said, taken aback. "I don't know." She took a step away. They were no longer touching and she was surprised how much she felt his absence. "I can't really go *out* with you. I'd like to but I can't. I . . ."

He hesitated, his expression becoming guarded. He crossed his arms over his chest. "You got a husband somewhere? One no one knows about?"

How could she tell him that she had no time for herself? That she wasn't really her own person. Suddenly she remembered she didn't have a job, or education . . . or a life of her own. She'd basically had to sneak away to meet him today.

Yesterday had never happened before. She didn't know what to do next. Or how to do it.

Duke straightened and seemed to turn into stone. No smile.

His lips a thin, hard line. "I get it that you don't want to go in public with me. I know I'm worth nothing. It's fine."

He turned toward his horse. "I like you, Peggy. A lot. But I can't be with someone who's too embarrassed to be seen with me."

She didn't know what was happening. Her cowboy was walking away.

How to explain her almost-life to him? That she still lived over her parents' garage and did everything the family asked her to?

She swiped at the tears filling her eyes. "Why are you leaving?"

"I don't own a ranch or drive a nice car, I'm not asking you to marry me. I just wanted to go out sometime."

He grabbed his reins again. Ready to bolt.

She knew in a second, he'd be gone. For once in her life, she had to talk before it was too late. She had to say what she really meant, not just what others wanted to hear. "I've never had a real date. I don't know how to do this. I've never lived completely alone or with a roommate. I've never left home. I've always been in my mother's shadow. I've never had time for my own life. Or done what I wanted."

He looked like he didn't believe her. Her face was probably pale. She couldn't tell if she was going to faint or run. "I don't know how to do this."

For a moment it seemed the world stopped moving. She didn't speak. She'd said all she could.

Duke moved away from the horse and approached her. The anger was gone, but he didn't look happy.

"Never?" he said so low she barely heard him.

She hung her head as embarrassment swept over her. "I'm twenty-seven. There was one guy that kept touching on me but that wasn't a date. That was a setup. In five minutes I knew I didn't want to talk to him, but he kept talking to me and touching me." She chanced a glance at him. "I wanted to date but the time wasn't right, or he wasn't right. I'm shy and it's not always easy for me to talk to people outside of my kin."

"You didn't seem so shy yesterday. You told me I had to kiss you if I came back."

She met his stare. "You were different. We talked and you were nice. I wasn't sure you would kiss me but I hoped."

"I still want to," he said. "It may have been a short while but I wanted to kiss you the moment I saw you."

"We needed to talk. I had to see the good in you first." She paused and looked down at her hands. "And I did."

He placed his finger under her chin and lifted her face to meet his. "I'm too tall for pretty much any woman. Most of the time ladies take one look and turn away. I don't have much money but I've got the best horse in the county. I worked hard until I met a beauty asleep in a grave. But she doesn't want to go out with me. And I don't know what to do about that."

Duke took a deep breath as Peggy held hers.

He suddenly looked very serious. "You've got to tell me the truth. Is there a husband hanging around? Or a boyfriend somewhere?"

She laughed. "No. Nowhere. I told you I've barely had a date." She grabbed his hand. "I'd like to go out with you, but I can't. I barely ever have time to myself. And if my family found out about you, they wouldn't like it—they'd start interfering."

After a long moment, he said, "If there is no husband and you won't go out with me, is there any chance you'll meet me here again? Or maybe kiss me again, lady?"

Peggy's yes came out as a whisper.

Duke suddenly seemed to understand. He lifted her off the ground. She kissed him several times. "I've figured it out. I'm afraid of everyone in the world but you. I hope you can handle my family." Feeling brave, she kissed him hard. "You better be a good man, Duke."

He laughed. "If you want to have our dates out here for the rest of our lives, I'll be fine. The kids can just run around and be wild."

Peggy smiled up at him, thinking about her new dream. Two lonely people had found each other, and two was more than enough.

Chapter 9

A New Chapter

Charlotte Lane

Charlotte wasn't sure whether or not she'd closed her eyes all night. Several times she got up and walked through the cluttered rooms of her new home. It was frozen in the fifties; nothing had changed except the junk that seemed to have grown like mold. But there was no time for her to redecorate or clean now. She had to get to work.

Before the sun came up, she was dressed and ready to step into the new chapter of her life. The last few years she'd felt she'd been sleepwalking on a treadmill that had been as slow and monotonous as combing through *Moby Dick* for the hundredth time.

In a few minutes Charlotte would walk out of her red door and become Crossroads's next English teacher. She was in charge of three high school level courses and two middle school classes.

After glancing in an old mirror to make sure all was in place, she caught sight of the small pink diamond earrings she always wore and shook her hair out to cover them. Then, she organized the satchel her mother had given her when she'd finished her dissertation. She looked at the dark leather and thought about how that had been the last time she'd seen her mom. Three months after Charlotte left Kansas, her mom, her only living relative, had died in her sleep. She'd left a note in her Bible.

> *When I die, I want no funeral. No flowers. No obituary posted. And, to whoever finds this: Tell my Charlotte that she was a good daughter and remind her to live and have fun.*

Charlotte looked around at her new home. "Sorry, Mom, this place doesn't seem like it's going to be much fun." She had never imagined being in a tiny town like this. She'd loved being in the big city, but at A&M she'd had the job but not the life. Now, she wanted it all.

She sighed, wandered into the kitchen and began rummaging through the stuffed cabinets, planning to fix herself a bowl of cereal. Two of the boxes had already been opened and they went into the trash. By the look of things, she couldn't tell if they were one year old or ten years old. But she finally found one that was still sealed and poured herself a bowl of Raisin Bran.

When she finished, she knelt and offered the milk to her cat. Baylor stared at the bowl, eyeing the remaining flakes floating around, and walked away swishing his furry tail. He was very particular. Charlotte laughed and added, "Like every male I've ever known."

At seven thirty, she stepped out onto her porch and into the sunshine, ready to turn to a new page of her life. She thought of all the first days of school she'd taught. The people at A&M, the professors, the administrators, even the janitors in her building, all seemed to be floating through her mind. She knew she would forget all of their names in a few months. She'd have a blank page where they'd once been.

Charlotte had forgotten the names of most of her students. New ones always came in each semester to replace the old students in her mind. Through the years, though, a few of them had shined. But she'd never really gotten to know any of them. Never gotten attached. Not even to the best ones she'd actually enjoyed teaching.

She'd thought of a class as successful if her students left the course understanding a thesis statement and knowing how to format citations. And as time went by, she became a well-oiled machine. Lecturing, grading, repeating. Maybe, just maybe, this time she'd remember to live in the moment. She'd dance and sing and stay out well past eight o'clock.

As she walked toward the school, she stared up at the biggest building in Crossroads. The three-story brick school stood tall and strong like a monument to education that had always been there and always would be.

How on earth was she going to learn how to live here when she'd spent her whole life pretending to live in fiction? But somewhere deep inside her was the blood of her ancestors who'd actually had the lives she'd only experienced in Western novels.

If she could have one wish in her lifetime, she'd want to live in the early days of Texas. Riding horses, sleeping under the stars. No clocks. No one telling her rules she had to follow. She'd go to California and pan for gold, or herd cattle to Dodge, or maybe follow rodeos across the West.

If only . . .

Charlotte paused for a minute. She knew she was stepping over a crevice of her life to try once more. She loved teaching so she could have time to read and dream of writing someday. To find a life full of adventure. There was no turning back now. This time, she'd make her existence more of a story and not just a paragraph in the margins of a book.

She raised her chin and smiled as a half-grown kid skipped out of the school building. He started waving at her excitedly, yelling her name as if he was the town crier. "You're Miss Lane, right?"

She moved toward the steps that led to the school's front door, and announced in her most confident voice, "I'm Dr. Lane."

The kid halted in front of her, offering his hand. "Wow, you're a doctor too? I'm Teddy. The head of the Crossroads K through 12 School welcoming committee."

She raised an eyebrow at the boy who looked like he couldn't be more than ten. "You can't be a committee if you're the only member."

"Sure can. Mr. Halls told me that I'm the whole committee for the day. And I've got lots to do." He puffed out his chest proudly. "The principal said that I'm to take you straight to him when you get here so he can talk to you. Then, I gotta take you to your room and tell Mr. Wyatt he doesn't have to teach your class. Oh, and you change rooms every hour, but don't you worry, I'll take you to the new rooms every period too."

"How old are you?" Charlotte leaned down to his eye level.

He grinned as if he always got that question. "I'm fourteen. I'm a freshman this year. I'm short for my age, but my pop says I'll grow. He's been putting fertilizer on me every night. It worked on the crops, so it'll work on me too."

Teddy offered Charlotte his elbow and led her through the door to the school's offices. No one was there except a round woman dressed in all pink.

The kid leaned toward Charlotte. "That's the secretary, Miss Butterfield. Mr. Halls says she runs the place," he whispered. "I heard him say once that if you want to go to Hell, you've gotta get Miss Butterfield's hall pass to get there."

Charlotte guessed the pink lady was about ten years older

than she was. She had two red pens sticking out of her hair and a pleasant smile plastered on her face. "Welcome to Crossroads K through 12. Now, before you do anything, I have papers for you to look over and sign. You can take them with you as long as you get them back to me today. And the principal, Mr. Halls, is waiting in his office to welcome you." She held up one finger. "Rule number one, never leave Mr. Halls waiting."

At that moment a tall man, dressed in a suit the color of dust, appeared in the doorway to the room behind Miss Butterfield. Charlotte wouldn't be surprised if he lived in his office, by the looks of him. No tan, but a grin that seemed to light up the room.

He waved her and Teddy in without another word, then started speaking before she crossed the threshold. "I have something to talk to you about before you get started, Miss Lane."

For the second time that morning Charlotte said, "It's Dr. Lane."

"Of course, it is."

She walked into a room that looked more like filing storage than a principal's office. He remained standing but waved at the metal folding chair in front of his desk. Teddy stood behind her by the wall.

"First, we are so glad to welcome you to our team here at Crossroads K through 12," he began like he was delivering a well-rehearsed speech. "But I may have forgotten to mention that teaching here also comes with extra duties. As we're a small community, some of our teachers have to stay after school and do bus duty. Some have lunch duty and some have counseling duties."

Charlotte was starting to get nervous. Mr. Halls was looking down at her like he was the last man standing at the O.K. Corral.

The principal continued. "But you'll have the best duties out of everyone. Mr. Biggers loved it. He always volunteered to coach our sports teams. And now that you're here, it can pass to you just until football is over. But don't worry about it taking too much time. It's only three afternoons a week during football season."

Coaching any kind of team was the last thing she had expected. But it was different. It might not be dancing or singing or even hiking, but it would be new.

Mr. Halls steepled his fingers and leaned toward her. "We've got a great team this year. We actually won four games, which is twice as many as last year. We're growing men in this community, not just football players, obviously. And the position has its perks. As the coach you get the coveted Crossroads High School jersey with your name on the back to wear at all the games. And during the season you get three hats allotted because, for some reason, the boys think it's fun to steal the coach's hat. But if you catch one stealing your hat, you come to me and I will deal with him harshly."

"Is wearing a jersey mandatory?"

Mr. Halls shook his head. "No, no, no. You'll also get a fine letterman jacket like the boys. Shows school pride and goes with everything. Plus, you'll get to wear jeans on game day."

Charlotte fought to hold her smile in place. Jeans were for laundry days or hiking. This would also be new. Jeans and a football shirt would be like a uniform—the ugliest one ever—purple.

"The board decided since you're our first female coach, you won't have to oversee wrestling. Our new history teacher, Wade Parsons, has volunteered to coach wrestling and debate, plus direct a one-act play contest," Mr. Halls explained.

Charlotte tried to speak through her tight throat. "Does everyone always have to do these extra duties?"

"Oh, no. You'll only do the extra duties until you have children or turn sixty. We understand that most women cannot stay after three forty-five once they marry and settle down or get . . . older."

Quietly, she said, "Then, I'd better start aging in double time or get married fast and pop out a few kids."

Charlotte decided she needed to get out of the office fast before they made her run the place or retire.

Teddy took her stack of papers from Miss Butterfield and pointed out the door with his head. "I'll show you to your first room. Our two new guys are rotating teachers. No room of your own."

She tried to smile. She'd never been a rotating teacher. At least she'd learn the campus.

As they walked down the hall, he prattled off all she needed to know about the school. Where the cafeteria was. Where the library could be found. Which were the best bathrooms. She asked him about her office, and the kid led her to the teachers' lounge.

As she opened the door to peek in, a book flew across the room.

Three doors down he led her to a room on the right side of the hall, and Charlotte walked into her first Crossroads classroom. Teddy put her papers on her temporary desk and said, "I've gotta run. As the head of the greeting committee, I've gotta go help the other new teacher before the bell rings. He got here last week but I don't know much about him. I heard he's retired from the Army. He never taught school but he's got the degree. It's like a war zone in his rooms and he's like you, always moving. The school is overcrowded. If you trip and fall in the hall, you better roll away fast because someone'll trip over you."

She looked at the boy and asked, "Are you afraid too?"

"Nope," he said. "I'm used to it; I play receiver on the football team."

"You play football?" Then she thought about it for a minute. She didn't know what a receiver was, but a four-foot-something kid thinking he could play football wasn't any weirder than her pretending to coach it.

Charlotte raised her head to thank him, but he was already gone. And in his place stood a sweet-looking woman who seemed like she was made of sugar.

"Good morning, Miss Lane. Welcome, welcome. I'm the home economics teacher, Miss Ollie. I'm out in the second portable." Her voice was like a falsetto that crescendoed at the end of each sentence. "I've been there for years, so I guess the building isn't very portable." She chuckled at her own joke. "Neither is the shop beside me. I wish it was, though, because I'd haul it off myself." Her bright smile disappeared under a frown as she seemed to chew back words Charlotte guessed weren't very nice. They must be for the shop teacher.

Then her smile was back. Miss Ollie walked toward the communal desk and dropped a loaf of some kind of bread on Charlotte's pile of papers. "I wanted to bring you a treat for your first day, Miss Lane."

"Dr. Lane," Charlotte said very properly.

"Oh, you're also a doctor? That's good because, between you and me, the nurse could use some help."

"No, I have a doctorate in English with a focus in postmodern Western literature."

"Well, that's a mouthful," Miss Ollie said. "My degree is in sewing buttons and baking sweets."

Charlotte looked out into the hall as she heard Teddy's voice rambling on about where to find the school's best water fountains. A tall man with one arm in a sling looked like he was marching through enemy territory. He followed the small kid past her first room.

The ex-soldier looked at her, and Charlotte sensed he was fighting down a smirk as he saluted with his good arm. "Morning, ma'am," he said, and moved on.

Her cheeks heated. She told herself it was because she had always hated when people called her ma'am. But she supposed it was better than "miss."

"That's the other new teacher, Mr. Parsons." Miss Ollie giggled. "Nice looking, isn't he? But he's probably scarred all over. What a shame. Mr. Halls said he's seen action and when he thinks no one is looking, he limps."

Charlotte had already figured he was the retired soldier. He walked like one. He may have one arm in a cast and a sling, but she thought he seemed more likely to be alive at the end of the day than she did.

Students filed in as Miss Ollie waddled out, and for a moment Charlotte felt like she was in *Little House on the Prairie*. Flannels, jeans, and pigtails filled the room. Everyone was dressed like a cowboy, except for the cheerleaders. As always, Charlotte was ready and prepared for her first lecture.

With every new class throughout the day, she gave the same talk. The rules of her classroom, her expectations, what they would all learn over the year. Then she had the students stand up and introduce themselves. At the end of the day, the only kid's name she could remember was Teddy's. He was like a jack-in-the-box, popping in every period to take her to another room.

When all was quiet during the last five minutes of lunch, she sat in her temporary chair behind her borrowed desk and wondered if she would still be alive by Christmas. She was used to giving only two lectures a day, a total of four classes a week. Charlotte was sure to run out of words by December.

By five o'clock the building was silent. She was too tired even to get up, find her satchel, and go home. High school teachers had to do this every day for forty years. She was thinking about getting married and having kids just so she could take time off, when Mr. Parsons walked through her doorway.

As he came toward her, he definitely had an ex-military way about him. He pushed his chest out as if he was proud to be serving the school. And his smile hinted that he was hiding something. Good-looking, but not in a way a high school kid would notice. At forty-three, Charlotte felt she might be having her first childhood crush. Maybe going back to high school wouldn't be so bad after all.

"You survived the day," he said with a grin. "I wasn't sure if you'd make it. You looked pretty green to me."

She straightened in her chair and smiled back. "I'm the veteran teacher here, soldier. I taught at A&M for fifteen years. I'm Dr. Charlotte Lane."

"Oh, pardon me, ma'am. I'm a veteran, too, served as a medic in the Army for twenty years. I'm Master Sergeant Wade Parsons."

"Oh, really? Have you been practicing on yourself?" She eyed the cast plastered on his left arm.

He patted his cast as if he was carrying around a pet. Then he sat down on the corner of her desk, swinging one leg. "No, but I could practice on you if you like. Are you hurt? Need medical attention? Maybe a drink."

She leaned back. "Are you hitting on me? I think that's against school policy. But I hear there's a bar on the other side of town where women are waiting for men like you to drop in. I'm sure there's plenty of people you could practice on there."

Was it possible he was flirting with her? Was she flirting back?

It had been so long since a man had noticed her that she had forgotten how this worked. She would have to do some research on it tonight. There was bound to be a book that explained how flirting worked.

"Yeah, I've been there. They have the best nachos to go with their beer. I feel like I could use a drink about now. You want to join me?" He ran his eyes over her as if searching for injuries. "I bet you could use one too."

"No, thanks. There's coffee in the teachers' lounge if I get thirsty."

But real food did sound good. There was nothing in her fridge at home, and who knew how old the food was in her pantry.

She was not looking forward to another gas station meal either. "Actually, sure. I'll go. But this isn't a date. I'm just hungry."

She ignored his smile and stood, gathering her things.

"Yes, ma'am." He saluted her. "That's fine with me. I'll even let you pay."

Well, that wasn't very romantic. Probably not flirting, then. Darn.

"Please don't call me ma'am. It makes me feel old."

He gave her a firm nod, his lips turning up at the corners. "You can call me Wade."

She eyed him, trying to decide how to deal with him. "Charlotte."

They walked in silence to the parking lot. A little too close for comfort. Wade's arm kept brushing hers and she seemed to stiffen with each touch. By the time they made it outside, she was wound tight.

He pointed to an old pickup. "Hop in."

"That's okay. We'll take separate vehicles. You look like the type to go over the speed limit." She needed some space and the freedom to flee if necessary.

He turned widely, making a show of searching the near empty parking lot. "I don't see another car. Around here."

Charlotte picked up her pace as she reached the sidewalk. "I'll walk home and get my own car. It's only a few houses down. I'll meet you there."

Ten minutes later, having driven there separately, they were sitting at a table. Within seconds a curvy blonde hopped over to take their order. He asked for a beer and an extra-large order of nachos with two plates. Charlotte got a Coke.

She couldn't help noticing that Wade didn't seem the least bit interested in their attractive waitress. She reminded herself that it didn't matter. Wade could look at a pretty girl. They were just colleagues, after all. And besides, they'd only just met.

The waitress brought their drinks and Wade lifted his with a smile for Charlotte. He clinked her glass. "You're my kind of woman, Dr. Lane."

She looked at him, surprised. She'd never been anyone's kind of anything. "What kind is that, Mr. Parsons?"

"The kind that's sober."

Charlotte laughed and felt herself begin to relax for the first time all day. They ate nachos and talked about their first day at Crossroads's school. And she watched him, thinking that she'd made her first friend in Crossroads. Her first friend in a long time.

When he walked her to her car, he politely said, "Thanks, Charlotte, for joining me. I'm glad we'll be working together. I'll see you at school tomorrow."

Wade held the door as she climbed into her car. When he walked away she sighed and almost said aloud, "Definitely not flirting."

Chapter 10

Windy Change

Tuesday

Staten Kirkland

Staten had meant to put on clean clothes, maybe dress up a little, or even wear his Sunday best. But as usual he didn't have time. School was almost out. He drove into Crossroads and to the only K–12 school in town, looking for Dr. Charlotte Lane.

Granny had just heard from Miss Butterfield that the ex-A&M professor was now teaching at his old high school, and he hoped she would help him. Surely, Dr. Lane hadn't forgotten all her lectures in a few months. Maybe she even had some old books lying around that could teach him to sound intelligent.

Who was he kidding? Teachers never tossed books. Granny still had her first lesson plan from twenty-five years ago. If this

Dr. Lane had a good book lying around and let him borrow it, Staten would start tonight. He could give up an hour a night to learn.

If he didn't start learning, it wouldn't be long before he'd be going backward. He knew a few cowboys who could only say "Yeah" and "Nope." And he didn't want to be like them.

Ten minutes later he pushed through the school's doors, suddenly feeling old. It had been less than a year since he'd been here, and he felt he was getting dumber by the moment. Oh, his grades had been decent enough, but he never took the advanced classes or did more than the minimum. Only six months ago he had walked through these halls as a student. Now he was running a ranch.

Folks in Crossroads respected the boss of a place. The work was hard but ranchers never talked about poets or scholars. Staten couldn't remember reading a book that wasn't assigned in high school. There were too many other things to do. Rodeos, sports, dates.

Except when he was with Jake, Staten didn't think about world problems. He had enough of his own. If the world was coming to an end, thirty minutes of the nightly news would let him know. Cowboys still got up by dawn and got to work. He didn't worry about anything but the ranch; he didn't have time.

As he passed the library, he tried to remember ever checking out a book for fun.

Truth hit him hard. He was dumb.

Staten reached the main office and decided to quit thinking.

He stopped at Miss Butterfield's desk, and the secretary, dressed in pink as always, smiled at him. "Well, hello there, Staten. I thought we already got rid of you. How's your folks?"

"Hi, Miss Butterfield. They're doing good." He grinned. "Granny told me about your new English teacher, Dr. Lane. I would like to talk to her if I can."

"Sorry, you can't do that. At least not for ten more minutes." The pink lady sat back in her chair and looked Staten up and down like she was counting each speck of dirt on his clothes. "But since you're all grown up and dirty as an outlaw, I'll help you a bit. She's upstairs in 307. The minute the bell rings, you can step into her room but not before. You better talk fast, though, because she's also the football coach. She'll be headed for the field after the halls clear."

"Thanks."

He left the office, turned to the stairs, and took the steps two at a time. He'd just hit the third floor as the bell rang. A few students nodded at him but Staten realized most didn't recognize him. They were all one or two years behind him. And Staten had changed a lot since high school. Now, he was dressed like a cowhand. Bigger. Tanner. His hair was months overdue for a cut, his beard was overgrown, and worse, he was dirty from work.

When he walked into the almost empty room, Dr. Lane turned with her eyebrow raised. "May I help you?"

Staten stared at the lady. She had to be almost middle-aged! Maybe in her forties. Neither pretty nor ugly. She was plain, one of those people folks never remembered details about. It crossed his mind that she'd make a great bank robber, then he considered slapping himself.

Stay on point, he told himself.

Staten took his hat off and said what he'd rehearsed on the way here. "I'm Staten Kirkland. I graduated this past May, and I was wondering if you'd be willing to teach me college freshman English."

The lady looked tired. "I'm a high school teacher now. You are in the wrong place. I hear there is a university about a hundred miles from here that you could try."

"I know. I was already enrolled at Texas Tech, but I had to leave to help my family. I know it's not your job anymore, but

I figure you probably haven't forgotten all you used to teach. I could really use the help. I plan to reenroll as soon as I can."

He paused, thinking of how to make her understand how important this was to him. "Since I left Lubbock, I feel like I'm dumbing up. I have a ranch about fifteen miles out of town and I can't leave it often. But I've got to feel like I'm learning about something besides ranching. I can pay whatever you charge. Consider it tutoring. I have to learn so I can grow."

She looked at him carefully. "Speaking of growing, you look about six feet, four inches. I'm just guessing, but I think you're as tall as you're going to get. How old are you, young man?"

"In three months, I'll be twenty."

She looked surprised. "I would have guessed twenty-five, maybe older."

Staten smiled. "I'm aging fast. I've got a full plate of work but I'll carve out time, and I know it won't count toward any college credit. But I don't care. It's the learning I need. I've got to talk to college people and not feel like an idiot. I'm getting dumber by the minute."

The teacher walked back and forth in front of her desk, gathering her things. "When do you plan to go back to college?"

Staten knew he had to be straight with this lady. "I don't know. I did one month at Tech. Then my folks needed help on the ranch. From the looks of it, I'll be needed for a while. I have no idea when I'll be able to do the college thing again."

He thought he saw sorrow in her eyes. Maybe she felt for him. "Dr. Lane, I just want to learn to talk to educated people. I love the land and working it. The job seems endless. But even so, I wonder if I can master ranching and college both. If you can't teach me, I'll find someone else. I just thought I'd start with English or history, if you'll take me on."

Dr. Lane folded her arms. "You seem wise beyond your age, Staten. I'll teach you what writers and poets have to say, but my expertise is in literature of the American West, so you won't be escaping ranching too much. We can start with a course I taught at A&M. About two hours a week. We'll discuss your lessons, and you'll have at least one book to read each week, but the price is high, I'm afraid."

Staten smiled. He'd won. "No problem. Name it."

"I know nothing about ranching or riding horses in the real world. If you have a horse I can ride, I'd love to learn how. I wrote my dissertation about postmodern Western literature, and I've always wanted to live out what I've read."

Staten pointed at the *Lonesome Dove* and *True Grit* posters covering her walls. "You like those movies?"

Her lips twitched. "They were books before they were movies. Have you ever read them?"

"No. I just watched the movies." Staten laughed. "I've got a horse at the Double K you can ride. Her name is Blue; she's old but gentle. Is Sunday afternoon a good time to start?"

"That is fine." She smiled for the first time since he walked into the room. "And, if you want to talk to highly educated people, mostly all you need to do is listen." She grabbed a worn satchel and threw it over her shoulder. "And now I've got to head down to the football field. I'll see you Sunday at two at your ranch. Where is it?"

Staten let out a breath.

"Just head west, and you'll run into it. Drive until you see the Double K gate, then keep going until you see the headquarters. Can't miss it."

He could barely control his excitement as he left the school. He wanted to run laps around the football field like he'd done the first time Amalah told him she loved him.

"Slow down there, Kirkland." Dan Brigman marched up to Staten's truck, his Eagle Scout uniform on and his backpack slung over his shoulder. "Every time I see you you're racing around."

Staten laughed. Nothing could spoil his mood. He clapped

Dan's shoulder. "You're right. We have to stop meeting like this, Deputy."

A red tint stained the junior officer's cheeks. He squared his shoulders. "Drive safe, you hear."

"Yes, sir."

As Staten got in his truck, he watched the future deputy rush to the crosswalk to help a group of younger students cross the street, whistling at a minivan that stopped an inch over the lane's white line. He would make a fine sheriff one day.

Maybe sometimes change was a good thing.

Chapter 11

Common Interests

Friday Night

Charlotte Lane

Charlotte was surprised to find herself excited Friday afternoon when she remembered she was going out to the bar with Wade again for more beer and nachos. Twenty years ago, a teacher would have been fired for doing such a scandalous thing in a small town, with another teacher no less. But today, the rules had slipped a bit.

As the last student skipped out of her room, Charlotte gathered up her satchel and work for the weekend. She'd been in Crossroads a whole month, and every day it felt more like home. Her whole career she'd thought of herself as an expert in her field, but high school curriculum wasn't watered down. To her surprise, she really liked teaching in Crossroads. Though she'd settled into a new routine, her students always kept her on her toes. Especially Teddy.

Wade Parsons popped his head in her room. "You ready?"

She stood and smiled. "Let's go."

They walked down the steps and out of the school doors like old friends.

"Wade, I've got to ask. What did you do on Friday nights before I got here?"

"Nothing." He shrugged. "Once in a while I went out and ate alone. You may not have noticed before, but most of the staff is older. I served twenty years for Uncle Sam and I was called the young teacher until you arrived."

As they drove together in Charlotte's car to the bar on the outskirts of town, she told him about Staten Kirkland and their deal.

Wade seemed fascinated. "Kirkland? I've been studying that family and the Double K Ranch since I got here. It's one of the reasons I found the area so interesting. You know their founder, James Randall Kirkland, was the first settler in the area? In the 1800s he bought his land out here for practically nothing and built the huge ranch out there today."

Charlotte tried not to laugh. She'd never seen him so excited.

He continued. "The story goes that he traded a broken watch for his wife, and rumor is she couldn't even speak English when they met. He wanted to see his land in all the seasons, so they lived in a cave the whole winter before he could build their house."

Charlotte smiled. What a great story. Exciting and dangerous, like some of her favorite Western books.

Wade continued. "No one knows where that cave is today. I wish I could find it. It's technically the first settlement in the area. I'm thinking that it has to be on the Double K Ranch. It must be out there somewhere. But the ranch covers over a hundred thousand acres."

"How big is an acre?" Charlotte asked.

"I don't really know," he said with a laugh. "But while you're out riding around, do me a favor and look for a cave."

"Will do. So do you know how to ride a horse?"

"Sure, I did it once. It's not that hard. All you have to do is stay on."

Charlotte suspected there was more to it than that. Maybe she'd show him the book on horseback riding she'd been reading.

After they were seated in the bar and had their orders in, Wade told Charlotte all the stories he'd read about the first Kirklands and how the owner now was named after his famous ancestor.

As they ate, their conversation shifted to school. They talked about their students and classes for almost an hour. Charlotte wasn't really interested in reliving the week, but it was an easy, relaxing conversation. Wade may not have been a date. But he was a friend, and when you had one good friend it made a place seem like home.

As they walked out of the bar after dark, he put his arm around her shoulders casually, not pulling her in too close. She liked that they'd settled into comfortable territory, and she'd have to be fine with that.

Chapter 12

New Season, Old Friends

Staten Kirkland

December slowly pushed its way into Crossroads with a few aging plastic signs dotted around town to remind everyone Christmas was almost here. One of the billboards of Santa Claus was missing a foot, and three of his reindeer had lost their horns. The little post office had paper gingerbread men strung across the only window. And, the school had a life-size manger and nativity scene.

Staten didn't find it strange. It was just Crossroads.

He enjoyed teaching Dr. Lane to ride on Sundays. They'd talk about the books he was reading and the essays people had written about them. Out on the Double K's open plains, it was the best class he'd ever had. He might not be earning credit for a course, but he was learning more than he ever had.

Staten didn't always have the time to give the teacher riding lessons though. As winter set in, work piled up and sometimes Jake Longbow would take over her lessons.

But no matter what, Staten always made sure he kept up with Dr. Lane's assignments. He loved sitting in the barn and studying freshman composition after having dinner with his grandfolks. His routine was changing. And he was changing again too.

Every night Staten spent an hour or two reading what Dr. Lane gave him. And the more he read, the more he got out of it. After studying the books that had been made into movies he'd watched before, he realized the stories were not the same. The books were so much richer. And he loved talking about them.

Amalah called less often than she had a month ago. By mid-December she was only checking in once a week. And usually only for a few minutes at a time. The good news was Staten and Amalah didn't argue at all. There wasn't time.

For some reason he didn't tell her about his tutoring with Dr. Lane. Maybe he was afraid she would find it silly. Or maybe he wanted to keep it a surprise. But Amalah loved sharing the details of what she was doing. She showed little interest in his life on the ranch. "I have to run" became her trademark goodbye.

The only other friend Staten talked to was Quinn O'Grady. At first she'd called to check on J.R., but recently, she had started calling more often. Maybe she needed someone to talk with too. She didn't say much about music school in New York, silently telling Staten the school was not fun for her. Which was a shame because he knew playing piano was her dream.

Although Amalah's calls had grown shorter, his conversations with Quinn had grown longer. Some nights Staten spent a whole thirty minutes telling her the plot of a book she'd probably never read, or describing the difference between a book and its movie. He'd known Quinn all of his life. They had been friends for as long as Amalah had loved him.

At first, they talked about all of the things Quinn liked

about New York, but then she didn't have so much to say about it anymore. She told him once that she still loved the city but she didn't care for the music school.

Quinn had always been much quieter and more reserved than Amalah and never shared her problems, but now the two of them had found a camaraderie in their unhappiness. Maybe it was because Amalah was too tied up in campus life to make time for either of them. Quinn was Amalah's best friend, and Staten couldn't help but wonder if Amalah was calling Quinn less and less too.

One December day, Quinn called him to ask if he could pick her up at the Lubbock airport and bring her home to Crossroads for the Christmas holiday. The music department at her school closed a week early because most of the students were performing at Christmastime. But for some reason she wasn't part of that, and Staten hesitated to ask why. Quinn was the best piano player he'd ever heard.

"Hey, Staten, I'm sorry to bother you for a ride," Quinn said, her voice small over the phone. "I called Amalah first and she was too busy to pick me up. She has to stay longer to get ready for next semester with her sorority sisters."

Staten didn't waste time with details. "Name the time. I'll be there."

"Thanks. I really am sorry to have to ask, but my father is out of town and Mom went with him for the first time." Quinn sounded like she had tears in her eyes.

Staten knew Quinn hated asking for help. "Don't worry about it. I've got you. What are friends for?"

When Staten talked to Amalah about it later, she had been full of excuses. "I'm just too busy to pick up my best friend. I don't have time. I'm too overloaded. I told her we'll have time after Christmas. When I get back."

Staten had stood like stone as Amalah had rattled on until he could get a word in. He tried not to give in to the resentment he felt brewing with each excuse. He thought about all of the things he wouldn't be able to do if he drove back and forth to Lubbock to get Quinn. The Double K was busy getting ready for winter, and there were extra hands helping out on the ranch. He could have asked one of his men to go into Lubbock and get Quinn. But Quinn needed a friend. She was alone in a big city a thousand miles away from home. Every time she called, Staten could tell she didn't want to hang up. Since Amalah wasn't stepping up, he would come through for her.

When Quinn called to remind Staten when her flight would come in, she was excited in her shy way to be coming home with him. "I'll get to see your Granny and J.R. and maybe ride for a few hours or more before my parents get back home. Would it be okay if I hang around for a while? I don't want to go home to a silent house. Maybe I could help Granny with the baking. I love her apple pies."

"Sure. If you've got time, you can help me count the cows."

Quinn let out a yelp. "No way. I haven't seen my folks for four months, and I don't want to smell when I do."

Staten laughed. "Well, maybe we can just go for a ride then."

"Absolutely." There was a smile in Quinn's voice.

He hung up the phone feeling happier than he had in days. He might not have his Amalah, but Quinn was a great friend.

The next week, when he picked Quinn up at the airport, he hugged her as he always did, but the minute she got in his pickup she broke down crying. Staten had never seen her cry before. She was usually so quiet, she never let anyone know when she was hurting.

Staten gently pulled her across the bench seat into his shoulder and let her cry it out. She told him all about how much she hated the music school in New York.

"I have no friends. My roommate barely even talks to me. I get lost at least once a day, and it's so cold up there. But worst of all is my professor. He seems to pick on me every time he gets a chance. Maybe he thinks he's making me stronger, but he's really not. It just makes me want to come home."

Staten patted her around the shoulders. "You want me to go out there and beat up that old man? I will."

"No, you'd get in trouble." Quinn giggled. "He thinks he's still young, but he's not. I bet in a few years he'll be scary. Maybe he wants to be. He flirts with some of the girls, but he just puts me down."

Staten pulled back to look at her. "Don't sweat it. He wouldn't last thirty minutes in a bar."

She smiled, settling into her seat and drying her eyes. "How would you know? Don't tell me you've gone wild since you got back."

He shrugged. "I pretended to be twenty-one a few times in Lubbock. The guy checking IDs was real busy one night and a head shorter than me. He waved me in. I've always looked older than I am." He softly tugged the braided blond rope of her hair. "With that braid I'm not sure you could even pass for nineteen. You know, Quinn, if you try to marry young, the county clerk will probably file adoption papers instead."

She pushed his shoulder but she was laughing.

He was glad he'd made her smile. Staten might outweigh her by fifty pounds, but Quinn was near his height and rod thin. Since about the fourth grade he'd called her "kid." She'd always be sweet, innocent Quinn to him.

A little over an hour later, they were out at his barn, saddling up. Staten strapped on his Colt as usual. His grandfather insisted the boss and the ranch hands never go out riding out of sight of the headquarters unless they were armed for safety.

Quinn put her foot in the stirrup. "You still think you need that gun?"

Staten didn't answer right away. He moved behind her and put his hands around her waist, then gently lifted her up onto the saddle. "J.R. always carried his old Colt. You never know what can happen out here."

He smiled. Lately Staten had been out riding for a reason, for some job that had to be done. But now he was going out for no reason at all except to enjoy the day with his friend. He almost felt like a nineteen-year-old kid again.

He knew Quinn would make it exciting. Horses usually got her out of her shy ways. She might not be a strong rider but she could stay on and keep up, which was more than Amalah could do.

They rode out to a point that Quinn had always loved. J.R. once told Staten it was the center of the ranch. No one ever measured it so they didn't know for sure, but it was a pretty vista. A quiet pasture with wildflowers in the spring. In the winter, they rode not on green land but rock-strewn plains colored in reds, oranges, and browns. They could see everything on horseback. Miles of gently rolling land interrupted by dried-up creek beds and twenty-foot rises.

Just as Staten turned to check on Quinn, six feet behind him, his horse slipped on some ice into a rocky creek bed. For the first time in years, he lost his balance. In a blink, he was tumbling sideways. There was no time for him to react. No time to catch himself. He fell.

Before he hit the brittle grass, he swore he heard his grandfather speak into his ear: "If you ride, you're gonna take a few falls sometimes, son, no matter how good you are."

Something hard smacked into the back of his head before he could respond to his grandfather, and the endless sky turned black.

Chapter 13

Quinn's Nightmare

Quinn O'Grady

For a moment, Quinn O'Grady just stared down at Staten lying on the ground. Fear rose in her chest. "Get up," she screamed louder than she ever had in her life. "STATEN!"

The one name echoed off the clouds as tears ran down her cheeks.

"Get up. You're scaring me." He looked like a huge cowboy doll whose eyes were closed.

He was tall and solid but asleep. He didn't look like he was hurt, only resting. Tanned. Young. Strong. He was not just Amalah's boyfriend; he was Quinn's friend too. He'd taught her to drive on back roads and how to ride a horse. She taught him math in the fourth grade and algebra a few years later.

"Staten, get up! This is not funny. We're too old to play games like this."

He didn't move. She'd seen him hurt on the football field

but he'd been conscious then, and groaning. Now he was still and silent.

Quinn climbed down off her horse and knelt to touch his cheek. Then she patted his face. "Staten? Staten, come on."

Nothing but shallow breathing.

Panic shot through her entire body.

She tried slapping him, as if that would wake him. "Get up, Staten. Say something."

His head rolled to the side but his eyes stayed closed. Quinn saw blood pooling at the back of his head.

She yelled his name again. He was bleeding. He might die and she had no idea what to do.

"You're all right. You're all right." He didn't move. She shook his shoulder. "You are going to be all right, Staten." He still didn't move.

Quinn gripped his arms, trying to pull him up. Blood was dripping on his shirt and the back of his coat. "Staten? Stop playing around," she whispered as tears filled her eyes. She stared as his face turned ghost white. "Staten. Wake up. You're scaring me. Wake up right now."

She took a few seconds to handle her panic. She tried to think. He was big and solid from work on the ranch. There was no way she could pick him up. But she couldn't leave him.

A river of tears almost blinded her. She looked around at the endless land and realized she wasn't even sure which way HQ was. North and South were sides of the Civil War to her, not directions. She'd tried to learn directions in New York by watching the buildings and still got lost.

There was no time to cry. She had to figure something out. Staten needed help. Ideas popped into her head. She couldn't pull him. The prairie had no trees to make a sled, even if she knew how, so that thought was useless. She could scream for help, but no one would hear her.

For the first time she realized how big this ranch was. When they were younger, she knew when they rode out, there was always a cowboy watching over them even if they couldn't see him. Later when they were in their teens, J.R. always said, "Stay in sight of the big house."

Now, as she knelt beside Staten, she looked in every direction. Nothing but yellow grass and a lonely mesquite tree dotting the land now and then. Amalah and Staten both had a great sense of direction. Quinn did not.

Maybe someone would come get them. But how would help find them? And how long would it take? If no one came, Quinn and Staten would probably be eaten by coyotes or worse, wild pigs.

Then, she remembered the Double K's emergency signal. When they were older, and they wanted to ride out farther, J.R. told Staten to take a gun along so he could fire three shots if they needed help. She opened his coat and saw the Colt at his side. After a few cuss words, she finally got the gun out of his holster.

Quinn stood and raised the Colt straight up, firing three times toward heaven. Staten didn't move. She replaced the gun in its holster, then she pulled the scarf from around her neck and reached for his head. The wound looked only a few inches long, but it was bleeding pretty badly. She placed the scarf on his cut, then sat down next to him and laid his head in her lap.

"Staten. Staten! Wake up." She put her hand over his heart and tried to let his steadily rising chest comfort her. But when he still didn't move, she quietly let tears fall. "You're all right. Help will be here in a minute. And I'm not going anywhere."

She waited and waited. Time seemed to stand still. She just kept whispering, "Staten. They will be here soon."

Quinn was about to shoot three more times when suddenly Staten groaned. Then she heard what sounded like horses racing toward her and a vehicle flying over rough land. One of the Double K's trucks skidded to a stop across from them.

Jake was the first one out of the truck. "What happened, Quinn?"

She tried to keep her voice steady as she explained what had happened.

The cowboys worked like a team of medics with Jake giving out instructions. "Lift him up and get him in the pickup bed. Watch his head. No doubt he has a concussion."

Jake kept yelling. "Four men get in the back. The other two grab their horses and ride as fast as you can to a phone. Tell whoever answers at the clinic that I'm bringing in Staten Kirkland, and someone better be there."

The foreman rushed toward the cab as the men climbed into the back and gently lifted Staten in. "The hay will ease the ride but you guys make sure he doesn't fall out. All coats piled over him. Quinn, you ride up in the cab with me."

There was no way she was leaving her friend now. She moved past him to hop in the back. "I'm going to hold his head. I'm staying with him."

Jake chewed a few cuss words as Quinn settled in the back.

While he started the pickup, Jake ordered, "Someone tell J.R. and Mrs. Kirkland I'll call as soon as I know something."

He was still yelling like his volume dial was broken while they headed toward Crossroads.

Quinn didn't say another word. She just did her best to hold Staten's head still. Silent tears slipped down her windburned cheeks as she kept whispering, "You're going to be okay."

Staten was coming to as the pickup hit town. He blinked slowly as if bringing the scene into focus. "Wha . . ."

Not one of the four men in the back said a word. They just had their hands around Staten's arms and legs.

"Shh." Quinn leaned in closer to his chest, stroking his head. "You're okay. Just rest now."

When they reached the county road, it wasn't as bumpy but the men didn't let up. They were all going to make sure Staten would make it to the doctor in one piece.

At the clinic, the men lifted him out as if they knew the routine. When Quinn hesitated behind Staten, Jake helped her down as if she weighed no more than ten pounds.

"Thank you," she whispered to Jake.

"No, young lady. Thank you. You may have saved the boss's life."

Quinn wished she could believe him.

Staten was rushed through to an empty waiting room. Jake walked, silent, beside her as the bossy head nurse took over. "I'll get him checked in. Then I'll call the doc. He'll decide if we should drive Mr. Kirkland down to Lubbock Hospital or keep him here."

The nurse tried to shoo everyone out of the exam room, and when that failed she started muttering that the ranch hands had better not trample the clinic's grass again.

Quinn couldn't stop a small smile as she heard Staten complain. "Get me out of here. I'm okay. I'm ready to go home. I . . ."

The nurse stopped him, then turned to the ranch hands standing still as statues, as if trying to make themselves invisible. "Well, if you're not going to vacate the room, at least make yourselves useful. Strip him, boys. Clean the wound and we'll see what we've got here."

"I'm fine. I'm going home." Staten swung one leg off the bed but everyone in the room knew he'd just used up all his fight. His face turned ghost white as his eyes rolled back.

Quinn moved to rush to him, but the foreman beat her to Staten's side.

"You're not going anywhere, Boss. Not until the nurse says you can," Jake ordered. "If I have to sit on you along with all four of these men, I will. Quinn, you might want to step out. If he fights us, someone could get hurt."

The silent nurse on the other side of Staten shoved a needle into his arm without warning and Quinn's heart squeezed. He managed to say, "Quinn," as she slipped from the room.

She looked back and saw him lying on his pillow. As the

door swung closed, the cowhands and Jake all stepped away as Staten shut his eyes.

As the minutes passed, Quinn wanted to storm the room, but all she could do was wait.

She moved to the closest phone she could find and called Amalah.

"Hello."

"Hey, it's me," Quinn whispered.

"What's up, Quinn?" A slight irritation colored Amalah's voice.

Quinn took a deep breath. "Staten is hurt."

All the noise seemed to fade in the hallway around her, and Quinn could hear Amalah's breathing quicken. In a low tone Quinn told her about Staten's fall and his head injury.

Once she started talking, all the facts came out. "The nurse said if there are no problems tomorrow, he might get to go home in a few days. But Jake is pretty sure Staten has a concussion. The traveling doc will examine him on his rounds later tonight to make sure nothing is wrong."

"Thank God he's okay," Amalah said. "Two days at the clinic and a week in bed at home. That doesn't sound so bad."

Quinn asked, "You are coming in tonight? Staten will want you here when he wakes."

Amalah hesitated. Then her words came slow. "No. I can't make it tonight. Besides, what could I do? He's in good hands at the clinic. The men will probably stay with him every second, too, and the staff will be there. After all, you said the doc was just keeping an eye on him. You've gotta remember he's a rancher. And ranchers are always getting beat up by nature." Amalah pleaded, "Quinn, you're my best friend, and I know you're Staten's friend too. I know it's a big favor but watch over him for me. I'll try to get home in two days, three at the most. I'm just so busy right now. And you being there is just as good as if I was."

Quinn didn't know what to say. She knew it was Amalah Staten would want when he woke up.

"Amalah, you should be here for him." Quinn placed her face against the smooth wall next to her, hoping it would cool her cheeks. "Of course I'll watch him, but you need to call and check in on him. Let him know you care. I'll be at the clinic until he goes home."

Amalah began to cry. "I do care. I'll call morning, afternoon, and night. If someone doesn't answer, I'll keep calling every hour until I get home. I'm just way, way too busy to come home unless something serious happens. I know I won't be much help anyway." She sniffled into the phone. "But please keep me informed. Stay with him and take care of him and let me know how he's doing every day. I'll be home as soon as I can. I promise."

Quinn hung up the phone wondering what she could do. What she could say. She had never felt sorry for Staten, but she was starting to feel sorry for him now. His girl wasn't coming home, and she knew that would hurt him.

She squared her shoulders and walked back to wait outside the door of his room. No matter what happened, she could be the friend he needed now.

Chapter 14

The Lone Coach

December

Charlotte Lane

The last home game before school was out for Christmas break would be crazy. And Charlotte was about to try to win today's match alone. Wade had taken over and done most of the football coaching through the season, and she'd mostly just kept the stats. But tonight she'd be the one yelling.

Mr. Halls and Wade were running the semifinals for the debate team. No more standing on the sidelines. She'd have to do something besides watch this time. She'd be in charge.

Dread worried over her. She felt like this was the first game of the year, not almost the end of the season.

The last couple of games, Charlotte had worn her letterman jacket and yelled "good job" a few times, cheering when one of her team ran the right way. But she never really understood what was happening.

She wasn't looking forward to halftime when she'd be alone, trying to read Wade's game plan for the second quarter. The players would go into the locker room and she'd wait by the doors. It was already getting too cold to stand outside. The only thing she was looking forward to was her first football game alone being over.

Teddy had continued walking with her to her classes, telling her all about the sport. And the minute Charlotte entered her classroom every morning there was Miss Ollie, the home economics teacher.

The plump woman would stand up from Charlotte's borrowed chair as if she was going to make an announcement. And she always did. "I thought I'd better come up here and give you some tips. I had four brothers and all of them played football. So, I probably know more about the game than Mr. Halls, but he'll act like he knows it all. Rule number one: Never stop yelling. Around here, football is war. Not just some game like soccer or baseball. Everybody in town will be watching you tonight."

This morning, Charlotte had taken a long breath and confessed, "I know nothing about football. I'd never even seen a live game before I came here. But tonight, I'm sure the boys are going to fight like lions."

Miss Ollie began to pace as she preached. "No one really knows anything about football; they just act like they do. Unless they've played the game for years, they just yell at the boys to do what they can. I'm sure you know the basics. Catch the ball and don't get tackled. But I wrote a few more rules down for you that most of the men don't know."

She handed Charlotte a packet of papers.

"Rule two: Don't ever let those boys see you or their teammates cry. Teddy does, almost every game, so just whisper to him 'Don't cry.' That's all you can do and then let him sit on the bench until he calms down. Not sure why that boy's so emotional.

"Don't worry, most of these boys know how to play. Their parents started teaching them before they came to school. They've been playing with their dads and brothers and uncles since they were little kids.

"So, rule three: If one of your players gets the ball, tell him to run. They should know which direction. And if the other team gets the football, make sure your guys knock them down. Like I said, they should know all this but sometimes they forget."

Charlotte nodded, trying to figure out which of Miss Ollie's rules to follow.

"The first thing you do when you walk on the field is tell them all to warm up. They'll get going. Just keep yelling, 'Do what you're supposed to do.'" Miss Ollie turned toward the door then spun back around. "Oh, and if one of your players gets a little yellow flag for a penalty, run up to the ref and tell him he's wrong. They're always wrong. That's what they say on the television. And at the end of the game, tell the boys to huddle up and that they fought hard and did great whether they win or lose. From then on, the boys will stop worrying about football and keep their eyes on the cheerleaders anyway. That's all I know."

As Miss Ollie walked out, Wade marched in. "You ready? First day of coaching alone. You'll be great."

Charlotte shook her head. "No, I'm not ready. I still don't know much about this game. And I'm more confused now than I was before Miss Ollie read me her rules. I don't know what to say or what to do, and now Mr. Halls asked me not to forget to walk the sideline in case anybody gets hurt. I keep telling people I'm not that kind of doctor."

"Don't worry. If there's an injury, just wrap the boys up and send them to their parents. Believe me, every parent will be there and most grandparents. They'll want to take care of their boys," Wade said.

Charlotte worried about the football game all day long, and by the time she had to walk out onto the field she thought she might pass out. But she'd come to Crossroads to start over and try new things. To live. She kept walking steadily to the rhythm of Miss Ollie's rules for the game.

As Charlotte slipped on her letterman jacket with COACH LANE printed on the back, she felt like a fraud. She *was* a fraud.

She walked up to Wade and pretended she might be able to do this. Only, looking like a head coach was a long way from being one.

"Good luck, Coach." Wade nearly shouted. "In the classroom you're Dr. Lane but out here you're the head coach. You'll be fine." Then he leaned in and whispered, "Who knows if there will even be another game after today. Just do your best."

He walked toward the debate semifinals being held in the school's small auditorium as she turned to the field.

When she was asked to go out for the coin toss to see which team would start the game, she whispered to herself, "It's time. Let's play some ball."

It seemed like when the coin touched the ground, everything happened at once. Her team rushed onto the field, and she began running up and down the sideline, yelling, not even sure what was going on or what to say. She made a point of telling her players to catch the ball. To run toward the end zone and to not get tackled.

She didn't have time to look at her watch. She had to keep moving and yelling and telling the boys they were doing great. Now and then she pointed at one of the refs and reminded him that he was wrong.

At halftime the boys went to the locker room and she sat outside and waited, hoping she wasn't dead yet.

The second half of the game seemed over in minutes. Like Moses parting the waters, she finally heard the last whistle and the game was over. Her players ran into the locker room again, and the parents and students in the stands collected their junk and headed to their cars.

She slumped onto a bench as a slow rain began to fall and darkness seemed to move over the field one yard at a time. She didn't even know who'd won the game. Everything was a blur.

The numbers on the scoreboard had seemed to bounce back and forth. All of her energy was drained. And like a storm passing over her, everything was suddenly silent. Everyone was gone but her.

Charlotte watched a shadow moving toward her and heard Wade's voice say, "You did great. We finished the debate half an hour ago and I caught the last few minutes of the game."

Charlotte didn't protest when he slipped his arm around her shoulders and pulled her in closer than usual. He steered her to the street heading toward her house. "How you feel, Coach?"

She couldn't answer. She felt like she'd lost all of her words while yelling during the game. She was exhausted and numb and relieved it was over.

They got to her house and without a word he took the key from her hand and unlocked the red door, leading her inside. He wrapped her in the blanket thrown over the back of a rickety armchair and led her to the ancient couch in the corner of the room. Then, he turned to the fireplace and started to light it. "You did good, Charlotte. You survived."

As the blaze sparked in the grate, her eyes filled with tears. She didn't even know why.

She'd done it. Lived outside the pages of her books and tried something new. Something daring. Something that had felt impossible.

Wade came to the couch and sat, lifting her feet onto his lap. He pulled off her shoes one by one, letting them plop to the floor. "There's no more games. You didn't make the finals this year, so the season's over. You don't have to coach football again."

She managed a nod.

He shifted, leaning over her and rubbing his hands along the blanket covering her arms. "You cold?"

"Mm." Charlotte shook her head. She was too numb to be cold.

He kissed the top of her head, still wet from the sudden rain she'd barely felt. "You hungry? I'm not really in the mood for beer and nachos, but I can whip something up."

"I'm not hungry, period." Her stomach still churned from the adrenaline she'd felt during the game.

"That's fine. But you've got to eat something, especially if all you've had is that salad I saw you picking at during lunch."

He got up to inspect the kitchen. She didn't have the energy to tell him that she'd cleaned out Mr. Biggers's pantry and now her kitchen had crackers and only two cans of soup. But a few moments later he walked back to her carrying two steaming bowls.

They ate in a comfortable silence, neither saying a word. When they finished, she leaned her head on his shoulder, his fingers lightly tracing her back. Before she fell asleep, she thought she heard him say, "You're one hell of a woman, Charlotte."

Her last thought before she drifted off was that she didn't want to coach football ever again. She'd lived enough of that story to last her a lifetime.

When she woke up at dawn, Wade was gone, but she saw a note written on part of a paper towel. It read *Don't forget. Today is Saturday, Coach. Get some rest. Good game last night.*

Charlotte came fully awake, trying to remember. "Did we win?"

No answer in the silent room. She looked down to find Baylor staring at her as if she had stolen his bed. She didn't have the energy to appease the cat.

Like a tree, she tumbled, face-first, back into the blankets and didn't move the rest of the morning.

Chapter 15

Ready to Live

Peggy Warner

For the first day in weeks Peggy May Warner had nothing to do. So close to Ashley-Lynn's due date, both grandmothers had driven in for the shower and planned to stay until the birth.

It wasn't long after Peggy had made her escape to meet Duke for their first real date that the newest Warner made her grand entrance, popping out in the middle of the baby shower. Turns out Ashley-Lynn's labor started around the same time the guests arrived, but she ignored it, thinking it was just another false alarm and not wanting to miss out on the cake. About half an hour later, she delivered a screaming bundle of joy.

Some of the women had still been arranging the nursery and putting out food when the newest Warner arrived. But no one thought to call Peggy or the clinic before the baby was cleaned up.

Peggy heard that after the head nurse finished her shift, she dropped by the Warners' house to make sure all was proper. Some of the ladies there for the shower claimed little Katie was already learning to talk. She was a whopping eight pounds and two ounces.

Auntie Ruth planned to stay a few weeks, and Fred's mother said she'd stay a bit longer if needed. Since the baby seemed healthy and the doctor wouldn't be in until Monday, everyone agreed to wait to make the one-mile journey to the clinic on Monday morning. So, for once, Peggy wasn't needed.

She wasn't surprised that none of her kin thought to tell her about the baby until days later. She had always been easy to forget. When her aunt came to the house to tell Peggy's mom all the details about the delivery, Peggy just listened with a smile.

Her aunt's story was like a dramatic retelling until she got to Fred and how calm he'd been this time when his wife delivered their newborn. He was a pro by now. The new dad wasn't much help, though, watching it all through the camera five feet away.

While several ladies circled his wife, Fred had watched and narrated for the group, describing everything that was happening. Which was pretty much nothing. The baby cried after she popped out. But soon she slept, and everyone told Fred he had a beautiful baby girl.

Peggy didn't say a word when her Aunt Ruth told all about her perfect new grandbaby. She just listened to the stories and kept refilling glasses while her mother oohed and aahed at the right times.

Ruth swore they could hear Fred breathing like a train at first, trying to hold back his tears. Then there were a few yells of joy mixed in. And suddenly everyone was giggling and laughing at the noise of a newborn. Auntie Ruth claimed it was a full five minutes before Fred said anything to anyone. He just stared at the new baby.

Someone finally said the baby was the most beautiful girl they'd ever seen and Fred yelled, "She sure is!" And then fell into awestruck silence again.

After her story, Ruth turned to Peggy. "You got to come see her. She's perfect."

"I'll try." Peggy's face felt frozen in place.

She'd seen this many times. Not the birthing, but the wiggling newborn and the recovering mama. When she would visit in a few weeks, she'd just be a guest. She wasn't close family, only someone who helped out when needed.

Besides, with Aunt Ruth around, no one else in the room would get a chance to hold the baby anyway.

Peggy learned years ago that grandmothers didn't turn their new grandbabies free, even if the diaper was wet. And visitors wouldn't notice the couple's two other preschoolers. In a matter of days, the older kids would wreck the house and break several of the new baby's toys. Peggy thought that was a rite of passage.

Peggy stepped back, letting her aunt talk to her mom. In a week they'd probably call her to drop in and wash the dishes, but right now she was perfectly fine having nothing to do. No one to help.

She walked to her car, reflecting on her lot in life. She hated her job. She hated being only the helper, always on the outside. Just moving around to tidy things up.

She had no education for a real occupation. No training for a career. At this rate she'd die poor with no space of her own. Living in her parents' garage apartment.

That's how she'd lived for as long as she could remember. Waiting for someday to arrive. She was tired of tasting only tiny bites of life. She wanted to spend her time with Duke, but she also wanted to keep him to herself, afraid that he would disappear, like a figment of her imagination.

Since their first date, she and Duke had planned to meet up again a few times, but something always got in the way. They couldn't find the time. After they missed each other two times in a row, Duke began leaving her notes hidden behind the big oak tree shading the graves. One or two words. *12 tomorrow* or *Monday lunch.*

    She parked along the hill that led to the cemetery and stared at the giant oak's branches waving in the wind. Duke was nowhere to be seen, but she knew he'd come along when he could. A sweet giddiness swept through her, and she got out of the car and headed up the hill. Pulling out the note, she stared at the words she'd written hours ago in her room. *Meet me here Wednesday at six. I'm ready for another date.* Peggy folded the paper and stuffed the message under the tree's roots where they'd broken free of the ground.

    Her moments with him were the only times she felt alive. And she was ready to live.

Chapter 16

Winter Changes

Staten Kirkland

Staten Kirkland stayed three days at the clinic. His concussion wasn't too serious. The head nurse said she would have sent him home sooner if other patients had arrived. Staten figured she just needed someone to care for and he was it.

By the third day, he had lost patience. "I'm ready to go home," he said to no one. He'd figured out Jake told the nurse to make sure Staten was well because he'd be riding full out the day he was free.

The three or four ranch hands who visited kept saying they had work to do at the Double K, but every morning they were back. Staten knew it was Granny's doing. She wanted her boy to get the best care, and she guessed they might have to sit on him to make sure Staten stayed.

Quinn was true to her word also. She was in his room by eight o'clock every morning and didn't leave until dark.

Amalah called every morning and evening but never stayed on the phone more than a few minutes.

Every night, he'd swear the next day he was going home no matter what the doctor said. He'd break out if he had to. Now he knew how J.R. felt with everyone hovering around him all the time.

The third morning Staten got his wish.

He and Quinn were both reading, waiting for his discharge papers, when Amalah rushed into his hospital room. She was the most beautiful thing he'd ever seen. She had presents for him and more sweets than would fit on the bed. Amalah acted as if he'd just come from war. Staten couldn't stop grinning.

He felt whole, as healthy as ever. He caught Amalah as she flew onto his bed and into his arms. Everyone in the room seemed to hold their breath but Staten held her solid. The aches faded. All he felt was her soft, warm body pressed against his battered and bruised one. They hadn't seen each other for more than a month, but she was here to take him home. A perfect Christmas present.

The nurse charged in carrying a clipboard and a stack of papers. "You're not going anywhere until you sign these." She passed a pen to Staten, then looked at Amalah. "He will get better if you take it easy on him. I'm sure he'll heal faster here, but the doc says he's ready to go."

"I'm fine. I just needed my gal."

Now that Amalah was here for winter break, they'd finally have some time together. His head still ached, but he felt as healthy as a stock horse.

Even the nurse could see this beauty of a young lady would bring him sunshine.

While he struggled to get his boots on and fill out papers, Amalah laughed at him. "Slow down. You don't want to be stuck here because you hurt yourself trying to put your boots on."

Quinn's quiet chuckle drifted behind him. Staten watched as

Quinn quietly slipped out of the room. Neither Staten or Quinn said a word, but their eyes met and held for a few seconds. She was a great friend. She'd stuck by him when he needed her, and he'd never forget it.

He handed the paperwork back to the nurse, who barely seemed to notice. She was watching the ranch hands gather Staten's things to load up in the truck outside as if she thought they'd take the clinic's furniture with them too.

Staten sat on the bed waiting for Amalah to come back. For a minute the room looked abandoned and bare. The disjointed melody of beeping machines had stopped, and all was quiet.

He heard a clatter of footsteps in the hall outside. It was Quinn coming back in the room.

Her shy smile broke over her face. "Forgot my book." She stepped to the armchair she'd sat in for the last three days and grabbed a worn paperback. "Are you glad to be going home?"

"Yes." He picked up the candy Amalah brought. "Glad Ama came home too."

"Me too." Before he could move, she leaned in and gave him a quick hug. "I'm glad you're okay."

"Thanks for staying with me, Quinn," Staten said.

She pulled away, a slight pink tingeing her cheeks. "No problem. Amalah told me to watch over you. But I would have anyway. You're my friend."

"I figured she did. You're a great friend. Always have been." He reached out to grab her hand and gave it a squeeze. "If that teacher in New York turns out to be a jerk, I'll go up there and knock him out for you."

She looked down at her fingers, and Staten wondered what she wasn't telling him.

"I mean it, Quinn. Don't let him pick on you. A teacher can still be a bully. And you deserve better than that."

"Thanks," she whispered as Amalah came back in the room.

"Ready?" Ama smiled.

"You bet." Staten let go of Quinn's hand and reached for Amalah's.

He was ready to get back to the ranch. The truth was he loved working the land as much as he loved the beautiful girl beside him. The Double K had always been part of him, and he was ready to get back to work.

Chapter 17

Dream Date

Wednesday

Peggy Warner

Peggy shivered and wrapped her sweater more tightly around her as the cold wind pricked at her. She'd been waiting under the cemetery's old oak tree for what felt like hours. But she knew in a few minutes it would all be worth it.

She hadn't made it back here since she'd slipped her note among the tree roots for Duke to find. In fact, she'd barely had a moment alone all week. Her mom had dragged Peggy along to help run errands. Then found extra chores to do around the house.

Mom's biggest fear was that Peggy would get restless on her free days and do something crazy.

Peggy laughed with the breeze. She'd been acting crazy for weeks. Dreaming of a life with her cowboy.

"I sure do love that laugh." Duke's low rumble sounded in her ear, sending shivers down her spine. But this time it wasn't from the cold.

She turned to stare up at him. "Hi. You made it."

He tilted his hat up and smiled. "Hi there, pretty lady. Sorry I keep leaving you waiting." He untangled her hand from her sweater and folded it in one of his. "Your hands are cold. What do you say we get out of here and warm you up?"

Peggy nodded. She'd been waiting to be with him, and he was finally here. She felt herself warm despite the chill. "Where to?"

Duke looped her arm through his and led them to his truck. "Wherever you want. As long as I can kiss you, I don't care where we go."

He planted a peck on her lips as if to prove his point.

Her cowboy opened the passenger door of his old Chevy and helped her in. Then he rushed to the driver's side and cranked up the engine. He turned the heater on full blast and pulled Peggy across the bench seat, into his arms.

She melted into him as his hand moved to stroke her hair. "I'm fine just staying here. I don't need a big fancy date or a night on the town. I just want to be with you."

Duke smiled down at her, his eyes glowing with excitement. "I've got an idea."

He put the gear in drive and swung the truck around. He turned down an old dirt road that looked like it'd been out of service for at least a decade. Then he threw the pickup in park and shut off the headlights.

"I want to show you something." He reached around the seat behind Peggy and pulled out a bundle of blankets. "Come on."

As she scooted to the edge of the seat to look out the driver's side door, Duke wrapped one arm around her waist and lifted her from the truck. Then he threw the blanket over his shoulders and folded her in, pulling her up against his chest.

Peggy snuggled in closer to her cowboy, placing one hand over his heart as she stared deep into his eyes, waiting.

"Look up," he said.

She did as he asked and gasped.

The sky was lit up and twinkling like the Christmas lights strung around town. It seemed like every star was visible.

Duke's lips brushed her ear. "Used to be, I thought this view was the best part of living in Crossroads." His mouth tickled the back of her neck. "And then I met a sleeping beauty and had lunch dates in a cemetery."

Peggy laughed softly as his lips trailed to her shoulder.

A shooting star flew across the sky, and he pulled her in closer. "Make a wish."

She turned in the circle of his arms and whispered, "No need."

She lifted her mouth to his, her heart exploding as he kissed her. She threw her arms around his neck and pulled him in closer. This was all she'd ever wanted. Time for herself. A life for herself. A good man for herself.

If her cowboy was everything he seemed to be, Peggy would never have to live on wishes again.

Chapter 18

Keeping with Tradition

New Year's Eve

Staten Kirkland

With Staten and J.R. both on the mend, Christmas had been a quiet affair. Granny had almost canceled their annual New Year's Eve party, but Gramps had insisted they hold to tradition. He may not have been the life of the party, but he seemed to enjoy himself as he sat in the corner of the big house, trying to hide the whiskey he'd snatched from the kitchen.

It was no surprise to Staten that his dad didn't show up. After all, there'd be no press on the ranch. There were too many big, important parties in Austin, and Samuel needed to rub elbows with the right people.

Granny was in her element. She loved having people over. And she hadn't gotten to see much of her friends since J.R.'s stroke. She mingled through the living room and sitting room, talking with everyone. She remembered everyone's names and asked after all their kin.

Staten was glad she could enjoy herself. Granny might not be out riding the land every day, but in her own way she worked just as hard as everyone else on the Double K.

Meanwhile, Staten might be sore all over, but he was going to make the most of his time with Amalah. Every year since the fourth grade, they'd slow danced at Granny's parties, and Staten couldn't wait to hold his girl on the dance floor.

Over seventy-five friends and neighbors showed up. The younger kids stayed in the barn playing games. A three-piece band played a dozen tunes every hour in the small sitting area off the living room of the big house. Amalah danced with everyone who asked her. There was no doubt she was the belle of the ball. Staten watched as she chatted with classmates she hadn't seen all semester. She was happy to be home, and he was thrilled to have her close.

Quinn arrived late, moving quietly through the crowd to Staten. "How's your head?"

"It's fine. Thanks to you. Jake told me about your quick thinking and waiting with me until help arrived. I appreciate it."

"You getting better is all the thanks I need. Besides, what else could I do?"

Staten gestured toward Amalah, dancing with a group of girls from the high school cheer squad. "You going to join them?"

Quinn made a face like she smelled a rotten egg. "No, thanks. I think I'll head out back and see what the kids are up to. Maybe go say hi to the horses."

Staten chuckled as he watched her sneak through the house like a burglar afraid of getting caught. Quinn had never been one for crowds or parties.

As the night passed, most of the older folks settled into talking. Reliving their glory days. The band had slowed to about five songs an hour. And the young adults had wandered outside to watch the ranch hands gather up the fireworks.

Granny and J.R. were relaxing in their comfortable chairs. J.R. had been quiet most of the night but he talked now and then to his wife. Staten wasn't even sure that anyone had noticed that his speech was slower. Staten knew his gramps was ready for the party to end, but it was good for the old man to sit among friends.

Staten didn't ask Amalah to dance until ten. He was having fun just watching her twirl around. And if he was being honest with himself, part of him hoped this would help her remember how nice things could be in Crossroads. How good it was to be home.

The melody of a slow, old Western song moved through the small room, and everyone in the house knew it was played for the two young lovers. Staten moved to Amalah's side, taking her hand and spinning her into his arms.

He still had a few fading cuts and sore bruises, but he was a healthy young man. And with Amalah by his side he felt even better. Like he could do anything. Even keep up the Double K. It seemed no one doubted Staten could handle taking over the ranch until J.R. recovered. No one except Staten.

Halfway through the song, he pulled Amalah in closer. A year ago Staten and Amalah had been kids, but now they moved as lovers. He knew every inch of her and he never wanted to forget.

They swayed through another song before Amalah reminded him that as a Kirkland he was the host and needed to mingle with the other guests. Unwrapping his arms from around her waist felt like prying open a ten-ton gate. He didn't want to let her go. But he knew his duty, and he'd do it like he always did.

Staten planted a swift kiss on her lips and was rewarded with her warm laugh as he moved through the guests, making sure to smile and thank everyone for coming. As the night grew later, he watched over his grandparents. J.R. was dozing in his green armchair. While Granny chatted with Miss Butterfield, she kept her hand on her husband's knee.

The younger children came in from the barn for milk and cookies, and by eleven most of the smaller kids had curled up near their parents. The music faded to background noise as neighbors and friends relaxed into comfortable conversations.

By eleven thirty, the home-care nurse rolled J.R. to bed, but everyone else stayed. It was almost like old times before J.R.'s stroke.

Those still awake began to bundle up and move outside to watch the fireworks show the Kirklands put on every year. Covered in blankets, the guests waited with hot cocoa as the ranch hands finished getting everything ready.

Staten found Amalah on their porch swing, huddled in one of Granny's old blankets. "This seat taken?"

Her response was to open her arms wide, inviting him to join her. He settled next to her and pulled her into his chest.

He slowly rocked them back and forth as they gazed up at the sky exploding in a rainbow of colors. He and Amalah may not have spent the semester together, but at least they would get to finish the year and start a new one wrapped in each other's arms.

Amalah sank deeper into his side as the last fireworks fizzled out and the smoke began to clear. The show wasn't long or big, but the fifteen minutes were grand.

All around them conversations were whispered in the dark. With low goodbyes, a few at a time, everyone left the big house and made for their vehicles. A long row of cars and pickups left the Double K Ranch and slowly drove toward town by starlight, headed for the school to ring in the New Year like they always did.

Staten knew those watching from town would think the line of cars was beautiful. Like a glowing snake slithering through the valley.

Amalah hopped off the swing to head to his truck, and he grabbed her hand. "Wait a second." He pulled her onto his lap and kissed her full out like he'd been dying to do all evening. When he pulled away, they were both trying to catch their breath.

She leaned her forehead against his and whispered, "I love you, Staten. I know a lot has changed lately. But that hasn't."

"I love you too. Always will."

For a second he crushed her to his chest, thinking they'd never be close enough. Then he lifted her to her feet and led her to the pickup. When Staten jumped into his truck, Amalah curled against his side, slipping her hand in his. He kissed the top of her head.

They followed the forty vehicles slowly moving toward Crossroads. The line of cars and pickups turned on their low lights so they could find their way to the school parking lot as the whole town seemed to turn off its lights and wait.

The night was silent, peaceful. Staten squeezed Amalah's hand as he saw the first cars reach the parking lot. He pulled up behind a dented old sedan and cut the ignition. Amalah seemed to hold her breath as they waited.

Then suddenly, all the town's bells began to ring as one. All around the valley, everyone knew it was New Years. Laughter blended with the bells as the whole town celebrated. Staten loved this tradition. He tilted Amalah's chin up and kissed her sweetly. Her first kiss of the year.

They watched as most of the cars circled the center of town

and then turned off toward their homes. In five minutes, Staten figured Crossroads would be asleep again.

As the parking lot emptied, he turned to his girl riding shotgun and smiled.

Even with everything that had gone wrong lately, this had been a moment of heaven.

Chapter 19

New Year's Wish

Charlotte Lane

Charlotte Lane poured herself a glass of wine and settled on the shaggy maroon rug laid out in front of the crackling fireplace. Throwing a blanket over her knees, she leaned against the arm of her couch and opened an old guilty pleasure. A tattered copy of *Lonesome Dove*.

She was ready to celebrate the New Year.

Baylor curled up on the cushion next to her, pretending she wasn't there. Charlotte didn't mind. They weren't a festive pair, but theirs was a companiable understanding.

When the doorbell rang, the cat eyed her as if she'd broken one of the house rules by waking him up. Charlotte had no idea who would be coming over at this time of night. It seemed the whole town was attending various parties, and she'd done her best to avoid them. After the craziness of the last semester, she'd hoped to end the year with a little quiet time.

She opened the door to find Wade with a bottle of champagne and a smile. Charlotte lifted her wineglass in salute.

"You started the party without me?" he asked.

She laughed. "What are you doing here?"

Wade walked past her as if he'd been invited in. "Celebrating the New Year. You know it's New Year's Eve? I knew you'd be holed up in here, so I thought I'd bring the fun to you."

Charlotte walked him into the kitchen and handed him a wineglass. "What fun?"

"Me, of course." He raised an eyebrow as if to say *Duh*.

"I guess you can be fun sometimes."

"Sometimes?" He followed her into the living room and joined her on the rug. "Admit it. I've made your time in Crossroads a blast. What would you do if you didn't go to the bar with me every weekend?"

If Charlotte was honest, she did love hanging out with Wade on Friday nights. The giant plate of nachos, the beer, and the soft country music playing in the background had been the highlights of her week. They'd become good friends. Talked about their school days. Joked about the wild things their students did. Even shared some secrets they'd never told anyone else before.

But they hadn't seen each other since school let out two weeks ago, and for some reason, she now felt like she was trapped in a blind date set up by a friend. She was on edge with no idea of what to say.

"So tell me—" Wade leaned back against the sofa, stretching his long legs across the floor. Baylor was wary but allowed the closeness. "What did you used to do at A&M to bring in the New Year?"

"Nothing much. I usually just read my book, had a glass of wine. Made up some ridiculous New Year's resolution." She shrugged.

"Oh, let's hear it. What was the worst resolution you ever made?"

Charlotte felt her cheeks go hot. She shook her head and took a sip of her wine. She wasn't embarrassed because she'd done some wild and crazy things. It was the opposite. She'd never done anything worth telling about.

Wade bumped her shoulder with his. "Come on. I won't laugh."

She knew he wouldn't. Charlotte shook her head again.

"I'll share if you do." He paused a beat. "Okay, once in high school, a buddy and me decided to gain twenty pounds of muscle by summer." He glanced sideways at her. "We ended up with fifteen extra pounds of pizza by April and had to seriously rethink things."

Charlotte giggled. "That's outrageous." She eyed his strong, lean body, trying to picture him overweight with a pizza gut.

"Hey, you weren't supposed to laugh."

"No, you said that you wouldn't laugh. I never promised anything."

He threw his arm on the couch cushion behind her shoulder. "You've got me there. But now it's your turn."

She took another drink of her wine, stalling for time. "Well, my resolution just about every year is to lose weight. But I guess no surprise there."

"What do you mean? You always look great."

Charlotte eyed her glass, wondering if she'd had too much to drink and misunderstood him.

Just then, a distant boom echoed through the town.

Wade looked at her, a huge smile lighting his face. "Fireworks." He hopped up like a five-year-old and rushed to the door. "Miss Ollie said the Kirklands put on a fireworks show for the town every New Year's Eve. Come on."

She couldn't stop the chuckle that slipped through her lips. His excitement made her feel like a kid again too. They rushed outside to the school parking lot across the street and watched as the sky crackled in a kaleidoscope of colors.

Back home, she'd never taken the time to watch the fireworks or celebrate the coming of the New Year.

The wind whipped around them as the grand finale erupted overhead, and Wade wrapped his arm around her shoulders, pulling her to his side.

As the last sparks fizzled in the sky, he looked at his watch. "They were a little early. There's still ten minutes till midnight."

"Look."

A winding line of what looked like dimmed headlights was slowly making its way through town. They watched as dozens of cars and trucks pulled into the school's parking lot and waited. Charlotte wasn't sure what they were all expecting to happen, but she found her excitement rising with each passing minute.

Then all at once, the bells of the school started ringing like a sweet symphony. Whoops and honks joined the melody as the town celebrated the start of the year. It was the most magical thing she'd ever witnessed.

She looked up at Wade, laughing, caught up in the atmosphere. He leaned toward her, and for one second, his lips pressed against hers . . . and her heart exploded like the fireworks that had just lit up the night sky.

"Happy New Year," he whispered.

Charlotte stared at her friend, shocked. After a moment, she smiled.

"Happy New Year," she said.

What now? She didn't want to read too much into this. They'd just had a little too much wine, right? That's all. Everything would go back to normal tomorrow.

Of course it would.

Chapter 20

Alone with Amalah

Staten Kirkland

Staten Kirkland's pickup was the last vehicle to join the short line of cars heading back to the Double K Ranch. As he drove through the night, midnight showered over them. Amalah settled against him and he wondered how long it would take her to fall asleep. She was never much for late nights. It was almost like old times. She was beside him. The way it should be.

His truck creaked over the back road leading to the Double K. This old trail was the first one he got to drive on by himself. Staten had felt ten feet tall that day. J.R. told him the dirt road had been the only way to town before the county road was built. If he ran off the road when he was a kid, the only thing that would have happened was he'd be in the dirt, but tonight Staten was very careful. He didn't want to wake the woman he loved. Not when she slept so peacefully.

Amalah stayed curled against Staten's side and he wrapped

his arm around her, pulling her closer. They'd driven down this road plenty of times. Meeting with friends to celebrate after football games. Sneaking a few kisses after dates in high school. Out here, away from the bright lights of town, the stars lit up the sky. It was a beautiful encore to the fireworks they'd watched earlier.

As he followed the winding road, Staten thought about his grandparents. Granny had told him several times that J.R. was her first and only love. The only man she'd ever wanted. She said she married him because the man never told a lie.

Staten tried to be like him. Honest, hardworking, reliable. He wanted Amalah to be able to trust him the way his granny trusted his gramps. He hoped their relationship lasted as long as his grandparents'. But if he was honest with himself, he worried that the distance between them would push him and Amalah apart for longer than just a few college semesters.

He feared other things on the ranch too. One was that his grandparents might die before he learned what he needed to know in order to run the spread. He'd known as a child that he'd be in charge one day, but he'd thought it would be years from now.

Amalah and Staten always knew they'd be laid to rest at the founder's cemetery someday. They'd had their future planned for as long as he could remember. Amalah wanted to teach grade school for a few years before they had their own kids. They could travel when she was off during the summers. They were going to see the world together, but they'd always planned to come back to the Double K to stay.

Once they had kids, Staten and Amalah had thought maybe Staten's father would retire and watch over the place for them while they vacationed. Maybe they'd build a cabin by the rapids when winter settled in Texas. Or maybe they'd remodel the big house one last time.

Now, he didn't think Samuel would ever come back to the

Double K to stay longer than a publicity shoot. Staten didn't believe his father would last even a full day on the ranch.

Staten and Amalah's dreams seemed far away now. So much had happened that they'd never planned for.

Staten couldn't think of vacations or time off now. Most ranchers worked year-round, and he knew he'd be no different. J.R. was still so frail. Granny rarely left him alone. Even with the in-home nurses. Her tea parties had gone. No more weekends at the farmers market. Friends came often but they rarely stayed for supper.

Staten would be stuck on the ranch for a while. It would take Amalah four years to graduate and probably a few more for him to finish too. Would she even want to wait that long for them to start a life?

The Kirklands were rich in land, but they worked hard from dawn to dusk. And they always would. Ranching and Ransom Canyon were in their blood. The plans of long vacations were just dreams. On a ranch, time was always too short. The job was never done.

He kissed Amalah as they bumped over the rocky road. He needed to get out of his head and focus on now. Staten would go crazy if he kept living in what-ifs and maybes.

He pulled her in closer as he saw the light that always burned over the barn. Staten remembered when he was little, he'd thought that light shined over the whole world. Things had been simpler then.

As he looked closer, the outline of a man stood still as a statue under the bright light. Staten stiffened, his adrenaline spiking. Was someone trespassing on the Double K?

His foot hit the accelerator. Then he blinked and the shadow was gone.

Shaking his head, Staten tried to clear his thoughts. Had he just been imagining things? He'd been so busy overthinking, he'd become delusional.

Staten put his truck in park beside the barn and lightly

brushed the silky brown hair away from Amalah's face. He kissed her softly, his lips feathering over her cheeks and eyes and nose. She would always be the most beautiful girl in the world.

"Wake up, sleepyhead."

Amalah grumbled, snuggling her head into his chest. "No."

He chuckled. "You want to sleep over? It's late. I can sleep on the couch. Though I'd much rather lay with you."

"Can't," she muttered sleepily, pushing off him to sit up and rub her eyes. "Quinn is waiting to take me home. I promised to spend some time with her. She is my best friend and I haven't seen her for months, so she's staying the night with me."

Staten opened his mouth but didn't say anything. Another thing she hadn't told him. Another plan she'd made without him. Another reason they couldn't spend time together. His hopes of talking her into them sneaking into his room for a while drained away.

When Staten opened the door of the big house, Quinn was there helping Granny put the last of the glasses away.

It took all his strength to muster a hello and thank Quinn. "You didn't have to wait and clean. You should have gone on the drive. I could have taken Amalah home."

Quinn shared a smile with Granny. "It's okay. I don't mind."

He reminded himself that he'd have the next two weeks with Amalah before she had to head back to Tech for school.

Granny stood next to him on the porch and waved to Quinn and Amalah. The romantic evening Staten planned had vanished when Amalah said goodnight.

When Staten woke at five the next morning, he was on the couch with no memory of how he'd gotten there. His grandparents were tiptoeing around him. Granny looked tired and J.R. looked like he wanted to go to work.

J.R. patted Staten on the head. "It's almost dawn, son. Better get to the barn. The men'll be waiting."

Staten didn't bother to change clothes. He went straight to the bunkhouse. Straight to work.

At almost eleven, he took a break. He took a shower and drove over to Amalah's place as fast as he could.

He didn't have much time. After he had lunch with her, he'd go back to work. But even ten minutes together was worth the drive into town to her house. He'd stop back about five and they could enjoy a real date. They could go out tonight. A nice dinner, maybe, then a drive and parking down in the canyon to watch the sunset.

Staten was smiling as he hurried up to Amalah's door.

Amalah's mother answered with sorrow in her eyes. "Hey, Staten. What are you doing here, hon? Amalah left hours ago."

Amalah left? Without coming to see him? Staten barely heard as Amalah's mom went on about Amalah's busy semester and her sorority sisters begging her to come home this morning.

"Is she mad at me?" he said with his head down.

He and Amalah hadn't really talked about what they'd do in the next few days, but he'd assumed they'd have another day together. More time.

"Hey, Mrs. Reed. Where do you want me to . . ."

Staten's head whipped up as Quinn stepped into the room with a bundle of what looked like dish towels in her arms.

Amalah's mom turned around. "Here, sweetie. I'll take those." She took the pile from Quinn. She lowered her voice, but Staten swore he heard her say, "Talk to him. He's upset about Ama."

Staten's heart pinched. He wasn't sure he wanted to hear what Quinn had to say. But she was a good friend; she'd tell it to him straight. And if Amalah planned to move on without him, Quinn would know.

He just looked at her, knowing the question sat in his eyes. And her obvious reluctance wasn't making him feel any better.

She moved next to him, crossing her arms over her chest. "Amalah left early this morning. She had some sorority thing back at Tech. I don't know why she didn't tell you. Maybe she didn't want to upset you."

Staten stepped out onto the porch and stared at the sky. He watched the thunderclouds rolling in and thought they matched his mood. He didn't know what to say. He didn't know what to think. Had he really become so unimportant to Amalah?

"Is she dating someone else?" He heard Quinn gasp but continued. "If she is, I can handle it. I just want the truth."

If Amalah wanted to move on, he'd let her. He would have to. But he'd always be here waiting for her to come home.

Quinn's small hand squeezed his arm. "She's not seeing anyone else, Staten. She loves you. She just had to get back."

He stared into her blue eyes and could tell she was holding something back. "What? You know you can give it to me straight."

Her voice got small. "It's just . . . I think college is a lot more than she thought it would be. High school was easy. Everyone loved her and she was home with all the people she grew up with. But when you left Tech, she was stuck up there all alone. She's having a hard time with that."

She looked so sad, for a moment Staten wondered if Quinn was talking about Amalah or herself.

Frustration gnawed at him. "I didn't want to leave her at Tech. I had to come back. J.R. needs me. I thought she understood that."

"She does," Quinn said quickly. "But it doesn't make any of this any easier. For either of you."

Neither does her disappearing without a word, he thought.

"Her classes have been really hard for her this semester," Quinn continued. "I know she's been worrying about flunking out. And the sorority is more work than she'd thought it would be. She's really stressed right now."

Staten knew a thing or two about being overloaded on

work. It seemed like his job never ended. He wanted to give Amalah the benefit of the doubt, but the truth was it felt like she wasn't even trying anymore.

Amalah never told him she was struggling in her classes.

Staten fought down cuss words. These few months he'd been playing a game like he'd wake up and this would all be over. He was a college kid learning ranching, but he hadn't accepted that his previous life was over.

Quinn's quiet voice broke through his thoughts. "Look, you're both just feeling lonely. Call her. Keep trying and be patient. It'll all work out the way it's supposed to."

He threw one arm over her shoulders and pulled her into a side hug. He hoped she was right. Maybe he did just need a little more patience and a lot more faith. But that was easier said than done. Amalah had a new life in a new place, and it seemed there wasn't any more room for him.

As Staten said goodbye to Quinn and walked back to his truck, the whole world seemed to dull. His plans for the night were over. He wasn't even hungry anymore. He might as well get back to work.

All his life he'd tried to live a good life. He'd tried to do the right thing. But right now, he wanted to disappear for a few days and go wild. Get drunk. Drive a hundred miles an hour. Blow all his money.

Get lost from the world for a while, but he couldn't, not when he was the boss. Like it or not, he had to do the right thing. He had to run the ranch. His gramps was counting on him.

He climbed into his pickup and headed back home. Like it or not, this was his life for now.

Later that afternoon, Staten pulled up near the bunkhouse and saw Jake.

He yelled at the foreman, "You done working today, Jake?"

"Yep, I got invited to a big dinner party, if you can believe it. Don't tell me you're getting back to work, Boss."

Staten kept his tone even. "I won't do much. I just thought I'd ride the fences. We've got four men out checking on the cattle. All is quiet."

"You want me to ride along with you for a few hours?"

"No, I need to ride alone. You go take a shower. If you're going to a party, no one will thank you for smelling like that. Besides, I was laid up for nearly four days last week. If I lay around too long, I'll forget how to sit on a horse." Staten headed toward the barn, yelling, "Take a day off. Go have a great dinner too."

"I think I will, Boss." Jake laughed for once. "You should come with me. You know, I think I've got a gal that can cook, and I plan on keeping this one. They are getting harder and harder to find these days."

"No, thanks."

"Suit yourself."

Staten jumped on his horse and got to work, pushing away the pain.

Chapter 21

Dreaming of Love

Peggy Warner

Peggy took her time getting ready once her mother and father were gone. Then she packed a basket of leftover sweets from the party last night and slipped sandwiches in. She had no hope of seeing Duke. Last night one of Staten's men said her cowboy drew the short straw and had to work.

Peggy drove out to the cemetery. She just wanted to sit among the trees and eat. She'd be home alone within an hour and then she'd watch movies and enjoy the quiet time.

As the day aged, she'd probably fall asleep on the couch.

It would be silent, but it wouldn't be lonely. When you're a "one," everyone wants to invite you to things. Many of the things Peggy didn't really want to go to. It took until she was almost twenty before she finally got up enough nerve to start saying no.

Two years ago, Peggy's school friends invited her to go out

to the local bar. She was twenty-five then. She decided to go. Why not? She had her own car so she could leave early.

When she walked inside, she was disheartened. The place looked more like a pizza shop than a bar. No band, just a radio playing, but everyone seemed happy. Conversation flowed easily.

But after a trip to the restroom, she came out to find the people she'd come with had already left. For a minute she panicked. Alone in a bar. Then she realized she lived three blocks away. Before she had time to calm, she saw her purse under her chair at the empty table.

No one in the bar noticed as she picked it up and slipped out. She didn't want to be seen sitting alone in a bar. This wasn't the wild place she'd feared.

The parking lot was well lit. No one passed in the street. There wasn't even any trash blowing around. Her old car was parked two places down from the door.

She almost laughed. All her life she'd feared a dark, unpaved lot at midnight. Bad thugs fighting or outlaws beating up drunks for their leftover beer money. But nothing happened until a few guys came out of the bar, talking about when to plant in spring. They walked to their cars without a single cuss word.

Still, Peggy ran and jumped into her car and was backing out before anyone could have gotten in.

She drove the proper speed. Before the car warmed, she was home. She ran up the apartment steps and darted in and locked both locks just in case one of the not-so drunks followed her home.

And then she laughed. What an adventure!

Peggy dreamed about walking into the place one Saturday night to find Duke there waiting for her in a booth.

They'd talk. Maybe he'd ask her to dance as they'd done at the New Year's Eve party at the Kirklands'.

When she'd danced with him at the party, she was happy. Proud.

She smiled. She loved living in her dreams.

The weekend had seen a dusting of snow, and by Monday, the cemetery was covered in a thin blanket of the freezing wet stuff. It had been too cold for Peggy and Duke to meet at their usual spot under the large oak that protected the graves on the hill, but Peggy found herself driving the few miles to the cemetery anyway.

She knew her cowboy wouldn't be there, but she wanted to brush off the inches of snow so he'd know she'd shown up and stayed as long as she could.

Ice patches dotted the hill, and Peggy had to catch herself from falling more than once. It was a slow climb up. By the time she joined her ancestors resting at the top, snow began falling again.

Peggy ran her thick gloves over the gravestones, brushing the small snow piles off the tops. She glanced out toward the rapids, remembering her time with Duke. Despite the chill, the white-painted ground shimmering in the sunlight was a beautiful sight. It would be even better if he were here.

She slowly made her way down the hill to the river, retracing the steps she'd taken with her cowboy a few weeks before. She didn't know how, but somehow in the short time she'd known him, the quiet, sweet ranch hand had come to mean so much to her. Peggy thought about him day and night and often imagined what it would be like to go out and face the world together.

Fat, puffy flakes fell on her nose, and she looked up to see a winter wonderland. White filled the air around her, falling faster with each second. In her daydreaming, she'd lost track of the time and the weather. It seemed a snowstorm was blowing in.

Peggy made her way back to the hill but could barely see

more than a few feet in front of her. Afraid she'd gotten turned around, she looked for the old oak swaying in the wind. Nothing. The huge tree seemed to have vanished. In a blink everything had turned white with the snow.

She lost all sense of direction for a few minutes. And the chill was starting to sneak through her winter coat. She looked back, searching for the rapids, but barely saw her own tracks. Peggy knew she was out there all alone. No one around for miles.

The snow was getting thicker. If she didn't move, she'd be stuck in this whiteout and maybe even freeze to death. She squinted her eyes, hoping for a clearer view. For a moment, there was nothing beyond the white flakes dancing in the breeze. Then the wind blew them away.

Tears rained down her face as the hill seemed to rise up in front of her. And racing down the side was her cowboy, bundled up in a thick brown coat with the Double K brand, his black hat tilted against the wind.

"Peggy. Thank God. I've been searching everywhere for you." He wrapped her in his arms. "I was afraid you'd gotten lost out here."

She snuggled her face against his chest. "Me too." She wouldn't tell him just how scared she'd been.

"Come on, let's get you out of here."

He grabbed her hand, nearly dragging her up the hill. As the graves appeared, relief melted through her. Duke led her to his pickup as the weather shifted to a slushy mist.

"I was waiting for you," she whispered.

He squeezed her tighter in his embrace, and she squeezed him back. For a moment all seemed right with the world.

Finally, they climbed into the truck holding one another. All she wanted to do was touch him. Every day he couldn't come, she'd missed him more.

A shiver racked through Peggy as the heater's hot air fell

over her. She hadn't realized how cold she'd gotten until her body tried to warm back up.

Duke pulled her onto his lap, rubbing his hands over her arms and her back. "How long were you out there?"

She shrugged, clenching her teeth to keep them from chattering. "I lost track. But I would've waited for you forever."

He tilted up her chin and lowered his mouth to hers. The kiss was slow and sweet, like he was trying to communicate with more than just words.

When he leaned back and breathed, Duke finally said, "I think I love you, Peggy. I know you may think this is crazy but I can't get you out of my mind. I'm not rushing into this. I told myself a hundred times to slow down but no one ever has kissed me the way you do. And I've never felt as alive as I do with you." He ran his thumb over her bottom lip. "This time I can't walk away. Not from you."

"I love you too, Duke."

This was the first time she found a man who cared. She couldn't wait to get closer.

Chapter 22

Riding in the New Year

January

Charlotte Lane

Charlotte loved her riding lessons at the Double K. She showed up at the ranch every Sunday, rain or shine. Staten wasn't always there to meet her, but if he wasn't there then one of his cowboys was, and he always had a horse saddled and ready for her.

She decided riding a horse on the Kirkland ranch was only the second wildest thing she'd done last year. The first had to be coaching high school football. And she was glad that was over.

At the Double K, Staten's men treated her like she was made of glass. Every one of them had a map with Staten's instructions written on the corners. Staten had her trained to ride on flat land at first and as the days grew colder the land became rough.

No doubt she loved every minute at the ranch, imagining she was traveling along an old wagon trail or preparing to round up cattle. Charlotte even convinced herself that she was born to ride, following in the footsteps of her ancestors and having been trained by her favorite books.

Most of the time the cowboys looked a little bored with her slower pace, but everyone was polite. Her favorite teacher was Jake Longbow, the Kirklands' foreman. His lessons always went over the time set aside for her, and he liked to talk about the history of the Kirklands' land. In great detail he told her about the first Kirklands and how they settled the Double K Ranch. The legend was that after James Randall Kirkland married Millie, the first Mrs. Kirkland ran away to her brother in East Texas.

Raised by the Natives, her brother asked if her husband had ever hurt her. Millie and her brother had both been captured by the Plains tribes as kids, and he would always protect his sister.

But when she told him that Kirkland had given up food to keep her fed and made their home in a cave to keep her warm through the winter, her brother thought it best that she go back home to her husband.

According to Jake, the story was that her brother had walked a few feet away from his sister and lit a fire. He wrapped arrows with cloth, lit them and kept sending them into the sky until her husband found them.

Kirkland was new to this wild land, but he didn't say a word; he just held his wife gently and comforted her as best he could. Finally, he lifted her on his horse and they rode home.

She never ran away again, but her brother always came armed when he visited his sister's house. Just in case Kirkland got out of line.

Charlotte wondered if the cave in Jake's story was the one

Wade had been looking for. But the foreman's stories were so interesting that she always forgot to ask.

Jake told her another legend about how the first Mrs. Kirkland loved the ranch and eventually learned to love her man. The first James Kirkland built their house with his own two hands, and folks said Millie always smiled when she opened the door. They called her a lady and a beauty and said there was never a mark on her from his hand even though she was a spitfire. When she got mad she would fly at her husband in anger.

Legend goes that James would just walk around with her beating on him until they finally found a bedroom. Then no one saw either one until dawn. She'd come out smiling and he'd come out bruised but happy.

Charlotte loved the stories. For generations, the Kirklands had lived and loved on this land, and she hoped to do the same one day in Crossroads.

"The founding Kirklands have such an interesting story. Why has no one written it?" she asked one day as their horses trotted back to the barn. She knew James's and Millie's love affair would make a great Western novel.

Jake shrugged. "Don't know. Maybe you should. The old papers and Kirkland's journal are in the safe at the school."

"I might do that." She'd always wanted to become a writer but had never found the time or motivation to make it happen.

She thought about the papers Jake had said were in the school safe. She wondered what she'd find in there. Had Wade looked in the journals for the cave's location? Did he even know about them at all?

She looked over the land. It seemed the love of the two Kirkland founders still whispered in the wind. She swore she heard the first Kirkland's laughter whistle in the breeze.

Charlotte and Jake rode for a while in silence before she said, "I'd like to keep taking lessons with you this spring. I feel like I'm living in your stories. And maybe writing my own."

The foreman pulled up his horse and stared at her. "Sure thing. You have met Staten, haven't you?"

"Yes." Obviously.

"Then you know he doesn't do something halfway and he won't want you to either. I don't know why, but he wants a degree and he'll get one if he has to do the classes one at a time. So, you might as well come out every week. We're going to be waiting for you. We won't stop until you're ready for barrel racing in the rodeo."

She laughed, swinging off the roan and grabbing a brush to rub her down. Charlotte wondered if the old cowboy would let her bring Wade out here sometime so he could hear the legends of the original Kirklands too. She thought about calling him when she got home to tell him about the journals at the school. Maybe they could spend the rest of winter break helping each other research the founding family.

Chapter 23

A Test for the Future

Staten Kirkland

The first few weeks of January were cold and rainy, but Staten was still out working before the sun brightened the sky. Since Amalah left, every day he pushed himself as hard as he could. He needed to do work. He rode horseback when he could and drove the truck when the weather was too bad. He was up before dawn and the last to call it a night.

Staten didn't talk much to anyone except to give work orders. No one objected. The men just got their jobs done. No one complained because the boss was working harder than any other.

At nineteen he made mistakes now and then, but no one said a word. He was a fast learner and never messed up on the same thing twice.

In the evenings, Staten was still reading the books Dr. Lane gave him, and he'd even tried his hand at writing a few essays for her to read. But after the last two papers came back dripping with red ink from all his mistakes, his confidence was shot. He wouldn't give up though. He'd just work harder.

Staten climbed into his truck and drove to town the first Tuesday the school was open. He saw the surprise in Dr. Lane's eyes when he walked through her door as the bell rang at three forty-five.

He spoke before she could. "I've been studying, and I read all the books you told me to. But I still feel as dumb as a bucket of rocks. Is there anything else I can do? I've decided to enroll in online classes next semester, and I want to make sure I'm prepared."

The English teacher raised one eyebrow. "You think you're ready to take another college class?"

Staten grabbed his determination by the horns and held on. "Yep. You've been a great teacher. I know I need to work on my writing skills, but I think I can do well enough with everything else."

When she didn't say a word, he added, "Ma'am, in one week I'll be twenty. I'm a man, not a boy. I've got to take things head-on."

Dr. Lane stood from her desk with a big smile lighting her face. "I'm glad to hear it, Staten. Truth is, you've been a great student and you're a lot more capable than you think. I know you'll do great."

"But my last paper . . ."

"You have things you need to work on, for sure. But you're a fine, smart young man. A hard worker. I have no doubts you'll go far."

Staten stared out of the window. "I plan to graduate, even if it takes me ten years."

"If you'd like, you can take one of my old finals from when I taught at A&M. It'll give you a little taste of the expectations college English professors will have."

She rummaged through a dark leather briefcase and pulled out a blue folder. She started flipping through the papers until she grabbed what looked like a thin packet.

"Here, take this exam. I'll time you just like I would if this were my real class, and we'll see how you do. If you bomb, at least we'll know what to focus on. And if you do great, which I suspect you will, you can move on to reenrolling in college with confidence." Dr. Lane passed him the test.

Staten hadn't expected to prove himself so soon, but he never backed down from a challenge.

She smiled as he took his seat. "You have three hours. Starting now."

Not another word was said for two hours and forty minutes. When he was done, Staten stood and walked to her desk. "I did the best I could."

"I would expect nothing less." Her red pen was out before he even reached the door. "I'll call you when I finish grading."

Staten headed to his truck, his mind buzzing with Robert Frost's poem about choosing the right path. He knew going back to school was what he needed to do. For himself and the ranch. Whether he passed or failed, he knew one fact. He wouldn't stop doing the best he could or keep trying until he passed.

Chapter 24

New Beginnings

Charlotte Lane

Charlotte watched the young cowboy walk out of her room with his head held high. In novels, there always seemed to be a moment for characters when they realized something important. And as Staten Kirkland had stood in the middle of her classroom, she'd watched wisdom grow.

She looked down at his test and did something she rarely had time to do while grading. Instead of just marking the questions he'd gotten wrong, Charlotte made a point of praising him on the questions he answered well. By the time she finished, the pages looked like they'd been scribbled on by a preschooler. Red colored the margins and small smiley faces dotted the test.

Staten had passed with flying colors, and she wasn't the least surprised. After watching him on the ranch and tutoring him through the past semester, she knew he was something special.

He was going to be a great man one day, and she wanted to stay around and watch him grow.

A light knock sounded on her open door, and as she looked up, her lips curved into a smile against her will. Wade stood in the doorway, leaning against the frame. What looked like a small grocery sack hung from his cast-free arm.

He spoke before she could. "You have any idea what time it is?"

Charlotte turned her gaze to the windows lining the left side of her classroom. Shock settled over her as she took in the already darkened sky.

Wade chuckled. "Yep, it's almost nine. What are you still doing here this late?"

She gathered Staten's test and placed it in her case. "I was working with Staten Kirkland. I gave him a practice test and just got finished grading it. I lost track of the time, I guess."

She stood, nervously sorting the rest of her things.

Ever since Wade had kissed her on New Year's Eve, things had felt different between them. She couldn't forget the feel of his lips on hers. It may have only lasted a few seconds, but she had replayed that moment in her mind a hundred times.

"What about you? Why are you still here?"

"Actually, I just got back. I poked my head in here earlier, but you were so focused on your papers you didn't even notice me. I figured if I didn't grab your attention, you probably wouldn't remember to eat dinner either." He dropped the plastic bag on the desk between them.

Charlotte tried to ignore the warmth filling her heart. "What's that?"

"Nachos. I ran up to the bar and got our usual. I even stopped at the gas station down the street and picked you up a Diet Coke." Wade smiled proudly, handing her the drink. He unloaded the bag and pulled a chair next to the desk. "Join me?"

She couldn't believe he'd gone out of his way to make sure she'd eat. It was so thoughtful. So sweet.

As they ate, they talked about the Double K Ranch and her riding lessons with Staten. She told Wade all about Jake Longbow, the foreman of the Kirkland ranch, and his stories about the first Kirklands to settle the area. "You should come out with me sometime. I swear that old cowboy knows more about this area than any of the founding families I've met. He told me that James Randall Kirkland left a diary behind that's supposed to be in the school's safe."

The ex-soldier sat up and leaned forward. "Here? In this school? In the safe downstairs?"

Charlotte couldn't help but laugh at the look on his face. "Yeah, he said it was stored here for safekeeping, since the school has one of the only libraries in Crossroads."

Wade jumped up off his chair. "Let's go check it out. Those journals might be what I was missing. They might hold a clue that will help me find the cave."

She stood up, too, and before she knew what was happening, he pulled her against his chest and hugged her. "You're a dream. You know that?" He planted a quick kiss on her cheek and bounded out the door. "Come on."

"Just a second. I've got to make a quick call."

Charlotte smoothed her beige skirt, trying to regain her balance. This friendship thing was a lot harder than she'd thought.

Chapter 25

A Land Man

Staten Kirkland

Staten pulled through the gate of the Double K as a dark sedan with tinted windows raced out. He watched the car, hoping to catch a glimpse of the driver, but he didn't see anything useful. It was probably another reporter wanting an update on Senator Samuel Kirkland's father.

He was still trying to push aside his irritation as he was walking into the little cottage. The wall phone rang, and he picked it up, raising it halfway to his ear when Granny rushed out of the bedroom.

"Staten!"

Panic stabbed at him.

"Hold for a moment, please," he said into the receiver and then dropped the phone.

"What's wrong? Is Gramps okay?" Staten didn't breathe. Everything was forgotten. Passing Dr. Lane's test. Trying to go to college. Running the ranch.

She took a deep breath, raising her hand as if to calm him. "Yes, dear. But I need help with that stubborn old man. He's been moving around all afternoon, trying to break out of this house. I can't get him to sit down for a minute. And when he told me that you were later than usual, he tried to get Jake to saddle his horse so he could ride out looking for you. Because he can't work, he's taken over the worrying for the whole ranch."

Staten relaxed, and then swallowed a chuckle as his gramps shuffled into the center of the living room. "Evening, J.R.," Staten said. "I see you're getting around. Maybe it's about time you did some work around here." Without giving Granny a chance to say anything, he moved past her to shake the old cowboy's hand. "I was hoping you could help out on the cattle count tomorrow. Some of the men can't seem to get more than ten."

J.R. frowned, thought a minute, and said, "I guess I could. I've always been good at counting. It's not hard but I did notice you boys were off by one last time. I'll find my jeans. Sounds like you need me."

"We'll always need you, J.R."

Staten turned into Granny's hard stare. She started to say it was too early to have Gramps step out of the house, but Staten disagreed. J.R. had enough of being locked in. He was slower and thinner, but J.R. was a recovering man and he was ready to work.

Granny would probably hide his work clothes by the morning, but Staten knew his gramps would be outside tomorrow if he had to go in his pajamas. J.R. didn't have to stay out long, and he'd have plenty of help getting to the gates, but nothing could stop him once he decided he was going.

Disapproval flowed off Granny. "No more than an hour," she said. "And, Staten, you stay there with him and have him locked in. I don't want a cow walking over him."

Gramps walked over to his wife of forty-seven years and

planted a kiss on her cheek. "Don't worry so much, Tabby. I've wrestled plenty of cows in my day."

"I'll take good care of him, Granny." He turned to his grandpa. "I'll have Jake drive the side-by-side over to pick you up at nine tomorrow, Boss. We're three men short this week. Haven't got back from Christmas. We could use some help."

J.R. grinned. "It's about time I get back to the land. I may not be able to handle everything but I'd like to see my grandson come in before dark now and then. If I don't do something, he'll be eating his supper and his breakfast about the same time."

Granny squeezed her husband's hand. "Promise me, no more than one hour, James. This first day I'll be nervous as all get-out unless you promise you'll come back in an hour."

J.R. laughed. "I'll just be counting. I'll be sitting on the fence. I was born and raised on this ranch. I can handle it just fine."

Staten was about to turn back to the kitchen when he remembered the mystery driver. "By the way, Gramps. Who was that in the sedan that pulled out of here a few minutes ago? Another reporter?"

His grandpa's smile fell flat. "No, a salesman. Claimed he was looking to buy up land in this area and wanted to check out the west pasture. I told him we hadn't sold in over a hundred years, and we weren't about to start today."

"That's odd."

"Not really, son." J.R. shuffled to his wife, placing a hand on her shoulder. "People come here at least twice a year trying to buy some of our land. But Kirklands don't sell. It's something I could never get your father to understand."

Granny huffed loudly. "All right, now. You've been running around long enough, James. You're meant to be resting."

As she walked him back to his chair in the bedroom, Staten remembered the phone.

"Sorry for the wait. Kirkland, here." There was silence, and Staten guessed whoever called had hung up by now.

He waited a beat, but just as he was about to hang up, he heard a very proper voice on the other line. "Staten, I wanted to tell you as soon as I could. You passed with a B," Dr. Lane said. "Great job."

He couldn't believe it. Maybe he wasn't so dumb after all. Maybe he did have a chance of getting his degree. "Thank you. Wow."

"I told you that you'd do fine. Hopefully now you will stop worrying so much. Save that for when you're my age."

"Thanks, ma'am, for all your help and not making it easy on me."

"I didn't, Staten. You earned this." She laughed. "I'd like to always make it hard on you because I have a feeling one day everyone in this state will be calling you Mr. Kirkland. You're going to be something great."

Staten was on cloud nine. He couldn't stop smiling. "I'll be happy if I can just learn a little more. Easy or not, I'm going to get that degree."

He hung up the phone feeling lighter than he had in weeks. Things were looking up. Soon he'd be back in college, taking online classes. J.R. was doing better every day. And Amalah would be home for spring break.

Slowly things were drifting back to normal. But one thing had changed for good. Staten was falling in love with the land, and as much as he loved Amalah, he no longer thought he could ever leave it.

Chapter 26

Blooming in Winter

Peggy Warner

Peggy huddled deeper into her jacket, trying to hold off the bite of the frosty wind. She tiptoed between the ice patches and small piles of snow dotting her cousins' walkway, pretending she was performing in a ballet. She'd never been much of a dancer, but lately, she seemed to want to break into a happy dance every chance she got.

The first month of the New Year had been a dream. She managed to sneak away for a cemetery date with Duke a few times every week. With all the snow blanketing Crossroads, it hadn't been hard to convince her parents that she was shoveling the sidewalks near the family plots.

But while the family expected her to maintain the cemetery for the county so no one else would have to, they didn't like when it took up so much of Peggy's time.

For the past week Ashley-Lynn had been calling Peggy asking for help with the new baby. Auntie Ruth had left, and Ashley claimed she couldn't handle all three kids on her own while Fred was at work. No matter how many times Peggy reminded her cousin that she didn't babysit, the stressed-out mama wouldn't take no for an answer.

Peggy knocked on the door, and it swung open almost immediately.

Ashley-Lynn handed Peggy the squirming Katie. "Thank God you're here." She pulled on her overcoat and grabbed the keys hanging on the hook by the door. "This one has already been fed; she just needs to be burped. Austin is taking a nap, and Mia is in front of the TV. I'll be back in a couple hours."

She jogged down the steps without so much as a thank-you and hopped into her car. Some things would never change.

Peggy readjusted the wiggling baby in her arms and stepped into the house. She peeked into Austin's room, making sure he was still sleeping peacefully in his crib. Then she settled into the armchair to watch cartoons with four-year-old Mia.

As she leaned the baby against her shoulder and began patting her back, Peggy felt a strange warmth flow through her. She imagined what it would be like to have little ones of her own. Babies to snuggle and take care of. Little Dukes running around the yard.

She smiled to herself. Maybe one day.

By the time her cousin returned, Peggy and the three kids were lying together on the couch watching TV. The children had all been fed, bathed, and were ready for bed.

Ashley-Lynn dropped a pile of shopping bags on the floor, her eyes wide. "Wow, Peggy, you should babysit more often. This is amazing."

Peggy jumped up, handing little Katie back to her mom. "Sorry, Ash, but I don't think I'm going to be available again for a long time."

She fled through the door before her cousin could react,

knowing exactly what she was going to do next. What she wanted to do. And she could barely contain her excitement.

Yanking her car door open, she jumped in and headed for the Double K Ranch. She'd been there many times before. Her folks and the Kirklands were good friends. But this was the first time she was going by herself to find a cowboy.

Nervousness flooded her, settling in her cheeks.

What if Duke wasn't even there? What if he was out riding? Or what if he got in trouble for having a female visitor? What if the Kirklands fired him for slacking on the job by talking to her? What if he got embarrassed that she showed up?

Before she finished thinking through all of the bad things that could happen, she turned onto the road that led to the headquarters. Anyone looking would see her coming a mile away. It was too late to turn back now.

She passed the big house and pulled up in front of the large barn situated a few yards from the bunkhouse. A dozen ranch hands stood around the corral, watching her as she slowed to a stop.

Panic started to rise in her gut. She was about to turn her car back around and speed out of there when she caught sight of a pair of steel-gray eyes.

Peggy watched with everyone else as Duke broke from the group and walked over to the beat-up green Pinto. She couldn't make out his expression in the dying light. She hoped he wasn't mad.

She held her breath as he opened her door with a loud creak.

He bent, leaning down to meet her eyes. "You okay, Miss Peggy?"

"Yeah, I just wanted to see you." She dipped her head. "I'm sorry."

Duke grabbed her hand and helped her out of the car. He stepped closer and lowered his voice. "I thought you didn't want people to know about us yet."

"I know. But I was just at my cousin's taking care of her kids, and cooking dinner and doing everything I've done a thousand times before, and..."

He tilted her chin up and she stared into the eyes of the kindest man she'd ever known. "And what?"

She grasped his hand. "And I want to be with you and I don't mind who knows."

Before she could say another word, her gentle cowboy crushed her to his chest and captured her mouth with his. He kissed her full out in front of everyone.

Hoots and hollers erupted from the ranch hands behind them but Peggy didn't care. She was ready to start living, and she wanted the world to know.

Before the cheers faded into background noise, Peggy heard Jake Longbow yell, "Guess those two aren't as shy as we thought. Looks like we're gonna have a wedding if we can pull them apart."

Duke moved away from her to glare at the foreman. "Shut it. I'm busy here."

He'd told her he was a Texan, but that didn't mean much to her. The state was so huge he could be a city boy, or maybe he grew up in the country. Though she couldn't really picture him on a ranch. If he'd had a Texas twang, he'd lost it years ago. She knew he'd been in the Army and that he was a medic, but he didn't talk much about that either.

Their two usual topics of conversation were either school or the history of the area. Almost every week he'd tell her to ask Staten something about his ancestors. But as far as she could tell, Staten didn't know much about the first Kirklands who settled the area.

As Wade walked with Charlotte to her car after school, she decided to avoid the subject of the Double K Ranch. "Do you want to try somewhere new tonight?"

The ex-soldier looked like he was confronting the enemy. "Why?"

She tried not to laugh as she added another thing about him to her list. The man was set in his ways. "Just to try something new. Nachos and beer are great and all, but I'm kind of in the mood for a good old-fashioned cheeseburger."

He watched her closely for a minute more before his lips twitched into a smile. "A cheeseburger, huh? I guess that sounds good. Where to?"

"This small place I found called Dorothy's Diner. It's not far from here."

Wade laughed as he settled into her passenger seat. "Nothing is far from here."

He was right about that. Charlotte chuckled with him. Crossroads might be small, but it was starting to feel like home.

As they walked into the cozy café, they were greeted by a wide woman with a warm smile. Her brown hair stood straight up like a spiky halo and she wore a nametag that said DOROTHY. "Hi there, folks. Would you like a booth or a table?"

Wade and Charlotte spoke at the same time. "A booth."

"Please," Charlotte added.

"Right this way." They followed Dorothy to a booth tucked into the corner. "I'm Dorothy. I own this joint and do all the cooking, so if you ever have a problem, you just come straight to me." She reached into the pocket of her floral apron and pulled out two small laminated squares. "Here's the menu. I'll give you two a chance to look over everything, but first is there anything you'd like to drink?"

Wade scanned the menu. "Actually, I think we already know what we want, ma'am. We'll take two cheeseburgers with everything. I'll have a decaf coffee, and she'll want a Diet Coke."

Dorothy collected the menus and smiled. "I'll have that right out."

A bell on the door jingled as it was opened, and Charlotte looked up to see Jake Longbow saunter into the restaurant. She patted Wade's hand across the table. "Look, that's Jake, the foreman I told you about. He works out on the Double K. He might be able to help with finding your cave."

She slid from the booth to invite him to their table. But as she took her first steps toward the old cowboy, Dorothy greeted him with a warm smile. Charlotte watched as Jake circled his arms around the curvy woman and kissed her sweetly on the lips. The spiky-haired owner backed away, swatting him lightly with a dish towel. Then she grabbed Jake's hand and towed him to the back of the diner, away from prying eyes.

Charlotte plopped back into her seat.

Wade whistled low and long. "I guess we'll have to try and talk with him some other time. He's a little preoccupied at the moment."

She nodded, speechless. She hadn't taken the rough old foreman for the romantic type. She smiled. She was happy for him.

Wade sighed. She knew his research hadn't dug up anything new. The first Kirklands' journals had been fascinating, but as far as she could tell, they didn't mention the location of the cave.

"You'll find it someday," she said softly.

"I hope so."

Charlotte knew he was frustrated that the heir to the huge ranch didn't know where the cave was that James Kirkland and his wife, Millie, originally lived in before any of the houses were built. She wasn't sure what he hoped to find there. Artifacts. Treasure. But Wade seemed determined to locate it, and she'd help if she could.

As they finished their meal, she asked if Wade would like to go to Staten's birthday party with her next week. Jake was sure to be there. Wade could ask about the settlers and the cave then. With all the legends Jake had stored up, she suspected the old foreman knew where it was. And if he didn't, he might know where to get more information.

"Sure," Wade said. "I'd love to go and get a look at the place. Maybe I'll go searching for the cave myself."

It was the first time she'd ever invited a guy out.

As they walked to her car, Wade asked how well she knew Staten.

"A little bit, not too well. He asks questions about his assignments sometimes, but most of the time he's busy with running the Double K. I love it when Jake comes along on my rides. He knows a lot about the ranch. I think he's been around all Staten's life. He likes to talk about the land and who has changed things over the years. He seems to know a lot of the history. I'm sure he'll help you if he can."

In his polite way, Wade took her hand at the driver's-side door and thanked her again for inviting him to the party.

As he walked around to the passenger side, it occurred to Charlotte that Wade might be a little too polite.

Chapter 28

Cloudy Day Birthday

February 1992

Staten Kirkland

At five o'clock Staten picked up his keys on his way out of the Double K's headquarters. He had less than an hour to get ready for a birthday party that he didn't want. Oh, he was excited that it was his birthday, but having a dinner was old-fashioned.

Granny had invited friends from all the other ranches. She even hired the town's only three-piece band to play. People would stand around for an hour, eat, and then talk for a while about ranching before going home.

The only good thing about having a party was Amalah. She would be on her way back to Crossroads and planned to stay the night at the ranch. Of course, Granny had reminded him twice that if Amalah was sleeping in his room in the cottage, then he would be staying in the big house.

Granny promised she'd wake Amalah at seven the next morning so Staten could eat breakfast with her before heading off to work. Twenty-year-olds might be spending the night together in college, but Granny wasn't going to make alone time any easier for them.

Halfway to his truck, Staten heard the office phone ring.

He thought about ignoring it, but he found himself turning around and heading back into headquarters. Glancing at the caller ID, he saw that it was Amalah.

Staten answered but all he heard was crying. It took a few minutes to understand what she was saying. She was not coming. She was sorry.

He picked out a few words. A wreck turning out of the parking lot on campus. Not bad but it would be two days before the right fender could get fixed. Amalah was not hurt but she was too upset to drive back to town alone. No, she couldn't find someone who could drive her somewhere a hundred miles away.

Staten's ears were ringing. He couldn't understand much besides the fact that Amalah was okay, but she was not coming home. "I wish I was with you. I wish there was something I could do to help."

"I wish you were, too, but I'm really okay. I just hate missing your twentieth birthday. I wanted to be there for you." The crying got softer. "I love you, Staten."

"I know. I love you too. You'll catch the next sixty or seventy birthdays. I guess one's not so bad." He sighed, trying to shake the gloom rolling over him. "The only reason I agreed to the dinner was because you would be sitting next to me."

The party hadn't even started yet and he was already dreading it. But he'd do what everyone expected of him like he always did. He'd show up with a smile and make the rounds, thanking everyone for showing up.

"I know," she whispered. "I swear, I'll make it up with the next one and the next, and the next."

Everything she said explained why she couldn't come. Why she'd stopped looking for a ride. He heard her. He was listening, but the words didn't make sense.

Why couldn't Amalah borrow a car or rent one? Didn't she understand that this was the birthday he'd been waiting for? He wanted to be a man. No. He was a man. He was running the ranch. Slowly restarting college. Working for his future. And he wanted his girl to be with him.

All his life he wanted to be a good man like his grandpa. Work hard. Be fair. Love his Amalah all his life.

But all he could think about right now was quitting. There was nothing he wanted more than his girl. If he couldn't have her, what was it all for?

In a rough voice he managed to say, "It's okay. Go to the dorm and get some sleep. You'll feel better tomorrow."

After he hung up, an anger rolled over him. He slammed the phone back onto the desk and turned toward the office entrance, ready to run. Staten made it one step through the door and crashed into a tall, thin ranch hand carrying a five-foot board on his shoulder.

Both men tumbled down the steps and collided with a huge pot full of dried-up dirt and dead ivy. Dirt clumps flew several feet up as the men lost the fight. After rolling, Staten and the cowhand called Duke Evans were spread out on the rocks.

The lanky cowboy grunted as he raised to one elbow. "You alive, Boss?"

"Nope, I think I'm dead on my birthday. Since the dead can't talk, you'll have to tell Granny."

Duke sat up, slapping blood off his face and inspecting his elbow. He ignored several other cuts. "We better get you cleaned up, Boss. You're leaking in several places. And I hear you've got a party to be at."

"Right." Staten staggered to his feet, aching in places he didn't know could hurt. "Let's get to the bunkhouse. Jake will clean us up and give us enough whiskey to keep us smiling."

Staten hurt so bad, he almost howled like a coyote. Duke was wincing as he stood. They helped one another to the bunkhouse. Hobbling like a pair of old men who'd had too much to drink.

Thirty minutes later both men were half drunk and smiling.

Staten was still hurting but a numbness was starting to settle in. He laughed with his men as they stood around teasing him. His left ear didn't seem to want to stop bleeding. A few of the ranch hands voted to cut the ear off. He was one of them now. He'd drunk enough to think about removing it. Others voted to brand it.

He'd done some crazy things on the ranch before, but he guessed that cutting off his own ear would make Granny mad. The thought of Tabitha Kirkland cussing mad was enough to veto both plans.

Staten took another sip of whiskey and began to feel better. He had no idea what the party would be like, but he knew it couldn't be as great as the bunkhouse.

Fifteen minutes later, all the men were cleaned up and someone had grabbed Staten's suit from the cottage. Staten showered and dressed, then looked in the mirror. He'd gained at least fifteen pounds of pure muscle since returning to the ranch, and his slacks and black blazer were a bit snug now. But that wasn't the problem. All his men had on clean work clothes. Staten stood out like a sore thumb.

He turned to Jake. The foreman always had a solution to everything. "I need something else to wear."

The old cowboy smiled. "Yes, sir." He turned to the ranch hands gathered around behind them. "Boys, the boss needs something to wear. Take out your best."

Staten began taking his suit off. "No, no. Nothing fancy. Some clean work clothes will do."

He didn't care about dressing up for the party. He belonged with his men and he wanted to look like it.

As he buttoned the blue plaid shirt, he yelled, "Grab those drinks, boys. We're all going to my birthday party."

Five minutes later, Staten's ear bandaged, twenty men marched behind the boss to the big house. The cowhands. The men who worked on the ranch. The ones who stuck with him from dawn till dusk. Staten's friends.

At the first step on the porch, Staten tripped, nearly falling into the post. Duke's hand steadied him.

"I've got you, Boss. But you might want to take it slow from now on."

"Thanks," Staten whispered.

Granny met him at the door and lifted her hand and gestured at his bandaged ear. "What happened to you?"

Staten leaned down and planted a kiss on her cheek. "Nothing, Granny. I'm just fine."

"You sure smell like it." She threw a hard stare at Jake and then spoke over her shoulder to the woman working at the stove. "Add some water to the gravy and cut more ham, please."

She turned back to the men standing around Staten like a group of bodyguards. "I expect you all to be on your best behavior."

Staten smiled. "Don't worry so much."

He was twenty. From this day on, he'd be a man! When trouble came, he'd handle it straight on.

Chapter 29

Staten's Birthday Party

Charlotte Lane

Charlotte sat in the passenger seat of Wade's old pickup, watching the sun dip behind the horizon as they passed through the gate leading to the Double K. So much rust covered the truck, it seemed part of the paint job. She decided the Chevy was a lot like the man driving it. A bit rough on the outside but still strong, solid, and dependable.

They stepped out of Wade's truck and followed the line of guests heading to what the Kirklands called the big house on the ranch.

The two professors had spent the past week poring over James Randall Kirkland's journals at the school but still hadn't found any solid clues to point them toward the cave. Now they hoped a conversation with the foreman would lead them in the right direction. It seemed the old cowboy had been here so long he'd become just as much a part of the land as the founding family.

They found Tabitha Kirkland waiting at the top of the steps to greet them. "Dr. Lane, I'm so happy you could make it. Miss Butterfield has told me so much about you. And so has Staten, of course."

Charlotte wondered what the school secretary had said. She hadn't talked to Miss Butterfield much except to turn in grades or paperwork for ordering supplies. "Thank you for inviting us, Mrs. Kirkland."

"It's my pleasure, dear." She leaned in and lowered her voice. "We know how much you're doing for our grandson. And we're very grateful."

"Well, Staten is a great student. And he's been helping me too. Riding has become a new passion of mine."

Mrs. Kirkland smiled. "And who is your handsome friend?"

Charlotte felt herself blush. "This is my colleague, Mr. Wade Parsons."

Mrs. Kirkland reached out and patted Wade's shoulder. "Ah, Mr. Parsons, I can't thank you enough for taking over my history class so that I can stay home with my James. Though some days it's harder taking care of one old man than a hundred students. I hope the kids aren't giving you too hard a time."

Wade straightened to military attention, looking like he was ready to salute his lieutenant. "No, ma'am. Most of my students are easy enough, although that Teddy . . . he can be a bit of a handful." He shot her a wink.

Mrs. Kirkland chuckled. "Has he grown any since last year? Poor boy thinks fertilizer will help him sprout up like the weeds."

Charlotte handed Mrs. Kirkland the banana bread she'd tucked under her arm. "This is from Miss Ollie. She couldn't make it today. She said something about blocking the vents from the shop teacher's room."

She shook her head. Not a day went by that Miss Ollie didn't complain about that man and all the noise coming from his classroom, insisting that his machinery shook the whole portable.

"Poor Miss Ollie," Mrs. Kirkland responded, amusement in her eyes. "Mr. Brody is always driving her crazy. I swear she enjoys hating him." She reached for the banana bread. "I hope I don't find any misplaced notes in my baked goods this time."

Before Charlotte could ask her what notes she'd gotten before, the mayor and his wife joined them on the porch to greet Mrs. Kirkland, and it was time for Charlotte and Wade to enter the house.

As they made their way through the crowded living room, Charlotte was surprised at how many familiar faces she saw smiling back at her. At first, the friendliness of the townsfolk had been overwhelming, but now Crossroads felt like home. Wade followed her through to a sitting room with a three-piece band playing "Tennessee Waltz."

"Would you care to dance?" Wade nodded toward the two couples swaying offbeat to the music as if their hearing aids weren't working. "We could show them how it's done."

"I thought you wanted to find your cave." Charlotte couldn't remember the last time she'd been invited to dance. She didn't really know how and couldn't exactly research that now.

"It's been missing for over a hundred years. It can wait another five minutes." Wade took her hand and pulled her onto the mostly empty wooden dance floor. "Come on. Live a little. Isn't that what you came here to do?"

Charlotte resisted the urge to make a face at him. He was right that she had promised herself she would try new things. If she could coach a high school football team, she could pretend to dance.

At a loss out on the dance floor, she tried her best to mimic Wade's outrageous moves, but she was pretty sure she just looked like a flailing balloon. On the other hand, he didn't seem to know how to dance any better than she did.

She wasn't sure she had ever laughed so hard or had this much fun.

As the band began a rendition of "I Walk the Line," Charlotte spied an old cowboy with a faded black felt hat sitting in a shadowy corner of the main room, sipping a glass of whiskey.

She pulled Wade away from the couple about to two-step into him. "I think I see Jake. If you want to ask him about the cave, now's your chance."

The man turned as they approached, and Charlotte realized the cowboy was not Jake; he was the owner of the Double K, James Ray Kirkland.

"If you're here because my Tabby sent you to take this drink away from me, you're gonna have to pry it from my fingers." Mr. Kirkland took an extra-long swig in defiance, as if to prove his point.

"No, sir." Wade sat next to Mr. Kirkland's chair, and Charlotte slipped into the seat beside him. "I'll even join you if you've got extra."

"Afraid you'll have to get your own. This was all I could manage to sneak away. But I can tell you where the supply is." He pointed to the antique cabinet by the doorway.

Wade laughed. "That's kind of you, sir, but I'm not much of a drinking man. I'll save the rest for you."

Charlotte resisted the urge to ask him if going against Mrs. Kirkland was a good idea. She'd only just met the woman, but Charlotte had seen a fire in her eyes.

"Well, if you two kids aren't over here to steal my booze, what can I do for you?" Mr. Kirkland took another sip of his drink. "Or are you just waiting for the birthday boy like everyone else?"

"Actually, sir, you are exactly who I want to see." Wade leaned forward. Clearly he thought finding the owner was just as good or better than looking for the foreman.

Mr. Kirkland's eyebrows lifted, and he settled back in his

chair to listen. "What is it you want with me, son? I've already told Samuel I won't be selling the ranch. It's Staten's now, and he's more than capable of running things."

"Oh, no, sir, I'm not interested in purchasing your land. I'm a historian. My name's Wade Parsons. I took over your wife's classes at the school, and I've been researching your ranch for months. I'm searching for a cave, a cave said to be the first settlement in the area. The place where your ancestor, James Randall Kirkland, spent the winter with his wife, Millie."

Mr. Kirkland's eyes widened. Charlotte couldn't tell if Wade's knowledge of the cave surprised the cowboy or if the whiskey was starting to kick in.

The owner of the Double K turned to look at her. "And who are you, darling? Another historian too?"

"I am Dr. Charlotte Lane. I'm teaching the high school English courses at the school."

"Doctor, huh? Now don't start preaching to me about the dangers of drinking. It can't be any worse than roping a wild steer and bringing him back to pasture. And I've done that a thousand times."

She laughed. "I'm not that kind of doctor. Really, we just want to hear any stories you might have about the first Kirklands. If you don't mind us poking around."

"Stories about my ancestors, huh?" He looked to Wade. "Sure, I've got plenty of stories about my ancestors, as you say." He looked at Wade before taking another sip of his whiskey as if it would help jog his memory. "I remember my great-grandma pretty well. She was a beauty in her youth. Loved sunflowers and the old creek that used to run through the ranch. But she was also a spitfire. Loved staying angry with her husband and bossing all the ranch hands around as if she thought their floppy hats kept them from using their heads.

"I never met my great-grandpa James Randall Kirkland, but folks said he was a hard worker and always fair. He must have been real patient with my great-grandma because she didn't even speak English when they met. But he stood by her through the years."

Charlotte loved hearing stories about the first Kirklands. Jake had told her several, and they always took her back in time to the old pioneering days like those described in her favorite Western books. "Your foreman told me that your great-grandfather built this house with his own two hands."

Mr. Kirkland sat back and tilted his head to the side. "Not this house, darling. The little cottage out back. He promised his new wife that he'd build their home where the first rays of the sun kissed the land. That way they could still watch the sunset over the cave where they'd survived their first winter."

Charlotte and Wade looked at each other. She could tell they were thinking the same thing. If what Mr. Kirkland said was true, the cave Wade was searching for would be directly west of the cottage. But would it still be out there after all this time?

Wade leaned toward the owner of the Double K. "This cave sounds like it was pretty important to your great-grandparents."

The old cowboy smiled. "Sure was. My great-grandma always said that it was good to let go of the past, but we should never forget it. Every night, as they watched the sun go down, they remembered the past they buried there, and let it melt away with the blackening sky."

This was like the beginning of one of Charlotte's Old West novels. "What do you mean they buried the past?"

"Well, no one knows exactly what or if they hid anything in there, but the legend goes that they left the pieces of their old lives behind, the ones they had before they found each other. James was a soldier in the Civil War. For a time, it defined his life. And Millie had been traded from tribe to tribe until my great-granddad found her. I imagine they didn't want to carry that baggage forever."

Wade grabbed Charlotte's hand and gave it a squeeze. "Could it be there's some kind of treasure in the cave?"

"Well, I don't know about that," Mr. Kirkland said thoughtfully. "I was never able to find their cave. Ranching doesn't leave much time for treasure hunting. But my great-grandma did tell me that she always loved bathing in the small creek twenty paces from their cave. I've ridden all over this land and never seen a cave along the creek bed."

Wade wasn't easily discouraged. "What if you just haven't found the right creek? A lot of things can happen to the land in more than a hundred years. Creeks dry up. Rock falls cause cave-ins. It could still be out there."

Mr. Kirkland shrugged. "You kids are more than welcome to go looking anytime. Just don't get in the way of the bulls."

Charlotte wished they could run out and search for the cave right now. She was ready for adventure. Ready to live out a storyline like the ones in her books.

The old man lifted his cup for another drink and his eyes locked on something behind them. "Oh, here comes Tabby. It seems she's found me. You two better go socialize." He motioned to Wade and whispered, "I suggest avoiding the dance floor. Your lady friend might leave you."

Charlotte did her best to disguise her laugh as a cough.

"James Ray Kirkland." His wife's voice came from across the room.

Mr. Kirkland downed the rest of his drink and thrust the cup in Wade's hand. "If she asks, this was yours."

Charlotte and Wade stood as Mrs. Kirkland barreled over to their corner. She felt bad abandoning him to his fate, but if she'd learned anything from Jake's stories about the fiery wives of the Kirklands, she knew the Kirkland women were not to be messed with.

Chapter 30

An Unexpected Gift

Staten Kirkland

Staten stepped into the huge room with forty guests in front of him and twenty cowboys behind him. Laughter mixed with the sound of a harmonica playing in the background as he moved through the crowd, thanking everyone for coming. He glanced around at all the familiar faces with a smile. He was surprised so many people had come out to celebrate his birthday. Amalah might not be here, but maybe it would be a good night after all.

The side of his face ached and he did his best to ignore it. But when the fourth guest asked after the bandage on his ear, Staten called for the attention of the room, thinking he might as well get his tale over with once and for all.

After a few moments of silence, he straightened the best he could and announced, "Well, hello, everyone. Glad you're all here." He raised his glass to the crowd. "A few of you may have noticed the bandage on my head, but rest assured, I'm fine. It's barely more than a scratch. I guess some of you have seen those big pots at the end of the HQ porch. One of my men and I plowed into them when we decided to roll down the stairs."

Light laughter moved through the guests.

Staten continued. "Today is my birthday. I'm twenty, a man now. I admit when I'm wrong and own my mistakes. And I'll probably make plenty more during this life. The truth is I wasn't paying much attention and caused the tumble. Sorry, Duke."

Duke patted his shoulder. "No worries, Boss."

He shook the cowboy's hand. "Now go mingle and have some fun."

The lanky ranch hand offered a rare smile. "Yes, sir."

Staten watched as he moved through the crowd as if looking for someone.

Another hand grasped Staten's shoulder. "That was quite a speech, young man."

He turned to find a group of old ranchers huddled around him. Surprisingly, they all kidded him about falling and then told their own stories. Rodeo mistakes. Car wrecks they lived through. Drunken falls. Fights they didn't remember. A few of the guys even showed their scars.

Staten suddenly felt like he was part of an elite group, and he was proud to belong among these tough cowboys.

As the last of the guests arrived, Granny and her helpers moved every chair in the big house to the huge tables set throughout the dining room and the small sitting area. When the folks sat down, they were almost touching shoulders, but no one complained.

Their conversations were loud and the laughter never stopped as everyone finished their dinner. Cheers sounded as slices of Granny's apple pie were passed around.

Staten was surprised to see Dr. Lane at one end of a table talking to the mayor and his wife. Mr. Parsons seemed to fit into the crowd too. The table kept erupting into laughter when he spoke.

There were a dozen or more old ranchers who'd dealt with major wounds but rarely had time to talk about them. But tonight they sat together and the scars came out like all were lifetime friends.

Several of the ranch hands took the time to mingle with the townsfolk tonight. Staten noticed Duke saying hello to Peggy Warner.

When Duke Evans first came to work for the Double K, for months Staten thought he was mute. When he finally asked a question, Staten was so surprised he couldn't immediately answer the cowhand. Now, it was great to see him socializing and having a good time.

Staten smiled as he watched his granny talking with a group of women she'd called her dear friends for years. He couldn't remember all their names tonight, but every one of the ladies had hugged him and wished him a happy birthday.

Looking around the crowded room, Staten knew he was home. Even without Amalah, this was where he was supposed to be. Crossroads, the Double K Ranch, Ransom Canyon. This place would always be his home.

About the time the tables were shoved to the corners and the food, except desserts, was moved to the long counters, the huge front door slowly opened, just enough to let a tall, thin girl with a long blond braid slip in.

Staten seemed to be the only one who noticed Quinn as she entered. He met her near the hall with a big smile. "Glad you could make it!"

"Of course I came. I'm not due in New York for another week, and I couldn't miss your birthday," she said. "Looking like a great party, but you look like you've been beat up." She lifted her fingers to his cheek. "What happened?"

He took her hand and gave it a squeeze. "Me and Duke

wrestled one of Granny's pots and lost." He laughed. "I'm fine, promise."

She smiled. "If you say so." She pulled a thin package from her oversized sweater and put it on a side table. "I won't stay long. I just wanted to give you a birthday gift. You can open it later!"

Staten pulled her in for a quick hug. "Thanks, Quinn. You didn't need to do that, but I appreciate it."

When she pulled away, her cheeks had turned pink. "Amalah called me to tell you she is not going to be able to make it home this weekend at all after that car accident. She had a whole plan to get the old gang together to surprise you and take you out tomorrow. Saturday night dancing and drinking down by the river where no one who isn't invited can find it. But we can still do it without her." Quinn chuckled.

Staten shook his head. "You can call that off. I wasn't into those things when I was a kid and I'm still not. That was always the kind of thing that Amalah enjoyed, not me. But tell me: Is she hurt? She said she was okay, but I can't tell if she's making light about this."

"She's okay, Staten. She's just shaken up."

Staten looked at the crowd. This was wild enough for him. He hadn't hung out with that gang from high school since he graduated. He felt he had nothing in common with most of his old buddies, and his close friends who did go to college were still away at school.

Quinn touched his ear covered by a bandage, then another on his forehead. "You're bleeding a little. Are you sure you're okay?"

He shrugged, knowing he'd have to tell her the whole story this time. "It's nothing. One of my men and me tumbled down the steps today. It's turned into a good story. When we got back to the house, we'd been patched up and drank too much whiskey. So, we came in and told our folks. Everyone started talking about when they almost died. No kids around, so the stories got kind of colorful. Then, Granny served wine. No one got drunk but they did seem to get rowdy."

He pretended to shudder. "I've seen more old scars than I ever want to see again. One old rancher had two scars on his butt." Staten grinned. "Trust me, no one needs to see those."

Quinn laughed. "I can't say I'm sorry to have missed that."

"You missed a lot. All through dinner folks talked about the dumbest things they'd ever done."

As the conversation had gone on, the stories had gotten more outrageous. Staten guessed that a few of the guys were just trying to one-up someone else.

Before he finished confessing his tale to Quinn, Peggy walked over and offered them a glass of wine. "Happy birthday, Staten." She grinned at Quinn. "How are you doing? How are things at that fancy school up in New York?"

Quinn smiled, but Staten could tell that it was forced. Her eyes looked haunted and her shoulders hunched over like she wanted to hug herself. "I'm fine," she said.

Staten felt the urge to protect her. He hoped things hadn't gotten worse with that teacher at her music school.

Before he could distract Peggy, Duke Evans came up and stole her attention.

"Hey, Duke. How are you feeling?" Staten asked as he sipped his wine.

The cowboy's attention was clearly on Peggy. "I'm good, Boss. I just want to ask this lady to dance."

Staten and Quinn shared a look. Her smile seemed to say she liked the idea of Peggy and Duke together, but he nevertheless leaned near the youngest Warner and whispered, "You want to dance with him?" She was about seven years older than Staten, but Peggy's parents and his grandfolks were close friends.

Without looking at Staten, Peggy took Duke's hand. "I'd love to dance."

Peggy and Duke walked to the center of the room and waited for the band to strike up the next song. Staten watched as the unlikely pair moved closer, staring at each other as if there was no one else in the world. They smiled at each other, laughing over their whispered conversation. He'd never seen either of them look so happy.

He bumped Quinn's shoulder with his and then winced. "I think something might be going on with those two."

Quinn chuckled as Granny stopped in front of Staten and poked him in the side. "Not a word, Staten. This may be your party but Peggy is Duke's girl. Let them have their moment."

"What? No one told me. How was I supposed to know?"

"You don't need to know everything, dear."

"Great, I grow up and now Granny's telling me to start unlearning things." He leaned toward Quinn. "Will you dance with me? I'm beat-up, half drunk, and the dumbest man in the room, but my feet still work."

She made a funny face. "All right. I'll dance with you for your birthday, but only if you turn your head away. Your breath is pure alcohol!"

As they joined the others on the dance floor, Staten saw Quinn nudge Duke closer toward Peggy. The lanky cowhand didn't hesitate a moment as he pulled Peggy into his arms.

Staten made an effort to at least act sober, keeping his mouth closed and dancing as best he could without stepping on Quinn's feet. His first day as a man wasn't going too great. His head was starting to pound to the beat of the music. Every one of his muscles hurt, but he kept dancing.

Maybe it would have been better to wait until he was twenty-one to drink so much, but it was too late now.

He danced with Quinn several times. She was tall and thin and easy to move with. Not at all the same as dancing with Amalah, but still fun.

During the last song he remembered something else about

Quinn that was different. Quinn was always honest. Amalah didn't lie but she was much more dramatic, whether things were good or bad. He loved how she could make anything more exciting. Quinn was great. But Amalah would have made his birthday a night to remember.

He wished she were here.

As the night wound down, he walked Quinn to her car. "Thanks for coming." The cold wind and hurting from dancing sobered him. "You made this birthday bearable."

She smiled in her quiet way. "I'll always be here if you need me."

He held Quinn's hands, turning serious. "You know, I feel the same. I'll come up to New York if that teacher gives you any more trouble. Just call and I'll be out on the next plane."

"Thank you, Staten. I don't have him this new semester, so I hope that's all in the past now." She smiled. "I'll miss you and Amalah until June."

"Me too." He stepped back from the car thinking he'd miss Amalah as always, but this time Staten knew he'd miss Quinn too. A real friend was a rare person.

When he went back inside, he caught sight of a thin box on the side table. Quinn's gift! He'd almost forgotten.

He picked up the package and shook it, trying to guess what it was.

He ripped the paper off like a child at Christmas. Opening the thin, rectangular box, he smiled. Inside was a bolo engraved with the Double K brand. Staten ran his fingers over the engraving and felt grooves etched into the back. He flipped it over and saw the word BOSS. He couldn't remember the last time he'd received such a thoughtful present.

Staten moved to the little mirror hanging on the wall opposite the doorway and put his new gift on. He loved it. He'd keep it forever. It was from Quinn, and that made it special. And someday he'd live up to the image Quinn had of him.

An hour later, most of the cowboys were in a group laughing. A few danced without a partner as the older folks slipped into their coats.

He realized Granny had been right about the party. He was a man now and he needed to get the town supporting him and the ranch. These people would help him grow and he'd always help them when trouble came. His gramps was right; this place was in his blood.

Staten glanced around the room. Tonight he'd learned all the guests' names. He knew his men, and with one hard tumble he'd made a solid friend.

Peggy's parents were talking to Granny as they'd settled into the kitchen. Then Staten realized Peggy had vanished. She was always so silent, people wouldn't even notice she'd left.

Staten would bet a hundred dollars he knew where she was. And with who.

Peggy and Duke were together, and not one person would miss them. From the way they'd been smiling at each other on the dance floor earlier, he knew they were exactly where they wanted to be.

Chapter 31

Peggy's Wish

Peggy Warner

Peggy drove as fast as she dared with icy conditions starting to dust the road. Excitement buzzed through her. Tonight, she'd danced with her cowboy in front of everyone, even her parents. And then they'd sneaked off before the party was over to be alone together. She didn't think her parents even noticed she was gone.

She felt like a wild teenager.

Pulling up by the garage, Peggy ran up the steps to her apartment, turned the TV on, and ran back down. When her parents got home, they would think their daughter was watching a movie or getting ready for bed. Everyone knew Peggy was the quiet one. The one who needed time to herself after socializing all day.

They would not climb the stairs after a party like tonight. Her parents would leave her alone, and after thirty minutes, they'd be settling in for the night.

With no outside light for the neighbors to see her, Peggy moved down the steps as quickly as she could. Duke's truck pulled up at the back of the garage. After she jumped in, he silently backed all the way to the county road before he turned the headlights on.

Neither said a word, but both were smiling in the dark.

After a few miles, he slipped his hand in hers and whispered, "I'm glad you're here with me."

She whispered back, "Me too." Then she laughed loudly and joyously. "Why are we whispering?" she nearly shouted. "We're alone. There's no one here but us."

Duke barked out a laugh. "I don't know." He lifted her hand to his lips. "Where are we going?"

It was so dark she could barely make out his face. "I don't care, Duke, as long as I'm with you. Anywhere is perfect."

He turned the radio on low, letting the sound swirl through the pickup as gentle background music. They just drove for several miles and traded stories about siblings and their first childhood jobs. She might not be able to see his kind gray eyes, but feeling her cowboy next to her was enough to keep a smile on her face.

After a while, Duke straightened in his seat. "I'd like to take you somewhere. We could stop at that pizza place, where the bar is still open. Or we could go to my folks' place. It's not much but it could be ours someday. We could fix it up and turn it into your dream home." He paused but continued before she could respond. "Honestly, I don't care where we go. I just want to be alone with you for a while."

Leaving the party had been easy. The problem was neither had thought of where they'd go after.

She slid over next to him. "I told you. I just want to be with you, cowboy." After another long pause, she whispered, "Show me your folks' place."

"I haven't seen it in months." He laid his hand on her knee. "It might look a little rough, but it's one of the few things that's mine." Their eyes met in the dim light of a streetlamp as they passed it by. "I'd love to share it with you."

"I want to see where you grew up."

"All right, Peggy. It's not far but it's over the county line."

She heard the smile in his voice and cuddled closer. Happiness settled over her, and she closed her eyes, soaking it in. Peggy was next to her cowboy. They were alone and sharing parts of their lives with each other. She couldn't ask for more.

Peggy was almost asleep on his shoulder when he finally slowed the truck into a turn. "Here it is."

She straightened and was surprised to see how big the old brick house was. Two stories with a chimney climbing up one side of the roof. Even in the dark she saw a two-car garage and another building big enough to be a shop. The fenced-in yard was the perfect size for a gaggle of growing kids. She could picture a swing set on one side and a pool on the other.

A few trees were down in the front. A few windows were cracked but boarded up. The railing on the porch was broken. The grass was overdue for a cut.

But Peggy was smiling as she bounced in her seat. Duke's house was just right to raise a family. "It's perfect."

He shook his head. "When my folks died fifteen years ago, the family came in one weekend. They all took what they wanted. No one fought over anything. Mom lived with practical things. She had no treasures. Dad didn't have much land to ranch. He didn't want to grow anything. Just wanted space from the neighbors."

Duke pulled to a stop near the large wraparound porch. "My dad worked hard and paid his taxes several years ahead. As far as I know, my brother and sisters never came back to this old place. No one wanted to keep it up. And when I turned thirty, the family signed the house to me as sole owner. I figured they thought I'd never marry so I might need a place in my old age."

He cut the engine. "I always carry a key just in case someone wants to take a look at it, but no one has for years."

Peggy squeezed his hand. "Can we go in?"

He hopped out of his truck and lifted her down. Slowly he pulled her into the unlit garage. "I know it's not much, but it's yours if you want it."

She cupped his face in her hand and brought his lips to hers. The kiss was soft and sweet. "I'd cherish it and you."

She nearly squealed as Duke swooped down and lifted Peggy up into his arms. "What are you doing?"

"Carrying you over the threshold, of course."

Peggy laughed as he carried her to the back door. The key needed a bit of wiggling before the door swung open.

For a moment all was in place. As if someone still lived here and forgot to come home. A kind of calm had settled inside.

Duke placed Peggy back on her feet, and she wandered around the family room as he moved to light a lantern. A layer of dust lay over everything, but the room was in order.

He stood, almost touching her, and whispered as if someone might hear his words, "I'm the youngest. The only one who didn't move away. My siblings all said they'd come back every summer for a reunion but no one ever came."

She recognized a loneliness in him that she felt in herself. She circled her arms around his waist and held him tight.

"The family met in Dallas once and another time we all went to Red River, New Mexico. A few Christmases in New England, but they never come back here. I come over and clean the place every summer."

He threw his arm over her shoulders and held the lamp high as they walked through the house. All the books were gone. The doilies were all gone too, if there ever were any on the tables. No toys. Nothing in the closets.

She took one step up the stairs and turned.

Duke waited.

"Can I ask for one thing before I see the rest of the house?"

"Yes. We can stop or not."

She waited for a while, then she said, "I love looking at the house, but, Duke, why have you never moved in here yourself?"

He glanced around the space. "This place is meant for a family. And just me alone, well, it's not enough."

"I think you're more than enough."

Duke set the lantern down with a thud and wrapped his hands around her arms, pulling her against him. For a moment she wasn't touching the ground. "Peggy May Warner, you make this house my home."

His kiss was not gentle. It was strong and hungry.

And she didn't mind at all.

He pulled her off the stairs but didn't let go. "I know I should go slow but I love you so."

They kissed for a while, then she said, "I love you, too, cowboy. I always will."

He laughed and said, "You shouldn't, Peggy. All I've got is a good horse and a house no one wants. I'll probably never have much money. A pretty lady like you could do better."

"I don't care. I want you. There is no better."

Duke's fingers ran over the wall, tracing imprints of pictures that were no longer hanging there. "My parents were happy here. I can never remember either one yelling at the other. But my dad would yell at us kids. If we started arguing, he'd say, 'Go outside and don't come back until you learn to act right. And don't forget the door locks at ten.'"

She laughed. "Did you ever have to sleep outside?"

"More than a few times with my brother. We hit each other until we hurt all over. Then we went to the door and it was locked. We had to lay on the porch, dripping blood, until dawn.

"Dad didn't look at us, but Mom said we had to clean up

and get ready for school before we set the table for breakfast. We were so mad that my brother forgot what we'd been fighting about. I remembered but it no longer mattered."

Peggy climbed the steps and slowly walked down the hallway. The parents' room. The girls' room, and the last room was the boys'. Two half-beds, both a foot too short for a full-grown man.

She stood near the window, looking out at the dead garden hugging the back of the house. "When did you leave home?"

"Right after high school to work the rodeo circuit. In winter I was a day worker. Mr. Kirkland paid great and he'd let me take off early in the summer for any out-of-town rides. Staten was just a kid then and most of the time in the way. But the old man paid him a day's wage if he worked with us until quitting time."

He sat on one of the beds, and dust settled over him. "After a few years I figured I'd never make it big in the rodeo. I told Kirkland I'd like to work full time. The old man didn't hesitate. He doubled my pay as well as my responsibility. Then he smiled and offered to hit me in the head now and then for free."

She laughed, sitting next to him on the bed. "Do you miss the rodeo?"

"Riding in it? No, not at all. But I like to watch when I have free time. I'd be happy to take you if you want to go. Houston has a huge one coming up."

"I'd love to see one big rodeo, but Mom said my older sister needs me soon. I sat for her with her last kid. I was babysitter to two children, house cleaner, cook, and caregiver. When I left, she paid me with a coat, not money. She said by not paying it would help me on my taxes." Peggy shook her head.

"Do you want to go help your sister?" He held her shoulder tight against him.

"No. She'd hasn't spoken to me for two years. No pictures. Not a word. But I know everyone expects me to help."

"Do you want to go with me instead? You could tell them you'll be out of town."

"Yes, but my mother won't let..."

He ran a finger over the seam of her lips. "Honey, you're twenty-seven years old. You can do what you want to do. It's okay to do things for yourself now and then."

They sat for a while on the little bed as she cried. She couldn't stop the tears. She felt helpless and hopeless. And the dam had broken. She wanted to be with Duke. To spend all of her time with him. To go to rodeos with him. To build a life with him. But she'd never told her parents no before. She'd never gone against what the family expected of her. She'd never done anything for herself.

Finally, Duke asked, "What do you want? Right now, Peggy? Name it."

She wiped her face. "I don't know."

His voice lowered, and the deep timbre of it melted over her. "Yes, you do, honey. What do you want? Tell me."

She couldn't say a word. A lump was stuck in her throat and she couldn't get the words past it.

He looked at her. "You are the prettiest, kindest woman I've ever met. You're always thinking and doing for others. But just this once, tell me, what would make you happy, Peggy? *You.*"

A tear slowly rolled down, over her cheek. "I want to be with you," she heard herself say.

It was true. She'd never wanted anything more.

When he didn't say a word, she touched the wound on his face.

"I'll heal, dear. But you can see that I'm not handsome. If I take my clothes off you'll see several other scars all over."

She smiled. "It doesn't matter. It's not your face I see; it's your heart. It was as clear as day when you laid next to me at the cemetery." She leaned in closer. "But for the record, you're perfectly handsome to me."

Duke crushed her to his chest and claimed her lips with his. When he pulled away, they were both struggling for air.

He stood and pulled a huge quilt from a box in the corner. He floated it over her, then climbed beneath it. "Peggy, nothing is going to happen here tonight but talking. If we're going to get married someday, we have to talk first."

"I agree, but you have to kiss me now and then. Since I had one, I can't get enough." She planted her lips on his cheek. "That is my demand."

He studied her with a smile and nodded once. "I am more than happy to meet it."

Chapter 32

Growing Up

Staten Kirkland

Staten sank onto the sofa in the little cottage, letting the smooth brown leather cool his skin. Granny and Gramps had gone to bed hours ago. Staten knew he should do the same. He had a long day of work ahead of him in the morning. He needed rest. His head pounded, his face ached, and his whole body was sore, but he was smiling.

Over forty neighbors and friends had shown up for his birthday. They'd toasted to him. Swapped stories with him. Shared scars with him. Supported and encouraged him taking over the Double K Ranch. He may have lived in Crossroads all of his life, but he'd never felt more like he belonged as he had that night.

Samuel hadn't made it, but that was no surprise. Staten couldn't remember the last time his father had been around for one of his birthdays. His son turning twenty wasn't newsworthy enough for the tabloids.

And, of course, Amalah hadn't shown up either. And while he did miss her, surprisingly, it hadn't ruined his day as much as he'd expected. In fact, it had been a really great night.

The phone in the kitchen rang, and Staten jumped up to answer it before it woke his grandfolks. Who would be calling at this time of night? In seconds he was wide-awake, adrenaline pumping.

"Hello, Staten here."

"Staten?" Amalah's voice sounded panicky.

"Amalah, are you okay? What happened? What's wrong?"

"I'm fine. I know it's late, but I knew you'd still be up. I wanted to tell you happy birthday again before you went to bed." Her voice was so low, he guessed she was whispering.

Relief hit him like a freight train and he suddenly felt more exhausted than he had in weeks. "I'm so glad you're okay."

Her soft laugh soothed him like a balm. "I was a little hysterical earlier, but I feel better now."

"Does that mean you're coming home tomorrow?"

Her second of hesitation answered everything for her. He spoke before she could. "It's okay. Forget I asked. I'm sure you're busy up there."

"Staten, I . . ."

She paused, seeming to search for words, and in that one moment, Staten saw things more clearly than he ever had. Her life was in Lubbock at Texas Tech. It might not be that way forever, but it was right now. And Staten's world had become the ranch and Crossroads.

He loved the Double K with every fiber of his being. It was a part of him. His family's legacy. Like his gramps always said, the dirt of Ransom Canyon was in his blood. He'd never give it up. Not for anyone.

And he didn't want Amalah to abandon her dreams and new life for him either. He knew she didn't want to, and she shouldn't have to.

Staten felt a tear slide down his cheek as he steeled himself for what he knew he needed to do.

"Ama." He stopped her as she started to speak. "It's okay. Stay there. Do what you need to do. Live your life. It sounds exciting and busy, just like you always wanted."

Her voice broke. "Staten, what? That's not what I meant."

"I just want you to be happy. I don't want to add to your stress. It's not fair of me. And I can't give you the support and help you need right now either. The ranch takes up all my time. All my energy."

A sob ripped through the phone. "What are you saying?"

Tears streamed from his eyes, but Staten held his voice firm. "You deserve someone who's going to be there with you. Everyday. Someone who can lighten your load, not add to it. So . . ."

"Staten, stop. I don't want this."

"I think we should take a break, Ama. That way you can focus on all the things you have to do at Tech without me pressuring you to come home."

He nearly took the words back as Amalah cried over the phone. "You don't bother me, Staten. I want to come home. I just haven't had the time."

"I know you haven't, and that's okay." He gripped the phone so hard he thought it would break. "I love you, Ama. And I'll always be here if you decide to come back. But for now, go live your life. I don't want to hold you back."

"But, Staten, I love you." Her voice was barely more than a whisper.

"And I love you, Ama. I always will, but things have changed. I'm not going back to Tech. That dream is dead. We have to grow up and move on."

She hung up without another word, and the click of the phone call ending echoed through his head.

A sob rippled through his chest, but he wouldn't let it out. He punched the wall next to the receiver. He hated change. He always had. But Staten knew he'd done the right thing. Amalah deserved to be happy. To live her dreams. Even if that meant he wasn't a part of them.

Chapter 33

Planning for the Future

Peggy Warner

Peggy smiled as the steady beat of Duke's heart thumped under her ear. She ran her hand over his arm, marveling at the strength she felt there. He rubbed her back as they stared up at the faded glow-in-the-dark stars dotting the ceiling of his childhood room.

They lay tangled together on his twin-sized bed, snuggling beneath an old quilt. The house's utilities had been turned off for years, but, wrapped in each other, they were comfortably warm.

The lamp Duke had lit earlier had burned out, and the night had settled around them. Tucking them in.

"I love your old house," Peggy said into the dark.

Her cowboy pulled her tighter to his side. "I hope you mean that because, someday, I want to give it to you."

Peggy smiled, though he couldn't see it. "Can we paint all the rooms?"

"Whatever you want, pretty lady."

She sat up in excitement and the cold washed over her like a bucket of water. She shivered and Duke gathered her back into his arms. "Where are you going?"

Lying back down, she tucked her head under his chin. "Nowhere. This is exactly where I want to be."

After a moment, Peggy said, "We can start with painting the kitchen. A sunny yellow. But the dining room has to be blue."

Duke kissed the top of her hair. "Planning on brightening this place up, huh?" He threw his arm behind his head, using it as a pillow. "You can pick any color you like. I don't care as long as you stay here with me." He spoke whisper soft. "I want you to turn this dusty old house into a home."

In the room, shadows danced. Peggy laced her fingers in his. "I'd like that."

Suddenly, Duke shifted, turning them both so they were facing each other on the small bed. He propped himself up on his elbow and traced Peggy's lips with his other hand. "Marry me, Peggy May. I don't have much, but I promise to love you with all that's in me for as long as you'll have me."

"Forever," she said. "I will, and I'll want you forever."

The gentle cowboy leaned over and kissed her, long and slow. She slid up against his chest and wrapped her arms around his neck, pulling him closer. He'd never be close enough.

He moved away, panting. But his eyes shined with happiness. "The bride gets to pick any color she wants. I'll always give you whatever I can."

"I won't ask for much. As long as you're kind and thoughtful and love me true, I won't need to ask for more."

"I will," he vowed. "I already do."

He kissed the tip of her nose and she giggled. "Can we have a wedding? I've always dreamed of being a bride."

"If you want a wedding, you can have one."

She rested her hand over his heart. "But what do you want, cowboy? I want you to be happy too."

"I'm already more happy than I ever thought I would be."

Peggy felt like she was living in a fairy tale. Like she and Duke were soulmates. Like it was love at first sight.

She'd never had anything all her own, but now it seemed she was getting everything she'd ever wished for.

Peggy stroked his face. "I don't need a big wedding, but I would like all my sisters to be bridesmaids and my brother to be a groomsman." She tried to picture how her family would act. "My dad will probably cry and my mother will say, 'Praise the Lord.'"

Duke's deep laugh melted over her. "When do you want to tell them we're getting married? In the morning?"

Peggy stiffened in his arms. "I need to wait a few days. Until I find the right time. I'm worried about how my mother will react, since it seems I was born to be her buddy. When I'm home she wants me to go everywhere with her. She doesn't even ask; she just says, 'We've got to go to.' Who is going to go with her once I leave her house?"

"Are you sure you want to marry me?"

"Yes!" she said fiercely. "I'm sure. We'll tell my family in a few days." She kissed his scruffy cheek. "I'm ready to start living my life with you."

Duke tucked the blanket in around them, and she settled next to him. The weather was blowing outside but she didn't feel the cold. They talked to each other, laughing and wrapped in each other's arms.

When dawn crawled into their bedroom, she smiled up at him. He looked like he hadn't been asleep all night.

Peggy laughed softly. "Did you close your eyes at all?"

"Nope." He pulled her onto his chest. "I didn't want to miss a moment being with you."

"If you work during the day and watch me at night, you'll be dead in a month."

"I don't care." A chuckle rumbled in his throat. "It'll be worth it. Now let's get up and go find a café. I'm starving."

She pressed her face against his chest. "Let's go out and have a real date."

Chapter 34

The Search Begins

March 1992

Charlotte Lane

The first weekend of spring break was perfect. Not a cloud in the sky and just a rare gentle breeze. Charlotte lifted her face to the sun, letting the rays kiss her skin as she and Wade made their way to the stables on the Double K Ranch.

She adjusted the Crossroads baseball cap she'd been given for coaching the football team. Wade was wearing a bright white Stetson hat, shining like a beacon in a sea of brown and red dirt, and actual chaps. She wasn't sure if he was trying to blend in with the ranch hands or honestly thought his chaps were necessary. And then there was the red plaid button-up shirt he was wearing.

They found Jake Longbow waiting for them next to the corral with two horses already saddled and ready to go. In his vest stitched with the Double K brand and his black felt hat dusted with dirt, he was the real thing. She wondered what the old cowboy thought of Wade's costume.

"Howdy there, partner," Wade yelled to the foreman.

Charlotte shook her head, wondering if it was too late to ditch him. She may not be a country girl herself, but she'd never once read of a character saying that in one of her books, let alone heard a real cowboy shout it.

Jake's wiry eyebrows lifted and his stern face cracked into a smile. He tilted his head but didn't say a word. She didn't blame him. The last thing they needed was Wade trying to play out some Old West reenactment. Ever since she'd told him that Jake would take them around the ranch to look for the cave, Wade had been practicing his cowboy accent.

Charlotte walked up to Blue, the docile old horse Staten had chosen for her to practice on, and patted the roan's neck. "Good morning, Jake. Thanks for taking us out."

"No problem, Miss Charlotte. It's always a pleasure." His spurs jingled as he moved toward them. He eyed Wade. "Ever ridden a horse before, Mr. Parsons?"

Wade looked nervous for the first time that morning. "Yeah, once or twice."

Charlotte couldn't help teasing him. "Don't worry, Jake. He knows the most important rule: Stay on."

The foreman didn't look reassured. "Well, Blue and Lady are the calmest horses we have. If you can't keep your seat on one of them, then you've got no business riding a horse." Jake passed the reins to Charlotte. "I've got to go saddle up Sadie. You two go ahead and mount up. It'll only take me a few minutes."

She swung up on her horse, pleased with how natural the motion now seemed. Jake was a great teacher, and after only a few short months, Charlotte felt like she'd become a part of the

West. This was her happy place. Sitting on a horse with miles of prairie stretched out in front of her and endless directions to explore. Here she wasn't stuck with just north, south, east, and west. Out here she was free to go where she wanted.

Charlotte turned to ask Wade where they should start searching for the cave and saw him struggling to put his foot in the stirrup. She thought about asking him if he needed help. What if getting onto a horse was how he'd injured his arm? But before she could ask, he managed to swing up and land in his saddle. He tilted but didn't tumble off. Maybe she should give him more credit. After all, he studied cowboys and the West just as much as she did. While she had read about it in her literature books, Wade researched the history and the old culture.

Jake walked out of the stables with his horse. The paint pulled against the reins. The old cowboy clicked his tongue and the horse calmed. Charlotte was always surprised at the power and strength that seemed to radiate from Jake's pride and joy. She knew she still had a lot to learn before attempting to ride a horse like Sadie.

"Ready to go?" Jake asked.

"Yes, sir." Wade straightened in his saddle. "Shall we start at the cottage so we can follow it due west? Mr. Kirkland said the cave should be in that direction."

"Sure thing, Mr. Parsons. This is your circus. I'm just a part of the show."

As they rode out toward the small cottage, the smell of apples filled the air. Charlotte spied a pie sitting on the windowsill and her stomach grumbled. Staten was sure lucky to have a granny like Mrs. Kirkland.

Charlotte wondered if she'd be able to get a piece once they got back but didn't think her chances were too high. She knew Mrs. Kirkland loved feeding the men on the ranch, and Charlotte knew how much they could all eat. She'd be lucky if a crumb was left in the pan.

As they steered the horses past the cottage to find a creek

bed heading west, Wade sounded off a list of questions for the foreman as if he were cataloging information for his research. "What kinds of threats can we find out here, Jake?"

"Not too many. Besides the snakes and coyotes, there's really only Senator Kirkland to worry about." The cowboy laughed at his own joke. "But I doubt you'll see any of them out this way this time of year."

"Too cold?"

"Mm-hmm."

Jake kicked his horse into a canter and Wade followed.

"I guess it does get pretty cold out here, especially in the wintertime. How do you make sure the cattle survive when it's below freezing?"

The foreman glanced over at the history teacher keeping pace with him. "The animals know what to do. There's windbreaks and things like that to help them ride out the weather. Mostly they just keep together to stay warm."

Up ahead of them the ground split, revealing the rocky bottom of a dried-up creek bed snaking through the land. The red dirt curved and swirled like the water that had once flowed over it. Wildflowers seemed quilted into the random patches of grass sprouting out around the rocks.

Charlotte decided to save the cowboy from Wade's never-ending questions. "Hey, guys. Look over here. Have you ever ridden down this creek bed, Jake?"

"Oh, yes, ma'am. I know this area like the back of my hand. I can't say I've found much interesting out there, but if you follow that almost creek west about three miles or so, it splits off in another two directions."

Charlotte wondered again how they were ever going to find the cave out here. The Double K Ranch was huge.

"Let's get going then. That cave's out here somewhere." Wade shot out in front of them and nearly fell out of his saddle as he rushed his horse forward.

Charlotte rode closer to Jake. "I never realized there were so many colors out here. Maybe it'll be an early spring. It's beautiful."

"That it is, Miss Charlotte. Wait until you see the sunflowers. Whole fields full in some parts of the ranch."

She smiled. "Mr. Kirkland told us that the first Mrs. Kirkland loved sunflowers. I wonder if they made her love this place more."

"Yeah, I reckon they did. Legend has it she's the one who brought them here." He pointed out in the distance. "They say she planted a patch of sunflowers out there somewhere. Her favorite spot was high up off a creek, where she could look out on the land and see for miles. And she loved them so much she planted more every year. Story goes she did it to help her folks and her brother find her if they ever came looking. But I think she just liked the view."

"Do you know where that spot is? Maybe the cave is there."

"That I don't know. The land is alive like everything else around here. It changes over time." Jake swept his hand out, gesturing to the dried-up creek they rode in. "About a hundred years ago this creek was as wet as the Brazos. Not as big, mind you, but it still carried water through this valley. Enough to water the animals. Now look at it."

Charlotte gazed at the creek filled with nothing but dust, rocks, and weeds. She knew what Jake was trying to say. Even if the cave was still out here, it probably wouldn't look anything like how it used to. It might not look like a cave at all.

Chapter 35

Future Decisions

Quinn O'Grady

Quinn flopped onto the iron daybed she'd had since she was a kid. Wrapping herself in her purple comforter, she begged sleep to take her away from reality, if only for a few hours.

After the five-hour flight from New York to Lubbock and the hour drive into Crossroads, Quinn was exhausted. She'd told her mother it was just jet lag. But the truth was she was tired from running circles in her mind. She needed to escape her head for a little while.

Her fists clenched around her blanket, and she winced as pain shot through both hands. She looked at her bandaged fingers as tears welled in her eyes. Quinn swiped at them angrily. She wouldn't cry anymore. This was all for the best. Lloyd deBellome had done her a favor. And now he could never get to her again.

A light knock sounded on her door, and she pretended to sleep. She couldn't face anyone right now. She'd been kicked out of school, labeled a nutjob. Worst of all, she'd failed at fulfilling her parents' dream for her. She'd never perform in public again.

Another lump formed in her chest, and she swallowed the sob.

She tensed as she heard her bedroom door creak, hoping whoever had opened it would leave her be. Quinn squeezed her eyes shut as her floorboards groaned under the weight of someone entering her room. Then her bed dipped as someone sat down and began rubbing her arm.

"Hey, Quinn. It's me. You all right?"

Quinn blinked Amalah's face into view. Her brown hair hung in loose curls over her shoulders, her dark eyes were crinkled in concern.

Before Quinn could understand her best friend's appearance in her room, she sat up, hugging Amalah as if holding on for dear life. "What are you doing here?" She wiped tears away as more rained down her face.

Amalah pulled back to catch Quinn's gaze. "Your parents called me and said you weren't well. That you had to come home from New York. I was so worried about you. I had to come check on you myself."

"But what about your sorority? All the stuff you have to do up at Tech?"

Amalah gathered Quinn's hands in her lap and stared at the bandages. When she looked back up, tears rested on her lashes. "You are more important than anything happening back in Lubbock. I know I haven't shown it enough this semester, but you're my best friend, and I would do anything for you."

Kicking off her shoes, Amalah crawled into Quinn's bed and settled next to her. "Now what's going on? Are you really okay?"

Quinn tried to say yes, but she found herself whispering, "No." And as the dam broke, Amalah pulled her in and began rocking her slowly back and forth.

She'd thought she was all cried out. That she couldn't possibly have any tears left after the weeks she'd spent crying herself to sleep. The endless insults and screaming. The pain and constant abuse. DeBellome had left Quinn a pile of damaged and broken goods.

But as Amalah held her, whispering that everything would be okay, Quinn felt safe for the first time in months. Safe enough to let it all out. To feel the anger and the fear, the shame and sorrow that had been choking her.

After what felt like hours, she wiped her eyes on her old pink T-shirt and settled back on her pillows. She stared at the ceiling, wondering where to begin, what all to tell Amalah. She didn't want anyone worrying about her. And she didn't want to relive what happened in New York. But she didn't want to hold it all in either.

Amalah traced the bandage covering three fingers on Quinn's right hand. "What happened?"

Quinn hid her hands under her blanket as shame washed over her. Everyone would look at her differently if they knew. They'd treat her like she was someone else. She would forever be the girl who was abused by her teacher.

"I broke them. A piano lid smashed on my hands. Three breaks, the rest is just swelling," she whispered.

"A piano lid? How could that even happen?" Amalah squeezed Quinn's hand lightly. "Are you okay?"

Quinn turned away as a single tear slid down her cheek. "I will be. Time heals everything, right? Besides, it was my fault."

She wanted to believe her own words, but how could time heal scars in the soul?

Amalah gently bumped her shoulder. "Well, this is just a temporary setback. Your hands will heal, and you can go back to school and become a famous pianist, just like you always talked about."

Anger simmered in the pit of her belly. "I'm never going back. I don't want to go to a fancy school in New York. I don't want to play around the world. I don't want to play piano ever again. I'm done. That was never my dream. It was my folks'." She closed her eyes, trying to calm down. "It was a mistake for me to leave home. I won't make it again."

"So what? You're just dropping out?"

Quinn stared at her best friend, determined to keep her voice steady. "Yes. I am." She attempted a small smile. "I want to help my parents sell the lavender and take care of the farm. I want to stay in Crossroads and build my own life the way I want it to be. The way that makes me happy."

There was a moment of silence before Amalah's face broke into a smile. "Good for you. It's time you do what's best for you and stop worrying about pleasing everyone else." She leaned back against the pillows and closed her eyes. She spoke so quietly, Quinn had to lean in to hear her. "I'm dropping out too."

"What? But you always wanted to go to Texas Tech and see the world outside of Crossroads."

Had something bad happened to Amalah too?

"I know." Amalah's sigh was so heavy, Quinn was surprised she didn't deflate. "But it's just not the same without Staten. Nothing is. It took me a whole semester to realize that life without Staten just isn't good enough."

Happiness swept through Quinn for the first time in months. "So are you staying home? Staten will be so happy."

"I want to come home," Amalah said. "But I'm not so sure Staten will take me back. These past few months we've drifted apart."

"Take you back? What do you mean?" Amalah glanced up at her, and Quinn saw the misery in her best friend's eyes. "What happened?"

Tears streamed down her face. Amalah shrugged. "Staten said he wants to take a break. He said we have two different lives now and we should focus on living them. Apart."

This time it was Quinn who gathered Amalah into her arms. "I know I haven't been around enough. Things have changed. We barely talk on the phone. We rarely see each other. He's changed so much, it's like I don't even know him." A sob racked through her body. "Staten's grown. He's settled into himself. I can see it. He's like a whole new man now. He's been getting by just fine without me while I've been miserable every day I've had to be without him."

Quinn brushed the hair out of Amalah's face. "Staten loves you. He always has."

"I know," she cried. "He loved me and was counting on me, and I was barely even there for him. You took better care of him than I did." She sat up, crossing her legs and facing Quinn. "I thought I wanted to go to a big college and get a fancy degree, but I don't think I do anymore. I just want to be Mrs. Staten Kirkland. Is that terrible?"

Quinn laughed softly. "No. You deserve to be happy, and that means doing what you really want. All you've ever wanted is to be with Staten."

"But what if I can't have it anymore? What if I ruined everything and Staten doesn't want me anymore? What if he's moved on without me?"

"That could never happen. You guys are made for each other." She pulled back to look at Amalah. "If you really want to make things right, you need to go to him and be honest. Tell him how you feel and what you want. And let him do the same."

"But..."

"No, listen to me. Staten is a good man. He's the kind worth fighting for. I'll spend the rest of my life looking for a man as good as the one you've got. So, if you want him, you need to go out and get him."

Chapter 36

Almost

Staten Kirkland

Staten sat atop his horse, riding among the cattle. He'd been coming out alone to this west pasture since he'd last spoken to Amalah and told her they should take a break. Since then, riding no longer seemed to ease his heavy heart, but something about the animals' low sounds and the click of their hooves over the scattered rocks calmed him.

He stared out over the land that had become a part of him. Wildflower patches broke through the tough red and orange dirt coloring the ground. Long prairie grass swayed in the wind while wrinkled mesquite bushes stood still as statues. The cliffs of Ransom Canyon spread out in front of him, offering peace. Solitude.

As a kid, Staten had spent many days hiking the canyon trails, staying out long after sunset to get out of posing for his father's photo shoots or pretending to get along with his stepmothers. Today, he stared at the uneven ground, the rises and valleys, the dried-up creek beds, wishing he could run away there for a few hours. To hike until his legs were sore. To climb the cliffs until his arms shook. To work his body until his brain couldn't think anymore.

He knew he'd done the right thing, letting Amalah live her life without him, but it didn't ease the pain in his chest.

The truth was he didn't know how he was going to live without Amalah. Loving Amalah was as natural as breathing. He'd known they were going to end up together since the second grade. Loved her since before he knew what love was.

But what Staten felt didn't matter. He'd do right by her just like he'd done right by the Double K by stepping in when his gramps needed him.

The sun dipped behind the clouds and a slight chill set in. He wished it would numb him to the ache that just wouldn't go away.

Sunset wasn't far off. As he turned toward the barn, he listed all the things he had to get done tomorrow. The work never ended, but for the first time he thought it was more of a blessing than a curse. Being busy would help him get through losing Amalah.

The sight of a dust cloud grabbed his attention. He'd always loved watching dirt devils as a kid, and he waited to see if it would turn into one. But as he looked closer, he realized the cloud was coming from a side-by-side flying over the land. Away from headquarters. He didn't know who would be out here at this time. Making a mental note to ask Jake about it, he headed back for the stables.

He swung down from his horse and entered the stables, then stopped short as he heard a sorrowful melody filling the air.

Slowly leading his horse in, he tried to make as little noise as possible. When he reached the last stable, there was Quinn brushing her favorite mare, humming her sad tune.

Staten dragged his feet the last few steps, trying not to startle her. "Hey there, Quinn. What are you doing here?"

Quinn gasped, raising her hand to her mouth and immediately wincing.

He stepped closer, the leather of his mount's reins pulling against his hand. She'd found her home and didn't want to take one more step. Staten dropped the reins and gathered Quinn's bandaged fingers in his. "What's this? What happened to you?"

She withdrew her hands from his and slipped them into her jacket pockets. "It was an accident, that's all. I'm fine."

She looked so miserable that he decided not to question her further for now. Quinn never shared her problems with anyone. She always stuck to herself, but he wished there was a way to let her know that he was here for her.

He softened his voice. "What are you doing home? Why aren't you in New York at school?"

Quinn turned back to the mare and started brushing her again. "I was released. Didn't make the final concert rounds, so I got to come home early." Her voice was flat and monotone.

Staten stepped up behind her and softly grasped her arms. He slowly shifted her to face him, giving her every opportunity to move away if she wanted to. "Is that teacher still bullying you?"

Her smile looked brittle, but she held it in place. "I actually came here to check on you. I talked to Amalah yesterday."

He dropped his hands. His throat didn't want to work. "And how is she?"

She dropped the brush in the cubby next to the mare's door and stepped past Staten into the walkway. "She's not good. She misses you. All she ever really wanted to be was your wife. She'd joke about needing to learn to cook like Granny, and dreamed of turning the big house into a warm home filled with kids." Quinn smiled. "You guys were always together. Could finish each other's sentences. Always knew what the other needed. It was like you could read each other's minds. We all thought you were meant to be together."

Staten's fists clenched. "That's all I've ever wanted too. But we've both changed. She has her life up in Lubbock, and I'm stuck here running the ranch. She deserves to enjoy college without me dragging her down."

Quinn moved closer, staring at him as if letting her eyes say what she couldn't. She cupped his cheek. "You are such a good man, Staten. You're kind and considerate. Strong and brave. Caring and honest. I swear I'll never marry unless I find someone like you."

Warmth filled his chest. His hand covered hers. "You'll find someone, Quinn. You're special, and you deserve to be happy and cared for."

She shook her head with a small smile. "Not everyone finds what your granny and gramps have. Amalah is lucky to have you, and you're lucky to have her. She loves you, Staten. She's not letting you go."

"What do you mean?"

"You'll have to wait for her to explain." She leaned in and kissed his cheek. "Don't give up on you and Amalah. Not yet."

Chapter 37

Taking a Stand

Peggy Warner

Peggy sat in Duke's truck, staring at the small white house she'd lived in all of her life. Memories flooded her as she examined the cluster of pots sprouting bluebonnets that she'd planted with her mother three years ago. A miniature windmill sat among them, creaking as its rusted rotors rocked back and forth in a half circle. Her mom claimed it was the best garden on the block, and she'd spend hours every other week, rearranging the pots to find the best design.

Scanning the red shutters, Peggy noticed the spots of white from the time her father and her brother painted the house themselves. Her dad hadn't wanted to spend the extra money on painters' tape. He called the white splotches part of his artistic vision.

She gazed up at the apartment over the garage, picturing the cozy space she'd made for herself inside. A lump grew in her throat. She would actually miss this place.

Duke squeezed her hand tangled in his. "You sure you want to do this? You can still change your mind. Don't want to push you into doing anything you're not ready for."

Peggy stared into the face of the man that had come to mean more to her than anything else ever had. The kind gray eyes. The almost crooked smile. The scraggly, unbrushed hair poking out from under a worn black cowboy hat. Her ranch hand may not be the most handsome man in the world, but he had a heart of gold. And that was more than enough for her.

She nodded and excitement took over. "I'm sure. I know what I want, and I'm ready to start living my own life."

He leaned in and traced her lips with his. A sweet, soft kiss to give her courage. "All right, then. Let's do this."

They hopped out of the pickup and marched up the walkway to her folks' front door. With each step, the tension in her gut grew. She could imagine what her mom would say. That Peggy was too young to know what she wanted. That she hadn't known Duke for long enough.

She lifted her hand to knock on the door, but it swung open before she got the chance. As always, Susie Warner's blond hair was pulled into a tight bun, with white streaks, like purposeful highlights, escaping around her ears. She wiped her hands down the daisy apron she wore most days. Her blue eyes looked hard as diamonds as she stared at Duke's tall, lean figure taking up most of the open doorway.

He tipped his hat with a smile. "Morning, ma'am."

Before her mother could say a word, Peggy spoke. "Hi, Mom. Can we talk to you and Dad for a minute? There's something important we want to tell you."

Susie glared daggers at Duke. "You coming here to say you're pregnant, Peggy May?"

"Mom!" Peggy gasped. "No. Of course not." She pulled her

cowboy into the house, headed for the family room where she knew her dad would be watching sports.

Benny Ray Warner looked up as his wife barreled past their daughter into the room. Annoyance sat on his face as she stopped in front of the TV. He didn't even try to peer around her. He was well aware that when his wife had something to say, she'd keep talking about it until he listened.

Peggy and Duke slipped into the room as her mom placed her hands on her hips. "Benny Ray, your daughter wants to talk with you."

He grunted. "Which daughter?"

They moved farther into the room. Peggy grasped Duke's hand like it was a lifeline.

As her father inspected the couple, his eyes got big, pushing his bushy eyebrows up to his wrinkled forehead. "What's this?"

"That's what I'd like to know," her mom chirped. "My youngest daughter running around with some strange man. And we know you didn't come home last night. It ain't proper."

Peggy was twenty-seven years old. She may not have gone to college, but she'd learned enough to know that letting Duke go would be the biggest mistake she'd ever make. It was time for her to make a stand and let everyone know she was taking her life back. Starting with her parents.

She laced her fingers in Duke's. "Mom. Dad. Duke and I are getting married."

Benny Ray abruptly shut off the TV and stood up from his brown La-Z-Boy recliner, muttering to the walls about the craziness of the times. Susie sank back on the matching sofa, clutching the pillows.

"What do you mean?" her mother cried. "We don't even know this man!"

Her dad poked Duke in the chest. "What's your name, son?"

Peggy moved to step between them but her cowboy held

her next to his side. "Name's Duke Evans. I ride for the Double K Ranch owned by the Kirklands. I've been a cowboy most of my life so I don't have much, but I do know how to respect a lady. And everything I have Peggy is welcome to."

"Oh!" Susie gasped. "That's right. We saw you at Staten's birthday party. You'd been drinking and fell down some stairs." She turned to her daughter. "This is why we need to keep an eye on you, Peggy. Why you should stay home. One dance and you think you're in love. What do you even know about this man?"

"I know everything I need to." Peggy's voice came sharp and hard. The room seemed to still as all eyes stared at her. "I didn't just meet Duke at Staten's party. We've been seeing each other for a while now." She looked up at him and felt herself soften. "He is the kindest, gentlest man I've ever met. And he understands me. Sees me for who I really am."

She looked to her parents, begging them with her eyes to hear her. To think about what she wanted for once. "Duke looks at me like I'm beautiful and special. He listens when I talk. And he treats me better than anyone I've ever met. I love him. And I plan to marry him whether you agree or not."

The tall cowboy pulled her into his arms along his side and kissed the top of her head. "I'll take care of your daughter, sir, ma'am. I'll treat her as an equal and make sure she always has everything she needs. You'll never have to worry about her being happy with me. I plan to treasure her everyday she'll have me."

Benny Ray seemed to assess him. "You seem like an honest sort of man. A hard worker, too, which is more than I can say for my other sons-in-law." He gave a sharp nod. "Well..."

Susie cut him off, her voice almost a whine. "Peggy, how can you leave us like this? I need you. You're my little mini-me. The one who's always followed me around and done just about everything with me. Can you really leave your mama?"

A small twinge of guilt pricked at Peggy. She moved out of Duke's arms to wrap her mother in hers. "I'm not going anywhere. I may not be living above the garage anymore, but I'll still be in Crossroads. This town is so small, you'll still see me every day and we can still do things together whenever you want."

She hugged her mom tightly and then stepped away. "But it's time I start living my own life. Do what I want to do and make myself happy. I've spent as long as I can remember taking care of everyone else. Now it's my turn."

Peggy held her hand out, and Duke joined her. "I'm going to marry Duke, and I hope we'll have your blessing. Because who else is going to help me plan my wedding and pick my dress?"

Susie swiped at the tears running down her cheeks. After a long moment, she said, "Of course I'll help you plan the wedding. We have to make sure it's right and proper. We can have it here, in the backyard. Right, Benny?"

Her dad groaned. "Then I guess I'll have to mow the grass." His mouth was stuck in a straight line, but Peggy could see the smile in his eyes. He understood.

He leaned down so she could kiss the top of his bald head. "Thanks, Daddy."

"All right, now." He sat back in his recliner and turned the TV on. "Let me get back to my game. It's not like you two are getting married today."

Susie looped her arm in Duke's. "Well, you just come into the kitchen and we'll talk things over without bothering Mr. Grumpy in there." She laughed at her own joke. "You're going to be my son-in-law. I can't believe it. And what a fine young man."

They spent the next three hours picking out a color scheme and choosing flowers and deciding cake flavors. Peggy and

Duke agreed on most things, but Susie seemed to have her own ideas. She'd even chosen the wedding date for two weeks out. Peggy didn't mind. She was just glad her parents had given their blessing. She was ready to be married, the sooner the better. And best of all, Peggy had stood up for herself, and the world hadn't ended.

Chapter 38

Spring Break Treasure Hunt

Charlotte Lane

Charlotte shivered as the frigid wind brushed over her skin. When she and Wade had left the Double K that morning to continue their search for the first Kirklands' cave, it had been nice and warm. But as the afternoon rolled in so had the weather. The sun had retreated behind the clouds and the sky had darkened to an early twilight. It seemed the rain was determined to find them. And looking out across the endless sea of prairie grass surrounding them, she knew there would be no shelter from the oncoming storm.

Next to her, Wade glanced at the sky, then turned to look behind them and muttered a curse. Clearly he was thinking the same thing she was. The rain would be coming in soon, and turning back to the Double K wouldn't help get them out of the storm any more than riding forward. They were at least three hours away from the ranch; that's how long they'd been riding anyway, and out here, there was nothing to hide under but half-dead mesquite bushes.

"Do you want to turn back?" Wade asked.

Charlotte knew that as much as he wanted to find the cave, he would retreat for her sake. But she also knew how much ground they would lose if they did.

They had spent the past three days searching for the first Kirklands' cave. The first time they'd ridden out here with Jake and followed the creek as far as the fork before they'd had to turn back because of the setting sun. Yesterday, the foreman had ridden with them as far as the fork before leaving to finish his duties on the ranch while Charlotte and Wade had followed the creek bed southwest. The scenery had been beautiful, with the wild colors of the canyon spreading out like a kaleidoscope across the land. But there had been no cave in sight.

This morning Charlotte and Wade had set off alone as the sun had risen in the sky. Their progress was faster now that Wade was more stable in his saddle, and they'd made it to the split in the creek with plenty of time to search the northwest part of the fork.

Charlotte and Wade had yet to find more than a few outcroppings, but as they traveled the rocky creek bed, they noticed small rises in the land. Sharp-edged hills sprinkled with rocks rose up about twenty or thirty feet and looked like miniature models of the canyon that the area was known for. If what Jake said about Millie loving an area that overlooked the creek was true, then the cave could be in this part of the ranch.

Charlotte didn't want to turn back now and risk not finding this place again. Especially if turning back wouldn't help them escape the rain anyway.

"I'm good," she replied. "Let's keep going. What if your cave is just around this bend?"

"All right, if you're sure." He straightened in his saddle. "Let's go. Yee haw."

Charlotte laughed to herself. She'd seen teacher Wade and coach Wade, but she had a feeling cowboy Wade would be sticking around for a while. He was definitely a character. One that was growing on her more and more.

The wind picked up and flung dirt in every direction. Her horse moved closer to Wade's.

Lightning sparked behind the clouds, and Charlotte's horse swung its head as if wanting to turn back. She patted the roan's neck and made cooing sounds like she'd heard some of the ranch hands do when their horses got skittish around the cattle. She might not be a real cowgirl, but she figured the horse just needed a little comfort like everyone else.

Raindrops began to fall as the dried-up creek curved out in front of them like a large S, disappearing slightly at one end as the ground swelled up again and seemed to swallow it. Charlotte lifted her face to the sky, wishing the rain would wash away the doubt that always seemed to haunt her, pushing her into safe routines, and into doing the same things at the same job with the same people over and over again for years. The doubt that made it easier for her to believe Wade was just a friend.

She closed her eyes against the droplets caressing her face. She didn't want to be that anymore. The plain girl with the plain life. She wanted adventure. She wanted to live.

Lightning flashed through the sky, highlighting the red and orange streaks in the rocks rising above them, and Charlotte thought she saw that one of the rocks toward the top had some kind of symbol etched into it. She guessed it was nearly a foot wide. The lines of the drawing were too perfect to have been sketched by nature. She nearly squealed with excitement.

"Wade, look. Up there. I think I see something." She swung off her horse and slid in the mud as the rain picked up. She made her way toward the closest boulder, trying to see if there were more carvings closer to the ground.

"Charlotte, wait."

She turned at the urgency in his voice, and immediately saw what was making him nervous. While Blue had stayed ground tied like Jake had told her it would, her horse had drifted slightly away from Wade. The horses were skittish, and her first-time cowboy was holding on to his reins for dear life.

She yelled to him, "Just jump down and come over here. The horses are trained. They're not going to go anywhere." She turned back to the rocks, trying to make out shapes in the dim light.

She ran her fingers over the stone and felt nothing but the smooth surface that had been sanded down over time.

"Here." Wade leaned over her shoulder, handing her a flashlight. "This might help. Now, do you want to tell me what the hell we're doing? What are we looking for?"

He turned on his light and ran the beam over the stones in front of them. Nothing. Charlotte looked up, trying to find the symbols she'd seen before, but she couldn't see more than a few feet through the rain now, even with the flashlight.

Lightning struck the sky again, lighting it up like fireworks on the Fourth of July, and illuminating the carvings, high above them on a rock near the top of the rise. As the darkness settled back around them, Charlotte began climbing.

"What are you doing? You can barely see. What if you fall?" Wade's shouts followed her as the wind screeched around them. "Let's just head back. We can come out here another day."

"I'll be fine. I have a medic with me, remember?" She winked but ended up just blinking water out of her eyes.

She knew she was acting crazy, but she didn't care. For once in her life, she wanted to be daring. Learning to ride and coaching the high school football team were the wildest things she'd ever done. They had been new and exciting, and if she was honest with herself, it hadn't been that bad. In fact, she'd loved every minute.

Charlotte's fingers dug into the loose, clumpy soil as she slowly felt her way up. The rough branches of mesquite bushes scratched at her. Sharp rocks stabbed at the heels of her hands. Once or twice she nearly slipped. But she'd never felt so alive.

"Charlotte, get down," Wade yelled from below her. "I'll never forgive myself if something happens to you."

She glanced over her shoulder and saw him making his way up to her. "What? Are you doubting your doctoring skills?"

His chuckle floated to her on the wind. "Never. Just hadn't pegged you for the mountain-climbing type. Have you ever had any training for this?"

She laughed with abandon. Maybe she really was losing it. "There's a lot you don't know about me."

"True, Dr. Lane." As she got back to climbing, she thought she heard him say, "But I want to know everything about you."

Charlotte didn't have time to analyze the excitement she felt, whether it was because she was climbing a slippery rockface during a rainstorm or because of who was following her up.

She pulled herself onto the next rock and saw that the surface leveled out into a narrow ledge. She grabbed the flashlight from her pocket and started searching the rocks for the symbol she'd seen from the ground.

Wade pulled himself up and stopped beside her. "I don't see anything. What did you drag us up here for? We could get struck by lightning."

"Will you just look? Trust me."

She ignored his grumbling and followed the light with her hand, running her palm over the smooth surface. Suddenly the ground was giving way beneath her, and her foot sank down. A scream burst out of Charlotte's chest as she felt a sharp pain stabbing through her leg.

"Charlotte!" Wade grabbed her arm, struggling to lift her out. "I'm not strong enough. I haven't worked out this arm since I broke it."

"Are you calling me heavy?" She tried to laugh through the pain, her heart hammering in her chest.

"What? No, no."

Her leg sank deeper, and she wrapped her fingers in Wade's shirt as the rain drove into her face. "Please, don't let me go."

"Don't worry. I don't ever plan on it."

He planted his feet on a rock stuck deep in the hillside. "Can you use me to climb out?"

Charlotte wiggled, trying to find some kind of purchase and realized there was nothing beneath her foot. No dirt. Just an empty space. Like she'd found a hollow spot. What if it was the cave?

Wade wrapped his arm around her waist, and she used her other foot to help him pull her out. Relief flooded her as her leg lifted from the muddy hole. They slumped against the rocks, panting as the rain soaked through their clothes.

She moved to step around him and gasped as her leg throbbed with pain. Taking her weight off of it, she leaned into him.

He pressed his lips to her ear. "Okay, that's enough adventure for one day. Let's go back to the horses and get out of here. You're obviously hurt."

"No, wait. There's something down there." She slid to her butt and then crawled to the edge of the hole she'd just made and shined her light in. "Look, it's hollow."

Wade crouched next to her. There seemed to be an open space that went down several feet. She couldn't tell how wide it was, but it seemed big enough for her to drop into.

"Why don't you lower me back down and I'll take a look around?" Charlotte asked, glancing up at Wade.

His mouth dropped open. "Are you crazy? We just got you out and you can't even walk right now. Plus, you don't know how far down it goes. What if the ground isn't solid and you fall through completely? Then, you'd really be stuck."

Lightning lit up the sky as thunder echoed over the hills.

Charlotte heard the horses whinny and looked up in time to see them run off in the direction of the ranch.

She turned back to Wade, trying to ignore her throbbing leg. She attempted a smile. "Well, it looks like we're stuck out here anyway. And if we want any chance of finding a shelter, we might as well drop down here and get out of the rain."

Wade cursed under his breath.

He removed the bright red plaid shirt he'd worn every day to the ranch like a cowboy uniform. And climbed to tie it to a mesquite bush a few feet above them. "There, if anyone comes out this way to look for us, they'll see that.

"Now, let me go first. We don't know what's down there." He lifted Charlotte up and pulled her into him. He held most of her weight as he circled his arms around her waist. "Trade places with me."

She could feel her heart thudding in her chest and wasn't sure if it was from a fear of falling again or Wade's chest pressed against hers.

They turned carefully, as if stepping out the beginnings of a slow dance. Wade released her, and she leaned against the boulders behind her, trying to steady herself. He dropped a few rocks through the hole to gauge how deep the underground space was. When the plop of a splashing puddle echoed through the space below them, they shared a smile.

"What a good idea. What made you think to do that?" she asked.

"Training. Army master sergeant, remember?"

As he jumped into the hole, Charlotte held her breath, listening for the thud that meant he'd landed safely. She shined her light down. He was standing in the middle of the space with his arms spread wide.

"I think this is it! At least, it's definitely a cave. Drop down to me. I'll catch you. You've got to see this place."

There was no way she was jumping to him. "That's okay. I can manage."

She sat at the edge of the hole and put her feet in. Then, she twisted until her belly was lying on the dirt and she could grip the edge. She tried to lower herself down but didn't think she had moved at all.

"You're good. Let's go." Wade's voice echoed in the space below her.

"No."

"I promise it's not that far." His fingers swept across her calves as if to prove his point.

Charlotte closed her eyes and dropped. Wade's hands slid over her body, slowing her fall. He pulled her in. "See, I've got you. You can trust me."

She felt the warmth of his touch against her cold, wet skin. He carefully set her down.

"We need to make a fire. We're both soaked, and it won't be any fun if we catch a chill."

"Do you know how to make a fire?" she asked.

"Of course I do. We learned all that survival stuff in the Army."

As Wade moved around the space looking for anything they could set on fire, Charlotte turned in a circle, aiming her flashlight against the walls. Unsurprisingly, dirt coated every surface. Loose in some places, rock hard in others. The reds and browns moved through the layers as if nature had run a paint brush across the walls.

"So you think this is their cave? The cave James Randall Kirkland and Millie survived in their first winter?"

"It could be. We'll probably have to excavate this place before we find any real answers."

"Maybe not."

Charlotte ran her hand over what looked to be a scratch on the wall. She traced it with her finger and realized that it was perfectly curved in some spots and straight in others. Like someone had carved it into the stone. She moved back, careful not to put too much weight on her leg. Shining her light where she'd just been, she saw the rough outline of the Double K's brand. The same symbol sat proudly above the entrance to the Kirklands' land.

"James had left his mark," she murmured.

"What?" Wade asked over his shoulder.

She pointed to the scratchings in front of her. "Look. This is it." She looked to him as excitement started to take over. "We found it. The first Kirklands' cave. You did it."

Wade stood up, wrapped her in both arms and swung her around. For a moment, Charlotte felt like a kid again.

He gently put her feet back on the ground, mindful of her injured leg. "Let's sit you down over here." He gestured to a spot on the floor. "I found a few old sticks and dried out tree roots and I'm going to try and start a fire to warm you up. If I can."

Wade took a thin metal rectangle out of his pocket. He flipped out a smaller piece of metal from the middle of it and started striking them together. They sparked, but nothing caught.

Wade lifted the white shirt he'd worn under his plaid button-up, revealing a small pistol holstered on his hip. Before she could ask him about it, he pulled the shirt off over his head to throw onto the pile of wood, and she was thoroughly distracted.

"What are you doing?" Charlotte nearly squealed. It had been a long time since she'd seen the naked chest of a man.

"I'm sorry if I'm offending your tender sensibilities, Charlotte. But this is the only thing we've got that isn't completely soaked. I've got to get this fire going and there's nothing else here to use for kindling. Unless you'd like to pitch in." His eyes grazed her wet shirt.

She crossed her arms over her chest. "Carry on."

"Yes, ma'am," he said, and even in the darkness, she thought she saw a gleam in his eye.

He struck at his fire starter again, and finally there was a little flame licking at the edge of his shirt.

Charlotte settled back against the cool wall and closed her eyes as he rearranged the wood over the small flame. She felt like she'd conquered part of the West today. She'd ridden on horseback over hills and through creek beds. She'd braved a storm and climbed over boulders. And now she was in a cave next to a crackling fire.

Wade sat beside her, his leg resting against hers. "I'm not sure how long that'll last. We don't have much else to light aside from a few extra sticks. But it's something."

He put his arm over her shoulders and pulled her into his chest. She opened her eyes as she felt his skin press against her cheek. The heat of him felt so good after the frigid rain of the storm.

As her heart beat in tandem with his, she noticed a faint pink scar twisting over his heart.

She ran her fingers over the coarse skin. "What happened here?"

"Oh . . . Just your typical broken heart." Wade laughed under his breath.

But Charlotte heard the pain hiding behind his smile.

Chapter 39

Reconciliation

Staten Kirkland

Staten sat on the porch of the big house, rocking back and forth in the ornately carved rocking chair mom number three had bought for a *Country Living* photo shoot years ago. He couldn't remember Granny and Gramps ever using the patio furniture, and now he understood why. Like everything else in his father's life, it was all for show. But he stayed in his seat, letting the wood poke at his skin. He hadn't been comfortable for a while anyway.

He watched the lightning dance through the clouds. The oncoming storm's performance wasn't enough to distract him from the thoughts swirling in his mind, but it lit up the countryside like a giant firefly playing in twilight.

The conversation he'd had with Quinn had been floating around in his mind for the past two nights, quieting only to let Staten relive his last talk with Amalah. He felt haunted by the ghost of what might have been, what should have been, and he couldn't get rid of the gnawing ache in his chest. Quinn said Amalah wasn't letting go, but he was afraid to think about what that might mean.

He stared out as the rain rolled in, pattering on the awning over the porch like an old country tune. He closed his eyes, remembering Quinn's sad song. He hoped she was okay. They'd been friends for years, but she never came to him for her problems. As far as he knew, she never went to anyone.

Most times, he couldn't even tell when something was wrong. But this time she'd seemed really shaken up. He just hoped Quinn wasn't alone. That Amalah was there for her like Quinn was always there for Staten and Amalah.

The crunch of tires moving over the graveled drive sounded, breaking through his thoughts. Staten stood, walked to the edge of the porch and peered through the curtain of water falling harder every second. He saw nothing but two small headlights getting closer.

They seemed to belong to a vehicle low to the ground, but he couldn't think of who would risk a drive to the ranch in the middle of a storm like this. The car stopped and then the door slammed as someone got out.

It was Amalah.

Staten stood frozen as she ran toward him and launched herself into his arms. A second later, he melted, running his hands over the body he knew so well. He molded her to him, wrapping his arms around her. He tucked his face into her hair, inhaling the familiar scent of her. The feel of her soft, warm body pressed against his chilled, hard chest was like the dream he'd had since he got back to Crossroads.

"Ama," he whispered, trailing kisses along her neck. He pulled back and caught her beautiful smile. "What are you doing here?"

She nuzzled his chest, settling her head under his chin. "I came home to you."

His heart seemed to pause for a second and then beat wildly.

He hugged her tighter and kissed the top of her head. "I missed you so much. I'm so glad you didn't listen to me. I didn't really want a break . . . I just—"

Amalah stepped out of his embrace but clung to his hand. "Actually, I did listen to you, Staten. I listened for probably the first time since you came back to the ranch." Tears filled her eyes and she blinked to hold them back. "You were right. About everything. We both changed. I was so busy and stressed out that I became someone I didn't even know."

The tears came thick, mixing with the drops sliding down her cheeks from her wet hair. "I haven't been there for any of the people I care about. I let my best friend down. I left you here to deal with so much all on your own. I've been so selfish, trying to live the exciting university life that I thought I wanted. Letting school overwhelm me. And the sorority take all my time."

She cupped his face with her hands. "I'm so sorry I haven't been here when you needed me."

He reached up to take her hands in his. "I haven't really been there for you either. I'm . . ."

"Shhh. It's okay. The truth is, we both still have a lot of learning and growing and changing to do. But, from now on, I want to do it here. At home. With you."

"What do you mean?" Staten felt hope ballooning in his chest.

"I dropped out of Tech. I'm coming home to stay."

Staten opened his mouth, but he wasn't even sure of what he wanted to say. Joy seemed to be lumping in his throat and he couldn't speak. But he was also terrified about what this might mean for Amalah.

"I've thought a lot about this since we last spoke," Amalah continued. "Everything I thought I wanted"—she shook her head—"I don't anymore. The fancy university. The bigger, busier city. The popular sorority group. All of it means nothing without you. And I realized that it wasn't even Texas Tech that I really wanted. All I've ever wanted was to just take the next step with you."

"But you're giving up on your dreams. I can't expect you to do that for me."

"My real dream was you, Staten. I love you, Staten Kirkland. None of that other stuff was going to mean anything to me without you by my side. My dream was to build a life with you."

He pulled her to his chest. He'd never felt so desperate to kiss her, and he let all of his passion out. She met him there, running her hands through his hair, down his back, over his face, showing him with every touch how much she loved him.

Staten had missed her so much, he felt like a starving man being fed for the first time. He was ravenous for her touch, her kiss. His girl was home, and he was never letting her go again.

Suddenly, the steady pounding of hooves beat in his ears, interrupting his perfect moment. He broke the kiss, trying to listen for the sound over their ragged breathing. Who would be out here riding in all this rain?

"Staten, what . . ." Amalah began.

He let go of her and stepped off the porch, looking for the rider in the heavy rainfall.

A moment later, Jake Longbow came into view, his eyes intense as he held tight to the reins of his paint. "Boss! We got a problem."

In all of the years his foreman had ridden for the Double K, Staten had never once seen the old cowboy lose his cool. He never got mad. Never worried. And definitely never panicked.

Adrenaline spiked through Staten's body. "What is it? What's wrong? Is someone hurt?"

"It's Miss Charlotte and that strange fellow she's been coming with. They rode out this afternoon before the storm hit. They went searching way out for that cave J.R. told us about." Jake swallowed hard. "The mares I let them ride, Lady and Blue, just made it back to the stables, but they had no riders."

Staten reacted immediately. The Double K horses never left their riders. They were trained to stay ground tied. The teachers were still out there somewhere. Were they hurt? Lost? Trapped?

It was too dangerous to attempt a search party in this storm. It was dark, and they wouldn't be able to see anyway. The rain was driving so hard, Dr. Lane and Mr. Parsons could scream at the top of their lungs and no one would hear them.

The Double K was huge. Even in perfect conditions, it would take hours to search just a few pastures, let alone the whole ranch.

He hoped the teachers were capable enough to find shelter from this storm somewhere safe until they could be found.

Even without the storm, the land was a wild and unforgiving place.

Chapter 40

Twenty-One Questions

Charlotte Lane

Over the last few hours, the faint pops of burning wood from the fire had settled into soothing background noise. The rain had slowed, though it still dripped steadily into the cave through the hole where they had dropped down. The wind howled above them and the occasional strike of lightning lit up their small space, making strange shadows dance along the cave walls as if they were spirits joining them from the other side.

Charlotte had removed her denim jacket, and she and Wade seemed tangled around each other and tried to keep warm. Somehow, through the night, they'd become impossibly close.

He seemed to think of himself as her personal space heater. When her teeth chattered, he'd turned to face her, then pulled her in closer and tucked her head under his chin. When she'd shivered after a draft had blown into the cave, he'd wrapped both of his arms around her waist and settled her entire body along the length of him.

She couldn't say it was an unpleasant feeling. And it was definitely something new. But she was having a hard time reminding herself not to turn and run her fingers over him.

Instead she kept her hands clasped under her chin and even curled her toes to keep from feeling too intimate. But he surrounded her, and the truth was she wished they could get even closer than they already were.

She just couldn't risk ruining their friendship by asking for something she wasn't sure he wanted to give.

"It's your turn, Charlotte. Or did you fall asleep?" Wade whispered.

Her heart stuttered. They'd started a game of twenty-one questions, though they were well past twenty-one by now. She'd learned so much about him: his favorite music, how many siblings he had, how long he'd been in the Army. And she'd told him about herself as they swapped embarrassing stories from their childhood and talked about all the places they'd each been.

The more they talked, the more she wanted to know about him. Tonight was different than their usual nights eating nachos at the bar. This time they didn't have the topics of students and school to keep them from discussing the real world. Something had shifted in their relationship. And she'd run out of simple questions she wanted to ask.

Uncertain of how to say what she really wanted to know, Charlotte spoke slowly, rethinking each word that came out of her mouth. "How did . . . I mean, did you . . . Were you injured while you were in the service? Is that how you got . . . you know, the scar on your chest?"

A low chuckle slipped through Wade's lips, but she felt how his body stiffened.

"I told you. It's nothing."

"You didn't get that from a broken heart," she breathed. She worried that she was crossing a line by pushing the subject, but something in her said this was important. "I understand if you don't want to talk about it. It's just that you've become a good friend, and when I mentioned it before I sensed there's more to the story. You can tell me anything."

For a moment he didn't speak.

Then, a deep sigh rumbled through his chest. His arms tightened around her, and he held her closer, as if using her as a weight to keep him grounded in the present. "About six years into my service in the Army, I decided I needed to help more than I'd been able to so far. I'd had friends who'd been injured in training ops or overseas, and I wanted to help take care of our guys. So, I enlisted to become a medic and got sent to San Antonio for training."

Wade took a deep breath, then let his words come faster. "Within a few days on base, I met this woman, Elena. Gorgeous, smart, hardworking, fast learner. Her mother was a doctor, and she'd enlisted to be a medic for the same reasons I had. We were like the same person. It was perfect."

He paused and Charlotte untangled her fingers to wrap her arms around him. "You okay?" she whispered.

Wade rubbed his chin into her hair. "Yeah. Well, anyway, we got serious pretty quick. Too quick. And soon I was proposing, thinking I'd never find another woman so right for me." He chuckled to himself. "I was young and dumb. I don't know what I thought would happen. I guess I was just living in the moment and hoping everything would work out in the end. But then the sixteen-week training course was over and we were sent to different bases.

"I went to California, and Elena was sent to Hawaii. I didn't think it would be a problem. After all, it's an easy plane ride to the islands. So, a few weeks later, I flew out to surprise her and found her in bed with another soldier."

Charlotte gasped and felt him shake his head.

"I don't know what got into me," he continued. "I charged the guy. But he saw me coming and *bam*." Wade pulled his arm back and ran his fingers over the scar on his chest. "He hit me with the closest thing he could find, a bedside lamp. The bulb broke and a piece of glass stuck me. I made it all the way through my enlistment without a scratch and it was a lamp that scarred me up."

For the first time ever, Charlotte's brain stopped working. She didn't know what to think or what to say. She heard herself squeal, "He stabbed you with a lamp?"

"Yep." Wade grasped her hand. "It wasn't really that bad. Not too deep. Not fatal. Looks worse than it was. Honestly, my pride was hurt worse than my body." He sighed again. "And that was the last time I saw Elena or her new boyfriend. I moved on. We got in trouble, and the military sent me to court of course, but the charges ended up getting dropped. I went back to California and moved on with my life."

Charlotte wondered if it was really as simple as he made it sound. She'd never experienced a grand love or a devastating heartbreak like the ones in her books, but she had seen the pain of rejection and betrayal up close. She'd watched her mom spiral fast after her dad left them to start another family with another woman.

Maybe that was why Charlotte found it so hard to let people in. Why forming and sticking to routines had become her habit. There was safety and stability in what was known. That was why it'd taken her so long to break away from her life at A&M.

Charlotte leaned in and kissed the scar over his chest. The symbol of his broken heart and the quiet pain he tried to avoid. "I'm sorry."

Wade had stiffened under her hands. "For what? For my tragic love tale or kissing me?"

She felt her face flush. She didn't know how to answer. "I . . . For everything."

He pulled back and lifted her chin, trapping her gaze with his. "Don't apologize, Charlotte. Elena was a long time ago. It doesn't bother me at all anymore. I'm not a heartbroken mess like the characters in your books. And you can kiss me anytime. Maybe next time try it on my lips." He winked.

She tucked her head back to his chest and thought about smacking him as laughter moved through him.

"No, seriously," he said, wrapping his arms around her like he'd done before. "All jokes aside. Thank you for the kiss. I know why you did it, and it was very sweet. I also know it made you really embarrassed and you shouldn't be. You genuinely care about other people, and I love that about you."

He ran his fingers down her spine and she tried to ignore the shiver that swept over her. "You're like no one I've ever met before. You're special. Intelligent. Daring. Passionate. Interesting as hell. I mean, you coached a high school football team with no knowledge of the game. You didn't do great, but you still did it."

Charlotte felt herself melt into him. "Maybe it was your game plans that weren't so great."

"What? Those plays were perfect." Wade pretended to be offended but she could hear the laughter in his voice. After a beat he whispered, "I love that sense of humor. And your quiet beauty. And the way you carry yourself with elegance and pride. I told you before, you're my kind of woman, Dr. Lane."

Surprise washed over her. His blue eyes were burning with a seriousness that made her giddy. Suddenly she felt as nervous as a teenager on her first date. "I . . ."

She turned away, untangling herself from the warmth of his stare and his body heat. She sat up, then got to her feet, balancing her weight on her good leg and pretending to stretch.

She'd moved to Crossroads to start a new chapter of her life. To find peace and make a change. Instead she'd found adventure and made her first real friend in a long time. One she didn't want to risk losing.

Charlotte had tried a few flings in college, mostly study buddies, but that felt like a lifetime ago. And every time she'd thought of getting serious with someone, she always found a flaw she couldn't overlook.

The guy from her British Literature class had slept through most of the course and tried to steal Charlotte's ideas for the rest of it. The one in her creative writing course had thought himself a reincarnation of Edgar Allan Poe, complete with binge drinking and disappearing for days on end. Then she'd tried dating a psychology major, but all he'd done was explain what was wrong with her. Charlotte guessed she'd been his personal research project.

If Wade wanted more, she didn't know what she should do next. What if they messed everything up and lost what they had now? What if the fear of a true heartbreak led her to making her life in Crossroads an inescapable routine like she'd done in College Station?

As she limped away from Wade, trying to sort through her thoughts, Charlotte realized the sound of dripping water was gone.

"Hey, I think it's stopped raining." She turned back to him, motioning him to join her under the opening where they'd jumped down.

"Yep, the storm's finally passed. Thank God. In a couple hours we can work on getting out of this cave. Now come on back here. I promise I won't bite... unless you ask." He smirked. When she didn't move, he said, "Seriously, you're going to freeze. And you should really get off that leg."

Charlotte crossed her arms over her chest and shuffled to him. "Why are we waiting to get out? Why can't we get out now?"

Wade settled on his back, using his arms as pillows and gazing up at her through barely opened eyelids. "Because we don't really know where we are. We rode for hours on this massive ranch, and we could be dozens of miles away from the Double K headquarters. Besides, it may have stopped raining, but it's still wet and freezing outside of this cave. But most importantly, we can't get out of here by ourselves. I could barely pull you out last night, remember? There's no way I can climb out by myself. We need help. And then there's the fact that it's still dark out. We need to wait for daylight."

He was right. They couldn't get out alone and even if they did, the horses were gone. How would they get back to the ranch on foot? The Double K was thousands of acres.

He patted the packed earth beside him. "Come get warm. I have a plan."

She sat down next to him and jabbed him in the ribs. "Care to share this brilliant plan?"

Wade opened one eye and blinked. "Come daylight, I'll fire three rounds into the sky." He patted the pistol still on his hip and shrugged like that explained everything.

"And?" She poked him again as his eyelids started to droop.

He raised an eyebrow. "And, the cowboys will know we need help. Didn't you hear that foreman explaining the emergency signal when we first started riding off on our own?"

"No." She flushed. She was usually so good at listening to instructions. She must have been distracted by Wade and his antics.

"Yep, as soon as everyone's awake to hear it, I'll shoot into the air and they'll all come charging in to save the day. Now will you lay back down so we can stay warm. It's survival rule one-oh-one."

As Charlotte lay next to him, she felt a shiver run through his body. Wade must be colder than he'd let on. If she was honest, a chill had settled over her skin too. She pulled her thin denim jacket back over them and prayed morning would come soon. They needed to get out of here. Their fire was out and right now lying close to each other was their only hope of staying warm. All they could do now was hope the night wouldn't get much colder.

Chapter 41

Dinner Interruption

Peggy Warner

Peggy rushed around her small apartment over the garage, checking for the third time that everything was nice and tidy. She fluffed the pillows on her couch. Refolded the blanket resting on her ottoman. Straightened the green and pink rug in front of her door that read WELCOME Y'ALL. She pushed her dining room chairs that she'd just pulled out back under her little table. And then did it all again.

She wanted everything to be perfect for her date with Duke.

It was the first time he was visiting her here. She'd seen his folks' house and now she wanted to show him her space. Wanted to give him an idea of what their married life might be like. She'd keep the house picked up, take care of the kids and the animals, and keep running her egg business at the farmers market every Saturday.

Duke wanted to stay on at the Double K while they fixed up

the place his parents left him. They would go to the big rodeos and travel around the states until the kids started coming. Then, they would settle down in Crossroads, and Duke would look to become the foreman on one of the other spreads in the area.

She smiled. She couldn't wait to start their life together. It may not be like the fairy tales most girls dreamed of, but it sure was magical to her.

Peggy stepped back into her little kitchen the size of a utility closet and checked on the rump roast resting on the stove. It smelled delicious. Her sisters had always said the fastest way to secure a man's heart was by feeding him. She already knew her cowboy loved her, but some good home cooking couldn't hurt.

The phone on the wall next to the fridge broke through the quiet, and she rushed to answer the call. Butterflies fluttered in her belly at the thought of hearing Duke's voice.

"Hello."

"Peggy?"

Staten Kirkland's frantic voice sounded through the phone, and a cold fear settled over her. She tried to squeeze out the words around the lump forming in her throat. "Is everything okay, Staten? Is it Duke? Is he all right?"

"Yeah, he's... Wait, you mean Duke isn't there with you? The guys in the bunkhouse said he was headed to your place."

"He was. We're having dinner together. But he hasn't made it here yet."

Staten groaned.

"What's going on?"

"Okay, look. There's trouble out here on the ranch, and I need all hands on deck. I'm sorry to interrupt your date night, but when Duke gets out there, I need you to send him on back as soon as possible."

A knock broke through the worry clouding her brain. "Hold on, Staten. I think he just got here."

She dropped the receiver before the new boss of the Double

K could respond and ran to the door. The air left her in a whoosh as she threw her arms around her cowboy. She held him tight, letting her heartbeat slow to match his.

Duke chuckled. "I like this greeting. I hope you're this happy to see me every day for the rest of our lives."

He leaned in to kiss her.

She met his lips in a too-short kiss and then grabbed his hand, pulling him to the kitchen. "I am happy to see you. But right now, there's someone who needs your help."

Peggy pointed to the phone hanging a few inches above the bright orange tile coloring her floor.

Immediately he straightened like an Old West cowboy ready to face a pack of rustlers. She could see his thoughts racing behind his gray eyes as he placed the receiver to his ear. "This is Duke."

Adrenaline raced through Peggy's veins as she watched her cowboy's eyes widen. One stiff nod was enough to tell her that whatever the problem, Duke was on board.

Finally, he said, "Yes, sir. On my way." Then he hung up the phone and gathered Peggy in his arms. "I've got to go, blue eyes. It seems two people are lost out on the Kirklands' land and need to be found quick."

She grasped his shoulders hard as panic bubbled in her gut. "But it's storming out there. You won't be able to see, let alone find anyone. It's dangerous."

Duke kissed the tip of her nose. "We're not going out into the pastures just yet. You're right. It would just cause more problems than we already have. We're meeting at the bunkhouse to set up a game plan, so we'll be ready at dawn. As soon as the sun climbs up over the horizon, we'll head out."

Peggy laid her cheek against the rough, worn cotton of his shirt. "How long have they been missing out there?"

She felt his shoulders lift in a shrug. "Not sure. A few hours at least. Jake says they were out riding before the storm hit. But then the horses came back in the rain with no riders. No one's sure what happened. All we know is we've got to find them and just hope no one is hurt."

"Okay." Peggy pushed off his chest, turned off her oven, and moved to the front door. She grabbed her brown jacket off a hook on the wall. "Let's go then. I'm ready."

Duke's hands grasped hers as she went to put her coat on. "You're not going out there, Peggy. It's too dangerous."

Squaring her hands on her hips, she stared up at him like her mom did to her dad when she was upset about something. "Are you telling me I can't go?"

He didn't say anything, but his eyebrows knit together like he was trying to find the words. Finally, he just shook his head. "All right. Let's go then."

As Peggy rushed down the stairs to Duke's truck, the rain seemed to find its way into her jacket. The cold settled around her like a blanket, covering her from head to toe. As she reached for the truck's heater, turning it on full blast, she hoped the folks out on the Kirklands' land had found some way to stay warm.

Chapter 42

The Boss

Staten Kirkland

The murmur of voices buzzed in Staten's ear like a gnat. He and the Double K's ranch hands were gathered around the large dining room table in the bunkhouse, organizing a plan to rescue the two schoolteachers.

Dr. Lane and Mr. Parsons had been out in the untamed land of the ranch for over eighteen hours now, and although the storm had finally quieted, the chill in the air made the situation increasingly dangerous, even without the ever-present threat of rattlesnakes, hungry coyotes, and other wildlife.

Jake ran his finger over the large map draped over the scratched wood like a tablecloth, tracing the line of an old creek bed that cut through the west pasture. "This is the creek they've been following for the past few days. That Wade guy seemed pretty certain the cave he was looking for was in this area."

One of the young bucks who'd joined the ranch for the winter season and stayed on spoke up. "But do you think they'd stay in that area if they've been searching it for several days and haven't found nothing?"

Another round of buzzing vibrated in Staten's ears. He pushed back from the table and started pacing. The adrenaline was rushing through his body and he needed to move. Staten felt his grampa's eyes on him. He knew Gramps was counting on him to figure out how to save the teachers, but right now, Staten's brain was drawing a blank.

With each passing minute, frustration grew in his gut. Keeping Dr. Lane safe had been his responsibility. He should have trained her more before letting her ride through the ranch without help. But he'd been too concerned with his own problems. He hadn't even been the one to teach her most days. Lately, Staten had passed that duty off to Jake.

But Staten was the one in charge. Everyone was expecting him to make sure things turned out okay. And that held true in spades for Dr. Lane and Mr. Parsons.

J.R.'s raspy voice broke through the muddled conversations. "Look here, boys. We've got to make a decision and stick with it. All this yammering isn't getting us nowhere, and it sure as hell isn't helping those folks out there."

He turned to his grandson with a look Staten knew well. The look that said Gramps already had the right answer but wanted Staten to solve it on his own.

J.R. lowered his voice. "Remember, son, you've got to work out the little problems before you can untangle a big mess." He settled back in his chair and steepled his fingers. Then he said loud, for all to hear, "Now, Boss. What do we do? Where do we start?"

Staten froze for a moment as all eyes turned to him. He placed his hand on his grandpa's shoulder, wishing some of the old man's wisdom would pass through to him. His mind raced.

In his experience, Dr. Lane was a straight shooter. She spoke her mind and did what she said she was going to do. According to Jake, she'd picked up riding pretty fast, so maybe that meant she'd climbed down off her horse on purpose. Maybe she'd found somewhere to escape the storm.

Staten stared at the map, searching along the terrain where Jake said the teachers had been traveling. If they'd gone to the northwest part of the pasture like the old foreman guessed, then maybe they'd found shelter among the boulders that outlined the rises that snaked through that part of the ranch. Staten glanced up at the clock above the bunkhouse door. Nearly dawn.

He looked around the table at the men he'd worked side by side with for the past several months. Staten may have been the first to rise and the last to quit every day, but each of his men had worked hard until the job was done.

"All right, guys. Here's what we're going to do." Staten pointed to his trusty foreman. "Jake, you grab a couple of men, whoever you need, and go saddle up all the horses. Make sure each is fed and watered and ready to go before sunrise."

Pointing to Duke and another group of cowboys not much older than Staten, he said, "You guys go fetch some blankets, then grab some biscuits and fill up some canteens with hot water and coffee. Make sure you have enough to share with Dr. Lane and Mr. Wade when we find them. We can expect them to be cold and hungry."

Staten looked at the remaining ranch hands around the table. "The rest of you gas up the side-by-sides, and let's get ready to go."

The sound of scraping chairs was interrupted by Granny's stern voice. "Now just hold on a minute."

He turned to see Peggy Warner, Granny, and his beautiful Amalah standing in front of the door like guards protecting the exit. Each had a tray filled with cinnamon rolls, eggs, and bacon.

And behind them, the Eagle Scout Dan Brigman held two steaming pots of coffee.

Each man stared with wide eyes, as if expecting an attack.

Granny moved closer. "You boys need to eat first." She placed her tray on top of the map covering the table as if it was just a placemat. "And get some more coffee in you too. You've all been up for hours. You've got to keep your strength about you."

Within minutes, the men were scarfing down food as if they were afraid it was the last meal they'd ever have. Staten watched as Duke pulled Peggy onto his lap and they shared a plate of bacon and eggs. Next to him, his granny was pouring J.R. a cup of coffee, quietly reminding her scowling husband that he would not be joining the search party.

Staten walked around to Dan, who'd settled at the table among the ranch hands and was eating his fill. He held his hand out to the scout. "Thanks for coming out here to help. We can really use it."

"No problem," the deputy-in-training said between bites. He puffed out his chest, letting the light from the small chandelier above them glint off of his Eagle Scout badge. "It's all in the name of duty. You know, I'm going to be sheriff one day, and that means I've got to start protecting the folks of Crossroads now."

Staten tipped his hat at the young man. "Well, thank you for your service."

Dan nodded, then turned back to stuff a pile of eggs into his mouth.

Amalah moved up behind Staten as he dropped into his chair. Wrapping her arms around his neck, her breath tickled his ear as she whispered, "You not going to eat, Boss? I made those cinnamon rolls myself."

Staten lifted one of her hands to his lips. "I will. I just want to make sure every man gets his fill first."

She leaned past him and grabbed a cinnamon roll. "Well, I

want to make sure my man gets his fill too. Who knows how long you'll be out there."

He took the roll from her and kissed her cheek. "Thank you."

Amalah straightened, wiping her hands on the floral apron he guessed she'd borrowed from Granny. "Well, it's a good thing I came back. Obviously you don't eat enough. I don't want you getting skinny on me."

He smiled at the likelihood of that. In the months since he'd been back, he'd put on at least fifteen pounds of pure muscle. He flexed and she giggled.

Then she settled into his lap, laying her head on his shoulder. She placed one hand over the Double K brand on his shirt. "Be careful out there. I don't want you getting hurt again." Her finger traced the back of his head where he'd been stitched up after falling off his horse with Quinn.

He inhaled the scent of her. His favorite smell in the world. "I will, I promise. Don't worry. As long as you promise to be here when I get back, I'll always have something pulling me home."

Amalah brought his head down and touched her lips to his. "I'm not going anywhere," she whispered.

After finishing the meal, everyone headed to the door. The sun was just climbing over the horizon, painting the sky in oranges, golds, and pinks.

"Hey, Boss." Jake pulled Staten aside. "One of the side-by-sides is missing. And the tracks seem to be heading toward the west pasture."

"What?"

Maybe someone had decided to start the search while the cowboys were eating breakfast. Staten scanned the yard to see if any of their group had gone off alone. Everyone seemed to be accounted for.

Staten turned back to his foreman. "The other night, about

four days or so ago, did you send anyone out to that pasture in the side-by-side?"

"No, sir." The old cowboy shook his head for emphasis. "Most of us like riding. And I rarely send anyone out alone. Your orders, Boss."

If none of the ranch hands took the side-by-side then that meant someone was trespassing on the Double K and stealing equipment. He had no clue who that could be or what he or she might want, but Staten hoped it had nothing to do with the teachers who were lost out in the wilderness.

Chapter 43

Burying the Past

Charlotte Lane

Charlotte ran her finger through the loose dirt covering the cave floor, drawing the old brand etched into the wall across from her. The morning sun had peeked into their cave hours ago, and she sat in its warm glow, appreciating the kiss of the sunlight on her skin. Her ankle had swelled through the night, but if she didn't move, the pain wasn't too bad apart from the ache that seemed to throb in time with her heartbeat.

Wade stopped behind her, staring over her shoulder.

"Do you think you should fire three more shots? Just in case?" she asked.

It seemed like an eternity since Wade had fired his pistol into the air three times. The Double K's signal for help. But they hadn't heard a response. She knew the ranch was massive. What if the cowboys hadn't been able to tell which direction the shots had come from? What if they were searching in the wrong area?

"I've only got a few shots left." He moved underneath the hole they'd dropped through and stared up. "My shirt's still out there, flying like a flag almost. It's bright red, so hopefully someone will see it and get the hint."

Charlotte tried to ignore her rising anxiety. What if it took days for them to be found?

He sat on the floor next to her and bumped her shoulder with his. "What are you doing here? Trying your hand at a little archaeology?"

A smile tugged at her lips. "No. That's one thing I've never wanted to do. Digging in the dirt to find old skulls and stuff." She shuddered at the thought of finding a dead body. "No, thank you. I've always preferred to get my information from books."

"I think you're just scared that you'll get one of your fancy dresses dirty."

She swatted at him.

"Here," he said, "just try something for me."

He pulled a small leather pack, slightly bigger than a wallet, out of his back pocket. He untied the strings wrapped around it and unfolded it. Inside were what looked like miniature tools. A chisel, a trowel, and a paintbrush, all small enough to fit in a child's archaeology play set. He lifted out the small chisel and dropped it into her hand.

Charlotte raised an eyebrow. "What is that? And what do you expect me to do with it?"

"Come on, Dr. Lane. You're smarter than that." He picked up the trowel and gripped it like a weapon. "I brought these, hoping we'd find the cave. Let's excavate this place. You're already playing in the dirt anyway." He winked.

"All right. Where do we start?"

He stood and reached his hand down to help her up. "While you were over here scribbling, I was walking the perimeter of the cave and I found something."

Charlotte glanced around the small space, wondering what more there was to see.

Wade threw his arm over her shoulders, helping her walk to the corner where he'd lit their fire the night before.

He took two steps to the right and Charlotte gasped as he disappeared. She moved to where he'd been and saw that he was standing in a small alcove, pointing down at something.

Dozens of stones were piled on top of each other in a small circle. It reminded Charlotte of the old stone burials Western settlers and Native Americans would make for graves. But this one was so small, it could hold only a child.

Wade dropped to his knees. "I think we should try here. Even if the first Kirklands didn't stack these, someone did. What do you think? We seem to have some time and nowhere else to be."

Wade started removing the rocks without waiting for her answer. She could feel the excitement flowing off of him.

Charlotte was worried, exhausted, and in pain, but in that moment, his excitement began to rub off on her. What an adventure this was. Before she'd come to Crossroads, every day had been like living on autopilot. But here, she looked forward to teaching each day. She enjoyed her classes, and the town had come to feel like home. She coached football and rode horses. And last night she'd climbed a twenty-foot rise in the pouring rain, only to jump into a hole without knowing what lay at the bottom.

She'd come alive lately, and she knew a lot of that had to do with Wade.

Putting her weight on her good leg, Charlotte picked up a flat orange rock that looked like it had been pulled from Ransom Canyon, and tossed it with the others Wade had removed. The work was slow and tedious, but it was good to do something other than sit and wait to be rescued.

It didn't take long to uncover the dirt floor. After that, Wade used his trowel to scrape away a few layers of dirt.

"What are you hoping to find?" she asked as she set to work on the dirt with the tiny chisel.

"Treasure," Wade responded.

A laugh burst from her lips before she could stop it. "Are you serious?"

Wade grinned at her. "I have no idea what might be here. Or if there's anything at all."

"Then why were you so obsessed with finding this cave?"

He sat back on his heels. "I just liked the idea of solving a mystery. I grew up not too far from here, and I always heard the legends about the Kirklands who'd conquered this part of the Wild West. As a kid it fascinated me. Then I heard about the missing cave the first settlers had lived in, and I just had to find it. I guess I always thought it'd be like living in part of history." He shrugged. "So, after retiring from the Army, I moved here."

She smiled. While she had been trying to live out scenes from her books, Wade had been wanting to experience the past. Maybe they weren't so different after all.

"Is it what you hoped it would be?" she asked. "The cave, I mean."

"It's better, because you're with me." His smile warmed her soul.

She turned her attention back to the hole they were making in the ground and continued chipping away at it. Suddenly, a hollow thud bounced off the dirt. They stared at each other for one split second before Wade began yanking the dirt away with his hands. Within moments, he had uncovered what looked to be the top of a wooden chest.

"I can't believe it!" he shouted, reaching over and pulling Charlotte into a hug. "We actually found something."

"You sound surprised, Mr. Parsons." Charlotte laughed.

"And here I thought you knew what you were doing the whole time."

"Oh, I do." He winked. "This is all part of my master plan."

"So, what now?"

"Watch and learn, Dr. Lane."

Over the next hour, they carefully freed the chest from the ground. Then Wade carried it into the larger area where they'd slept. With the light now pouring in, Charlotte ran her hands over the rough wood and noticed that the Double K brand etched on the wall was carved on the lid.

The chest was beautiful. It looked handcrafted. Made out of a light wood that was now stained with the red and orange dirt of the area. An antique brass latch held it closed.

"How old do you think this is?" Charlotte sat down and spun the box around to examine the craftsmanship from all sides.

"It looks to be from the mid to late eighteen hundreds. After the Civil War."

The smell of wet dirt filled her nose as he lifted the lid and pulled out a bundle of old cloth.

Sitting back on his heels, he held the material to his chest. "They buried the past," he said. Charlotte could have sworn he had tears in his eyes.

"What is it?"

He carefully unfolded the clothing in his hands. "It's an old Confederate uniform." He stared at it as if he was seeing the ghost of a precious loved one.

Charlotte looked at the faded gray and blue material. At Staten's birthday party, Mr. Kirkland had told them that the Civil War had affected James Randall Kirkland's life until he found his wife, Millie. He'd buried the past here. Buried his uniform and his soldier's lifestyle in this cave to be lost to time.

She saw Wade clutch the uniform and wondered if he wished he could do the same. If he could bury his past like the

Double K's founder. She wondered if it was the memory of his ex-fiancée's betrayal that caused the pain in his eyes. Or was he haunted by the numerous soldiers he'd tried and failed to help?

Charlotte brushed her hand over his leg next to hers, unsure of how to comfort him. "What else is in there?" she asked after a moment. "What else did Millie bury?"

Clearing his throat, he refolded the uniform and sat down to place it back in the chest. Then he pulled out what looked like a worn blanket. Almost every inch of it was frayed, and it was so thin Charlotte doubted it would have kept anyone warm. The red, orange, and black designs stitched into the material were interrupted by various holes of different sizes.

"I don't blame Millie for wanting to let this go and never remember it again," Wade said. "I can't imagine what she went through as a Native captive."

She stared at the contents of the chest, seeing the story of the first Kirklands like never before. "They both seemed to have suffered. And I'd bet they were both afraid of going back to those dark memories. Why else bury these things? But why not just burn them or throw them away?"

Wade returned the tattered blanket back to the chest.

"Fear isn't always a bad thing. It protects us. Helps keep us alive." He wrapped his arms around her waist and pulled her next to his hip. "But sometimes, too much fear can also keep us from living. I think they buried these things because they were ready to let the past go and start their future together."

"I feel like I'm always afraid," Charlotte said. "Afraid of getting hurt. Of messing something up. Of being wrong."

She stared up at him as the dam broke and tears streamed down her cheeks. "I'm afraid of being alone. I stayed at A&M because it was my safe place. I followed the same routine, spoke to the same people, even taught the same courses. I knew what to expect there. It took me half my life to realize I wasn't really living."

His thumb trailed across her jaw, catching the tears before they dropped. "Then why don't we bury our own pasts? Just like James and Millie Kirkland. We both have things we need to let go of to move on. Let's drop it all here. Everything we're afraid of. Everything we want to forget. And when we leave this cave, we'll step into a new kind of future."

Charlotte stared at him as what felt like love filled her whole body. "Okay." She may not know what the future held, but she was willing to face it with him.

Keeping hold of her hand, Wade pulled out his wallet and opened it, grabbing something silver from the part that usually held money. His military dog tags dangled from his fingers before dropping on top of James Randall Kirkland's old uniform.

Charlotte's eyes widened.

"I'm letting go of my survivor's guilt. I saved everyone I could and served my country the best I knew how. And the service brothers I lost. I would stand with them if I could. They'd want me to move on." He squeezed her hand. "To find someone special."

He looked at her expectantly. "What are you going to let go of, Charlotte? What's going to help you start living?"

She thought about all of the things she'd let hold her back. All of the things she'd run away from and all of the things she wanted now.

As she dug inside of herself, she finally found the answer. She lifted her hands to her ears, running her fingers over the small pink stones she wore every day. The earrings had been a gift from her father when she was six. The last thing he'd ever given her. Thinking back now, she didn't know why she'd kept them, but she knew she didn't need them anymore.

As she pulled them from her ears, she felt peace settle over her.

She threw the earrings into the chest and gripped Wade's hand tighter. "I'm finally ready to forgive my father and every bad relationship along the way. I know now that not every man is the same. And some things are worth taking a chance for."

A warmth settled over her, and Charlotte almost expected to look into a corner of the cave and see Millie Kirkland nodding in approval. Today was a new day. And as soon as Charlotte got out of this place, she planned to live her life to the fullest.

Wade set the lid on the chest and carried it to the little alcove at the back of the cave. They reburied James and Millie's box and placed the stones back where they'd found them, letting the past stay buried. Never to haunt them again.

Afterward, they settled on the floor in the main room of the cave and lay back together as they had last night. They looked through the hole that had led them down here and stared up at the clouds floating overhead. They might not have been rescued yet, but she felt that in some way they had rescued each other from all that had held them back in the past.

Charlotte turned to Wade and wrapped herself around him. So close their legs tangled together.

"I knew you'd warm up to me." Wade breathed into her hair.

"I'm still hoping we get out of this hole," she said. "But there's one thing I've got to do before we're saved."

She lifted her face to his, her heart fluttering. And she kissed him. Pressing her lips to his softly. Then Wade took over, crushing her to his chest and kissing her full out. Hot and hard. His hands ran over her body, settling in her hair to angle her head so he could deepen the kiss.

Charlotte didn't know how long they sat pouring their feelings into each other, but after minutes or hours, he pulled away suddenly, as if he had regained his sanity. Panting, he placed his forehead on hers, waiting for them both to catch their breath.

"You're an incredible woman, Charlotte Lane." Wade's finger stroked her bottom lip. "Does that kiss need to stay buried here too?"

"Not if I have anything to say about it."

She ran her lips over his again. This kiss was slow and sweet. Two new lovers getting to know each other.

A cough sounded from above.

Jake Longbow stared into the hole. "You two lovebirds want to stay in there? We can come back another time if you're busy."

Staten Kirkland laughed from behind. "I sure am glad we found you two and that you're in such . . . good condition."

Wade shouted up at them. "All right, enough with the wisecracks. Get us out of here. Charlotte's hurt."

It took three men to get Wade out of the hole. Charlotte had been pulled out pretty quickly, but Wade was solid and heavy. Then they followed the cowboys to a pair of horses and a side-by-side. Wade carried most of her weight as they slowly hiked back down to the dried creek bed that had led them here.

Patches of dried sunflowers dotted the land as far as the eye could see.

"Why do you think Millie planted sunflowers out here?" she asked to no one in particular.

"The sunflower is a symbol of marriage to some Native cultures," Staten said.

She looked at him, a clear question in her eyes.

The young cowboy laughed. "I read about it when I was doing research for one of the papers I wrote for you last semester. Maybe she planted so many sunflowers to show James Randall Kirkland her love."

Pride washed over Charlotte. Staten would turn out all right. She just knew it.

She and Wade settled into the vehicle with a lanky ranch hand named Duke. As they drove towards headquarters, the frigid air pierced the blanket Staten had given her. She shivered, and Wade pulled her in closer. She laid her head on his shoulder and closed her eyes.

"You folks find anything in that cave?" Duke yelled over the wind.

She peeked up at Wade and caught his smile.

"Nope," he said. "And we won't be looking for it anymore either. We've decided to let it go."

Charlotte laughed under her breath. They were burying the past, and from now on, they would focus on the future together.

Chapter 44

Blessed with Change

Staten Kirkland

Staten stepped onto the porch of his grandparents' small cottage and breathed a sigh of relief. He looked out at the endless sea of prairie grass, mesquite trees, and wildflowers. From here, the Double K Ranch spread for miles in almost every direction, and somehow they had been able to find Dr. Lane and Mr. Parsons despite the thousands of acres that made up the Kirklands' land.

The teachers were in the house with Granny and Peggy Warner, getting warmed up and fed. Staten was grateful neither of them was seriously injured.

The rumble of tires on the gravel drive caught Staten's attention, and he looked up to see the sheriff's cruiser picking up dust as it headed to the Double K's entrance. Before confusion rattled Staten's brain too hard, Dan Brigman walked up.

The Eagle Scout placed one foot on the bottom step of the

porch and pushed his hat back to stare up at Staten. "I caught the perpetrator who stole your side-by-side. He didn't want to come quietly, but I was able to subdue him. Sheriff's taking him in now."

Rust-colored dirt stained the junior deputy's usually spotless uniform, and what looked to be a twig from a sticker bush clung to his pant leg. They must have had a hell of a tumble. Staten wondered what the other guy looked like.

"Any idea what the guy was doing out here on the ranch?" he asked.

"I don't know. The man said something about a legend and a settler's cave." Dan laughed at the confusion on Staten's face. "The perp's not making too much sense to me."

So that's who Staten had seen sneaking around the ranch. He hated trespassers, but they caught people out here poking around every once in a while.

Staten chuckled. "Well, he was searching for a part of Texas that doesn't exist. He wasted his time and got himself in trouble for nothing. Mr. Parsons said there wasn't anything out there but a few carvings on the rocks. This place is full of legends. Half the cowboys who work here make up their own stories. Not sure which one he was chasing. There's a popular tale about James Randall Kirkland burying his money, but no one's ever found it. And I doubt there's any of it left if it was out there at all. Any treasure James and Millie might have had was buried with their love."

He walked down the steps and shook the junior deputy's hand. "Thanks for coming out here and helping. If you ever run for sheriff, you'll have my vote."

Dan tipped his hat. He walked over to his old blue pickup and drove off.

J.R. stepped out onto the porch and clasped Staten's shoulder. "You did good today, son."

Staten looked at his hero and felt pride swell in his chest.

The old cowboy might be a few inches shorter than him now, but Staten would always look up to the man who'd raised him.

"You've been doing great with the ranch," his gramps continued. "You work hard. The men respect you. You've become a fine boss."

Staten tried to talk around the lump forming in his throat. "I couldn't have done it without you."

J.R. coughed out a laugh. "Yes, you could. And you have been for a while now. You don't need me looking over your shoulder anymore. The ranch is yours. You're its caretaker now. Granny and I already signed all the paperwork."

Staten saw tears filling the old cowboy's eyes as he blinked away his own. He pulled his grandpa in for a hug. "Thank you, Gramps."

Clearing his throat, J.R. pulled away and turned for the house. "You're a great man, Staten. The best kind of man. You've got honor and integrity. You keep your word. Never let anything break you of that."

As Gramps entered the house, Staten dropped down on the step. He felt his exhaustion all the way to his bones.

He watched the sun dip on the horizon and felt a protectiveness burn through him. The ranch might be his, but he belonged to the land. It was a part of him. His legacy. Like Gramps always said, the dirt of Ransom Canyon was in his blood. And he would protect it and cherish it for the rest of his life.

It was a saying of the Kirkland men to leave the land better than the way they found it, and Staten intended to do just that. He would take care of the Double K until the day he could pass it on to his own kid.

Chapter 45

A Day of Her Own

Peggy Warner

Nervous excitement grabbed Peggy and wouldn't let go of her all day. The past couple weeks she had been planning for her wedding. It was small, and most of the decorations were homemade, but for her and Duke, it was perfect. Her mother made most of the decisions, but Peggy didn't mind. She was just ready to start her new life with her cowboy.

She hadn't seen much of Duke since they'd rushed off to the Double K to help with the search and rescue of Charlotte Lane and Wade Parsons. He'd spent most of his time fixing up his folks' place so they could move in on their wedding night. She remembered how surprised he'd been when Staten and the other ranch hands had offered to help.

The men had worked through the night after long, hard days on the ranch, and gotten the house in decent shape in a matter of days. There was still a lot of work to do, but it was theirs.

Peggy smoothed the flowing white lace of her dress and glanced up at Duke sitting beside her in his truck.

He turned to her with a smile. "You all right, Mrs. Evans?"

A thrill shot through her. Today she'd become Mrs. Duke Evans. She was no longer the youngest Warner or "Hey you, kid." Now she had a new name. One all her own.

"I'm perfect, Mr. Evans."

"That you are, Peggy. You're even more than perfect." He kissed the ring gracing her left hand. "Was the wedding everything you hoped it would be?"

She smiled. "Everything and more. I wouldn't have changed a thing."

"Well, I would have." Peggy's gaze whipped to his, but he was laughing. "I would have made everyone leave as soon as we said 'I do' so it was just you and me. I've been trying to get you alone all night."

Anticipation swept over her. She might be inexperienced, but she knew being with Duke would be amazing.

The whole day had been a blur. Walking down the aisle. Reading her vows. Running through rice amidst an eruption of cheers. Slow dancing in her parents' backyard, which had been turned into a dance floor. Cutting the cake. Family and friends surrounding them with hugs and congratulations as they'd left.

It felt like she'd blinked and it was all over. Now everything was moving in slow motion. And she wanted to remember every moment.

Her heart was bursting as they pulled into the driveway of their house. Theirs. She smiled. She may not have gotten a place all her own, by herself. But Peggy had found the perfect man to share her life with, and she was ready to start living.

Duke's hands circled her waist and he lifted her out of the truck and into his arms. She wrapped her hands around his neck and kissed him slow and long.

"I love you," he whispered as he carried her over the threshold.

She kissed him again and again, showing him how she felt with every touch. The best she knew how.

"I'll love you forever," she said. And forever started right now.

Epilogue

Staten stared out at his land from the highest ridge on the Double K. He looked up as Amalah settled next to him on their blanket covering the ground. Her warm smile melted through him like it always did. Staten opened his arms, and his girl laid her head on his shoulder.

"You okay?" she asked. "You've had a long day."

Staten kissed the top of her head and watched the sunset make her flawless skin glow. "I am now."

She laughed, bumping him with her hip.

"No, really, Ama." He pulled back to stare into her chocolate eyes. "With you here, I feel like I can do anything. Like we can do anything. And I never want to lose that. Never want to lose you. I want to get married and fill this place with babies, like you always dreamed."

Amalah smiled. "Is that a proposal, Staten Kirkland?"

"Yeah, I guess it is. Will you marry me, Ama?"

"Yes," she whispered.

Staten kissed her like a drowning man finding air for the first time.

When they broke apart, her carefree laugh filled his heart. "I want a small wedding. Here. On the ranch," she said.

"But I thought you always wanted a big, fancy wedding. Something you'd seen in those big-city magazines."

She smiled. "I've changed. We've changed." She looked out at the pinks and purples painted in the sky. "This is what I want. This is where we belong. When we get married, it should be here. Right here at the Kirklands' cathedral."

Staten pulled her back to his side. Maybe change wasn't so bad after all. The past few months had been crazy and difficult and unlike anything they'd ever imagined, but they'd survived. They'd survived it together.